GOLDEN STATE

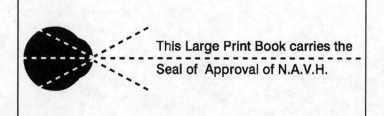

This Large Print Book carries the
Seal of Approval of N.A.V.H.

GOLDEN STATE

MICHELLE RICHMOND

THORNDIKE PRESS

A part of Gale, Cengage Learning

GALE
CENGAGE Learning·

Farmington Hills, Mich • San Francisco • New York • Waterville, Maine
Meriden, Conn • Mason, Ohio • Chicago

GALE
CENGAGE Learning·

LIBRARY OF CONGRESS CATALOGING-IN-PUBLICATION DATA

Richmond, Michelle, 1970–
    Golden state / by Michelle Richmond. — Large print edition.
      pages ; cm. — (Thorndike Press large print women's fiction)
      ISBN 978-1-4104-6911-3 (hardcover) — ISBN 1-4104-6911-5 (hardcover)
      1. Women physicians—Fiction. 2. Sisters—Fiction. 3. Large type books.
    4. Domestic fiction. I. Title.
    PS3618.I35G65 2014
    813'.6—dc23   2014003213

Published in 2014 by arrangement with Bantam Books, a division of Random House LLC, a Penguin Random House Company

Printed in the United States of America
1 2 3 4 5 6 7 18 17 16 15 14

For Kevin and Oscar

Where is Nirvana?
Nirvana is here, nine times out of ten.
— HỒ XUÂN HƯƠNG,
"Spring-Watching Pavilion"

PROLOGUE

Tell me a story, he said.

So I told him about my first morning in San Francisco. It was July, summer in the city, foggy and cold. I was tired and jet-lagged and had yet to unpack, but I wanted to see the famous California coast. I took a bus over the Golden Gate Bridge to San Rafael, where I boarded a shuttle to Point Reyes.

Alone, I wandered along the cliffs in the freezing fog, out to the lighthouse. I stood gazing at the roaring Pacific, a crazy-looking ocean, infinitely more dangerous and dramatic than the Gulf Coast waters I knew so well. On a small hill above a meadow, I followed a picket fence for several hundred yards, curious where it led. And then, without warning, the fence abruptly ended. A narrow ditch split the ground in two; on the other side, the fence continued on its way.

A middle-aged man stood with a boy of about seven. The man was on one side of the ditch, the boy on the other. They held hands across the divide. "We're on top of the San Andreas Fault," the man explained to the child. "This used to be one long, straight fence. When the earthquake hit in 1906, it broke the fence in half and moved it sixteen feet."

I imagined the earth moving in one swift, startling motion, rearranging everything in an instant. Battling a sudden feeling of vertigo, I placed a hand on the fence to steady myself. What was I doing here? California might as well have been another country. Back home, we had hurricanes and tornadoes, thunderstorms so violent they shook the house to its very bones. But this was different.

1

12:41 p.m., June 15
The reception area of the tiny hotel is eerily empty. On the desk, a coffee mug smeared with red lipstick sits beside a small television, the volume turned up high, blaring news of the vote. Eleanor's mug, Eleanor's lipstick. Famously difficult Eleanor.

I leave my crutches behind and use the rail to pull myself up the stairs. At the top, I turn left. The first room is empty, the door open to reveal two twin beds, an old dresser, blood on the floor.

I continue along the hallway. The second door is closed. Room 2B. Heather's room. Early this morning, while I was still sleeping on the couch of a radio station at the other end of the city, my phone began to vibrate. It was Heather, texting: *It's time.* It seems like a lifetime ago.

"Heather?"

I try the knob, but it doesn't budge.

"Heather?"

I knock. Again, no answer.

Finally, a scraping sound, furniture moving across the floor. The knob turns, the door opens a few inches, and there she is — red in the face, her T-shirt drenched with sweat, her eyes strangely calm. Her gaze takes in my wrecked face, my filthy clothes, the hastily wrapped bandage on my foot.

I squeeze through the doorway. On the opposite wall, a bureau is shoved against a tall window that opens onto a balcony. To my left, as far as possible from the window, stands the bed, the sheets twisted and wet.

"When I saw him coming toward the hotel," she tells me, "I barricaded the door. When he left, I barricaded the window."

She shuts the door behind me, then locks it. Together we shove the desk back into place.

"What happened next door?"

"He had Eleanor," she says. "Sounded bad."

Heather doubles over in pain, moaning. I limp to her side. She grips my arm so tight I can feel her fingernails through my sweater. Seconds pass before her face relaxes. She catches her breath, lowers herself onto the bed. "What's the difference between a pregnant woman and a lightbulb?"

she asks.

"Got me."

"You can unscrew a lightbulb."

I smile, happy to see the Heather I know.

In the bathroom, I wash my face and hands. I smell terrible and look worse. The skin under my arms is bleeding, rubbed raw from the crutches. Rummaging through Heather's cosmetics bag, I am grateful for the small miracle of a rubber band. I gather my hair into a ponytail, drink cold water from the faucet, and rinse my mouth with toothpaste.

I scan the bathroom for anything useful. There's a small bar of soap, two towels hanging beside the stained tub, an empty waste bin beneath the sink. I grab the towels and bin and hobble into the darkened room. I drag a chair up to the end of the bed and drape a blanket over Heather's knees.

"Are there any cops out there?" she asks.

"Just one terrified kid."

She clutches the sheets as another contraction seizes her. Her face registers the pain, but she is silent. Thirty seconds pass before she collapses back onto the pillow, panting.

"Where's the National Guard?" she asks.

"Sacramento and L.A., I guess."

A foghorn wails in the distance — that familiar, soothing sound. "Scoot down," I say. "Here comes the fun part."

"When I said I didn't need the bells and whistles, I didn't quite picture it like this." She moves toward the end of the bed.

"The baby's going to be fine," I say, mustering my calmest voice.

I lift the blanket to examine her. I'm not an ob-gyn, I'm a general internist. This is not what I do. Of course, I did it during my residency years — a month on the maternity ward at San Francisco General — but I was relieved beyond measure when my time was over.

Just to the west of us, beyond the barricaded window and the empty parking lot, is the Veterans Administration hospital. The six-unit hotel is normally booked with veterans' families, waiting out heart surgery and organ transplants, but today the place is deserted. All but the most crucial surgeries have been postponed, and the whole campus is running on a bare-bones staff.

Both of us are startled by the footsteps on the stairs. Our eyes lock.

A knock on the door. I open my mouth to answer, but Heather brings a finger to her lips.

The knock again, more insistent this time.

"Dr. Walker?" I recognize the voice — Greg Watts from security. Relief washes over me. I shove the desk away from the door just enough to let him in. At sixty going on forty-five, Greg has the slim, athletic build of a runner. He looks me over quickly, grimacing.

"You okay, Dr. Walker?"

"Fine."

He glances at Heather. "What about her?"

"We're managing. It would be great if we could get a nurse and supplies."

"Nobody wants to cross that parking lot," he says. "Not after Eleanor. Not after he shot at you."

"*You* crossed the parking lot."

Greg holds up a cellphone. The blue Mute light is flashing. "Special delivery. He wasn't going to shoot his own messenger."

I look at the phone, uncomprehending. "What?"

"He wants to talk to you."

"Shit."

"He says if he can't talk to you, someone's going to get hurt."

"Where is he now?"

"He broke into your office."

I take a shaky breath. My office. I think of the photos on the desk, the art on the walls, the radios from Tom, the sand dollar from an afternoon on the beach with Ethan. If he wanted to get inside my head, he's done it.

15

"Anyone else?"

"Betty Chen."

Betty's worked ICU for twenty-six years. A nice woman, a gifted nurse, very calm, four kids and eleven grandkids spread out all over the country. Every year, she and her husband travel by RV to Florida, New Jersey, Ohio, and Montana to see all of them.

"Better staff than patients."

Greg shakes his head. There's something he doesn't want to tell me. "He's got Rajiv."

My heart sinks. Twenty-seven years old, in his final year of residency, Rajiv is my chief resident and my favorite student. In a couple of months, he's getting married. I've been looking forward to the wedding.

I press the Mute button and take a deep breath.

"Hello?"

"So," a familiar voice says, "I finally got your attention."

2

For several moments everything seems normal — the smell of bacon from Lee's, the streetlamps on Spear Street, the damp air against my skin. Then a plume of smoke to the west catches my eye. A fire. I try to calculate the distance from here to there, try to draw a map in my mind.

A curb — such an ordinary thing: five inches from sidewalk to street. I've stepped off this particular curb into this particular street hundreds of times, and yet today, in my distraction, I misjudge its location. My right foot comes down hard, twisting inward. A snapping sound. A jolt of pain from ankle to knee.

I move quickly, counting steps to distract myself from the pain: a full step on the left foot, a half step on the right. Suddenly, my run-down Jeep Cherokee, the one I can't bring myself to get rid of, seems like a luxury. Once I get to the Jeep, everything will be fine. It's only seven miles across the city, from one end to the other. Seven miles to Heather, who texted me minutes ago: *It's time.*

Customers are already seated at the counter of the deli. Lee's usually doesn't get busy until later, but on this day, people want to be together. The door is open, the small television above the cash register is tuned to CNN, and CNN is tuned to California.

I limp down Spear Street, across Folsom, grateful for the sun glinting off the tall glassy buildings, the briny smell drifting in from the bay, the rumble of traffic moving over the bridge. How many times have I walked these two blocks at precisely this time of morning? In the first year of our marriage, I did it once or twice a week, after spending the night at the radio station with Tom, keeping him company before my own workday began. He stowed a blanket and pillow in the closet for just this purpose, and I would fall asleep on the couch, the sound of his voice a pleasing background music to my dreams. Later, there were the years with Ethan, when the station was the furthest thing from my mind. In those days, I would tuck Ethan into bed, lie down

18

beside him until he fell asleep, then curl up on the sofa with a book or, more often, a medical journal, listening for the sweet, miraculous sound of his breathing. Those nearly perfect years, when we felt, so briefly, like a family.

Up ahead, the Jeep comes into view. Just one more block, and I can rest my ankle. I've sprained it before — last year, in fact, running a half-marathon — but this is different. The snapping sound, the feel of something ripping beneath the skin. A level 3 sprain, at least; more likely, it's fractured. The initial treatment is simple, straightforward, one of those medical school basics you never forget: RICE — rest, ice, compression, elevation. But there's no time now.

As I hobble forward, I imagine how my ankle would look in an X ray: the ligaments stretched and torn, blood from the ruptured vessels spilling into the surrounding tissues. Visualizing the X ray gives me comfort — a point of reference, a matter of perspective. Every pain has its cause. That's what I tell my patients when a diagnosis is elusive. For most, it comes as welcome reassurance: something specific is making them suffer, and I will do my best to find it.

Later, at the VA hospital, after all is said and done with Heather, I'll have one of my

19

colleagues set the foot. There will be a cast or boot, the awkward fact of crutches. Any other day, I'd take something strong to reduce the swelling and dull the pain, but today, Tylenol will have to do. I don't want anything to blur my mind or blunt my senses. I want to be fully present, absolutely alert, for the task at hand.

The drive should be a straight shot down California Street. Normally, it would take half an hour, tops. Now there's no telling. The most unsettling part of all of this is the uncertainty. At this time tomorrow, where will we be? I mean this in the broadest sense: not just my husband, my sister, me, but also our state, our country.

A thundering racket fills the air. It's a helicopter, wobbling overhead like some big, clumsy bird. A white bundle drops. My breath catches; a baby is falling from the sky. But then the bundle breaks apart, and the sky is aflutter with something white and snowlike. The chopper shifts; a second bundle drops. The helicopter moves inland in its jerky, graceless way. One of the snowflakes drifts down and settles at my feet. A rectangular piece of white paper, printed with the image of the California flag. Beneath the flag, a slogan is printed in thick red letters: VOTE YES FOR SUCCESS!

The smoke in the distance has grown darker, taller. Where is it, exactly? How far might it spread? And how fast? No good jumping to conclusions. More than likely it's a garden-variety emergency — a kitchen explosion, a cigarette left smoldering on a mattress. There have been rumors, of course, predictions — riots, destruction, looting — but I have to believe that the whole thing, whatever its outcome, will go off in an orderly fashion. I'm not alone in this thinking. "This is, after all, a reasonable state," our governor said last night, "and we are a reasonable people."

But there's something wrong: glass on the ground, lots of it. It looks as though some- one has taken a baseball bat to the line of cars parked along the curb. Three cars in a row, all vandalized — the Prius in front of me, the BMW behind, and in the middle, my humble Jeep. The windshield has been smashed, a sunburst of broken glass. The driver's door is open. The stereo — just a year old, a gift from Tom — is gone. Both back tires are flat. Despite all the dire warn- ings, I envisioned a day of relative calm, the voters going peacefully about their business. It's true that what we're doing here has polarized the nation. "Save the Union" ral- lies in other states have degenerated to

21

angry shouting matches. A pro-secession organizer was shot dead in New York, the campaign office of a sympathetic congress-woman was torched in Florida, and the governor of California has been deluged with hate mail. For the past two months, it seems, the whole country has been simmering. Still, deep down, I wanted to believe that California could get through this without a hitch, that in the midst of the storm, we could be civilized.

I dial my husband. "Call me when you get there," he said when I walked out the door. One of those matrimonial habits that will be so hard to break. The constant communication, the endless mundane updates: I'm here, or we need bread, or I'll be home late, or I'm safe.

Last night at the station, he used my cell-phone to call his, which he'd lost again. He was always asking me to help him find his keys, his watch, some novel he was in the middle of reading. How many hours have I reclaimed since he moved out, by not having to help him find his lost things? What I've done with those hours, I can't say. You think you're so busy until you're alone, and then you discover the disconcerting phenomenon of time on your hands. Last night when he dialed his number a song started playing, muted, from another room, and we followed the tinny music to the staff lounge, where we found the phone buried beneath a sofa cushion. "When did you change the ring tone?" I asked. For years his ring tone for my number had been set to Steve Forbert, "Romeo's Tune." He chose it for that line about southern kisses, and because Forbert is from Meridian, Mississippi, fifty-eight miles from my hometown.

Last night, it played a different song — some instrumental I didn't recognize. "It's Ryuichi Sakamoto," he said. " 'Put Your Hands Up.' "

"Going mellow in your old age?"

"You'd like him," he promised. "I'll make you a CD."

He will, too. In a few days, I'll come home from work to find a padded envelope in the mailbox, a CD with a playlist, something on which he's spent hours, each song containing a message I'll be tempted to try to decipher. "It's just songs," he's told me a hundred times. "There's no secret message."

I imagine him sitting at his new desk — a small, sleek, modern affair — writing our address on the envelope. The desk came with his loft, a six-month lease south of Market, fully furnished. The place looks like

23

a midcentury-modern showroom, everything tasteful and angular and somewhat cold, none of it scaled quite right for Tom. At six foot five and solid, he has a knack for making ordinary tables and chairs look like children's furniture.

Last night, over Thai take-out at the radio station, he made a proposition: "We can start over. Dinner, movies, late-night games of Monopoly and Life."

What I was thinking, but didn't say, was that we'd already played the game of life. We'd had a nice go of it, too — the house, the sex, the dinner parties, the risks and rewards, even, for a while, the child. I imagine the board game, the colorful spinning wheel and the clunky buildings, the hopeful couple in a little plastic car, a blue peg in the backseat — a happy family. In the end, though, it didn't hold.

Tom answers the phone. "Everything okay?"

"Someone broke into the Jeep. Glass everywhere. Can I take your car?"

Add that to the list of matrimonial habits that die hard: communal property.

"It's not here," he says. "I took the bus. For what it's worth, I don't think you'd get far. I just heard there's a police blockade at Stockton — a protest turned violent, and now they're dispersing the crowd."

"How do they do that?"

"Tear gas, apparently. It's ugly."

So much for being civilized in the midst of the storm.

"Your best bet is to walk to California and Davis," Tom says, "catch the cable car to Van Ness, then pick up whatever bus is heading west."

"That's not as easy as it sounds. I just busted up my ankle."

"Seriously? Hold on."

Some clicking and whirring in the background as he changes the song, and then his voice is so clear through the phone that he could be standing beside me: "A little Chris Isaak to get us in the mood this morning, folks. Quintessential California."

For as long as I've known Tom, there have been two of him — the public and the private — and I have felt by turns proud and grateful to be a part of his real and secret life, the one lived off the air. Although sometimes, it's true, the boundaries have blurred. Like when a colleague at work would ask how I'd enjoyed my meal the night before at such-and-such restaurant, though I was certain I hadn't told anyone I was going to eat there. Or they'd mention my problems with the roof, which had to be

25

replaced.

"I never reveal anything too personal," Tom used to say when I protested. Still, I felt exposed. Now, Chris Isaak is singing "San Francisco Days," and my husband is back on the line. I half-expect him to spill out the details of our divorce on the air, to list, item by item, all the ways we failed to make it work.

"Want me to come down and get you?"

"And do what? Carry me across town?"

"It'd be just like old times. Except, of course, it wouldn't. You never needed me to carry you anywhere."

"End on an up note," I say.

"Jules."

"Hmm?"

There's a pause on the other end, a sigh, while Chris Isaak croons, *I still love you, I still want you.* The message is one of surrender, of complete devotion; but the words never quite fit the moment. There's always something lost in translation between lyrics and real life.

"Jules, are you sure you want to go through with this?"

Tom always could speak my name in a way that drowned out all the background noise. It's that voice, bred for the radio. His father is a natural crooner, a successful businessman who sings Johnny Cash tunes at local fairs and corporate events in his spare time. He sang a couple at our wedding — "I Walk the Line" and, because he's not without a sense of humor, "Folsom Prison Blues." My husband doesn't sing, he talks, but it doesn't matter what he says. He could be reciting the alphabet or reading the phone book, and people would listen. Even me. Even when he's just saying my name. Especially when he's saying my name.

"Jules, are you still there?"

End on an up note. It's what my residency adviser, Dr. Bariloche, used to say on rounds. No matter how bad the news, exit the room with a smile, she would tell us. In the early days, I took her advice as gospel, but over the years I came to realize she'd been mistaken. Sometimes optimism is not called for. Sometimes, what is needed is an acknowledgment of just how bad things are, and how much worse they might get.

"I'm here."

3

Today, the people of California are voting. The ballot boxes are ready; the citizens are poised to act. What once seemed like an outlandish notion has become, almost overnight, a real possibility.

In retrospect, is it possible to pinpoint the moment when things began to change, the event that set all of this madness in motion? I remember certain headlines, vaguely anxious conversations with friends and colleagues, a growing sense of excitement coupled with an equal measure of unease. I remember twenty-somethings in leg warmers and bomber jackets, dressed as if they'd just discovered the ironic eighties, standing on street corners with their clipboards and ballpoint pens, shouting, "C'mon, people. Let's put it on the ballot!" Even their anthem was a throwback to a time when they were toddlers: the Scorpions, "Wind of Change," blasting from portable iPod speakers.

"Boy, that takes me back," Tom said one night several weeks ago. We were sitting at a sidewalk café in Noe Valley, having just come from the mediator's office, where a young woman in an exceedingly tight dress had assured us that our divorce need not be rancorous.

"Are you married?" we asked her in unison.

"No, but I know a great many married people — divorced ones, too," she answered brightly, as if that made her an expert. Anyway, her assurances were unnecessary. The end of my marriage to Tom has been sad and exhausting but never rancorous. We don't despise one another. Between us, there is no lack of mutual respect. Neither one of us did anything specifically to hurt the other. Instead, something happened to us, a wound from which our marriage was unable to recover.

That night at the café, "Wind of Change" blasted from the window of an apartment across the street. I heard the soaring notes and thought of Berlin in 1989 — the dramatic events on which the song was based. "I was glued to the TV, watching the wall come down," I said to Tom. "I wanted to be over there, in Eastern Europe, where the world was changing."

"It's changing here, now," my husband said. "These kids, they're on a mission."

True enough. "The student volunteers are the real heroes in this fight," our governor has said. You have to admire their righteous aggression, as if daring you to pass them by without signing up for the cause. And I did sign their petition, standing in front of the Safeway across the street from Ocean Beach, chatting amicably with the good-looking college kid in a SURF MAVERICKS T-shirt, who offered me his purple pen and proclaimed "Awesome" with such conviction, I longed to share his enthusiasm. It was so easy to scribble my name on the page, never bothering to read the fine print. After all, a signature seems so harmless until one considers the fact that, in California, the number of signatures required to put an initiative on the ballot is laughably small, a tiny drop in the bucket of our state's population. And once an initiative is passed, the state legislature is powerless to reverse it.

After the success of the petition, the campaign began in earnest. There were editorials in every newspaper, commercials on television and radio, town hall meetings across the state. The new president of the United States weighed in ("foolish"), along with the minority whip ("ludicrous"), not to mention every D-list celebrity who could book five minutes on cable news.

And yet, if there were some way to revisit these moments, to watch myself and others, eavesdrop on the conversations, I think I would be bewildered by our collective apathy. Until a few weeks ago, it all seemed like so much babble. Few of us believed that anything would come of it. After all, one becomes accustomed to a certain level of security, a certain level of, well, certainty. We understand the possibility of change up to a point. What we are not prepared for, what we lack the capacity to imagine, is a seismic shift. The wall going up or coming down, the decades-old dictatorship falling, the familiar boundaries disintegrating.

As a doctor, I regularly experience that moment when I sit across the desk from a patient and tell him or her the news — cancer, heart disease, diabetes, Parkinson's — that moment when, with one utterance of a phrase, I turn someone's world on end. After all these years, it's still the part of my job I dread the most. There is a look of confusion, a flicker in the eyes, as the diagnosis takes shape in the patient's mind. Everything must be reevaluated according to this new knowledge, which the patient will carry around like a thorn in the side, a stone in the shoe, until the day he dies. The seismic shift writ small, in the bedrock of an individual life. No one is ever quite prepared for it.

One morning three months ago, I was standing at the bedside of Mr. Luongo, a quiet man known throughout the ward for his habit of addressing everyone, even the youngest orderlies and volunteers, as "ma'am" or "sir." My residents were gathered around me, trying to get to the bottom of Mr. Luongo's recent seizures, when he grabbed the remote control and turned up the volume on the television mounted on the wall. "Call the cartographers," a familiar voice said. "We will have to draw a new map." I looked up at the screen. There was the governor standing on the steps of the capitol in a sharp gray suit, his signature hair holding its own against the wind. It was a rather melodramatic thing to say, but he is that kind of politician. Before he was the governor, he'd been the mayor of San Francisco. Most had assumed he'd soon be making a bid for the White House, that each office he held in California was only a stepping stone to something bigger. Which was why almost everyone was stunned when he

threw his hat into the ring with the secessionists.

"There comes a time when 'states' rights'
must be more than a catchphrase," he
continued. "That time has come for California. It is our right and our destiny — our
responsibility — to become a sovereign nation."

"Fucking idiot," Mr. Luongo spat.

"It's about time." Debbie, a first-year
resident in podiatry, was gazing up at the
television with a look of undisguised admiration. She'd met the governor once at a
fund-raising event in Berkeley. He'd
touched her back while moving through the
crowded room, his hand lingering a moment
longer than necessary.

"What happens to you — to everyone at
the VA — if this goes through?" asked Rajiv.
I wanted to tell him not to worry, that
everything would be fine. Instead, I
shrugged. "I have no idea." It occurred to
me what a strange limbo we would be left
in, should the initiative succeed.

In the days that followed, the governor's
performance was played ad infinitum on the
national and local news, parsed by the
pundits, analyzed by the lawyers, and much
maligned by other politicians, even those of
his own party. He was called a traitor, a

hero, a fool. One powerful southern senator said, "Is it really surprising, coming from that immoral, elitist hotbed of wacko liberalism called California?"

Many Californians were enraged, but a great many were inspired. Before his announcement of support, the secessionists had been considered a fringe faction, percolating their extreme ideas on the sidelines for decades, not to be taken seriously. The governor's speech, combined with a perfect storm out of Washington, D.C. — a tide of radical conservatives elected to Congress, an impending attack on Iran, a legislative ban on stem-cell research, a dismantling of basic gun control legislation, a federal rollback on offshore drilling regulations, a constitutional amendment that struck down gay marriage — changed all that. To top it off, California was on the verge of bankruptcy.

"We sent $315 billion to Washington last year," the governor wrote, in an open letter that was published in every major newspaper in the state. "We received $245 billion in services. That's $70 billion that we paid to build roads in Juneau and fighter planes in Huntsville, while we're forced to fire teachers, close schools and nursing homes, release violent offenders from our prisons, and gut social services. And let's not forget Crystal Springs."

Crystal Springs Reservoir, which lies on top of the San Andreas Fault twenty miles south of San Francisco, had been in need of seismic repairs for decades. Last summer, during a 4.2 magnitude earthquake, the dam finally collapsed, as geologists had long warned it would, putting an elementary school in the small, wealthy town of Hillsborough underwater. Forty-seven children who were attending summer school that day drowned, along with three teachers. Their photographs were all over the news for months, as were the pictures of two dozen runners, hikers, and mothers with strollers whose bodies had been washed off the adjoining Sawyer Camp Trail when the dam broke. The Crystal Springs repair was part of a planned $4.5 billion overhaul of the Hetch Hetchy Aqueduct system, largely funded by the state, but the project had been put on hold due to budget cuts.

"We had the money to fix that dam," the governor wrote. "But we sent it to Washington instead."

If the governor was polarizing, he was also charismatic. By the following morning, vendors were already hawking secession merchandise in Union Square. T-shirts and

bumper stickers and key chains and under-
pants declared, CALIFORNIA IS <u>MY</u> COUN-
TRY.

I bought one of each. Not that I really
wanted California to secede. Not that I
thought it could ever really happen. But I
did appreciate the historical significance of
the moment.

Today is the day, then: democracy in action. It's up to the voters to decide whether
we will stay or go. Whether we will protect
the union or destroy it. In the past three
months, Roger Harte, a tech billionaire
from Palo Alto, has poured tens of millions
of dollars into the campaign for secession.
The opposition was slow to organize, even
slower to pony up funds for a fight they
didn't believe they could lose. Just as they
began their anemic counterattack, Congress
allocated $12 billion to erect a gigantic
electric fence along the entire border between Mexico and California.

"When they sealed the border, they sealed
our fate," the governor proclaimed, standing before an energized audience of thousands, wearing a tie striped red, white, and
green, the colors of the Mexican flag. At a
rally in the area known as Tehrangeles in
L.A., he posed this question to the crowd of
Iranian Americans: "When the drones fly

over your relatives' homes in Tehran, do you want them dropping bombs bought by *your* taxes?"

Meanwhile, behind the scenes, certain members of the state legislature were busy drafting a constitution, and it was rumored that the governor of the world's eighth-largest economy was meeting with prime ministers and presidents. Less than a decade earlier, another governor, Arnold Schwarzenegger, had sat down with then prime minister Tony Blair at the Port of Long Beach and signed an accord between California and Great Britain on global warming.

"I call California a nation-state because of the diversity of our people, the power of our economy, and the reach of our dream," Schwarzenegger had said in his second inaugural address. "The commerce and trade of the nations of the earth pass through our ports. The world knows our name. We are a good and global commonwealth."

When the new governor came out in favor of secession, rumor had it that Schwarzenegger called to offer his support. As it turned out, belief in California's independence crossed political boundaries, created whole new allegiances, and dissolved old alliances that had once seemed set in stone.

Other lawmakers were getting nervous. "The last time states attempted to secede," a leading Democrat in the California senate warned in a news conference, "the result was a full-blown civil war."

"This is a different time, and we are a different country," the governor replied. He eschewed the traditional press conference and instead posted his reply on Twitter, with eighty-four characters to spare. He refrained from mentioning the obvious: certain states were salivating at the thought of a California secession, dreaming of a nation unfettered by our left-leaning electoral votes. Meanwhile, scholars and politicians squabbled over whether or not states have a constitutional right to secession, or merely a right to revolution.

Years before, in the rural Mississippi church that swallowed up the Sunday mornings of my childhood, the thickly toupeed and eternally sweaty pastor had been fond of delivering sermons on hedonism, in which "the dark cavern of Hollywood" and "that modern-day den of iniquity they call San Francisco" were equated with Sodom and Gomorrah. "It would do us no harm," Brother Ray once said, "if the whole godless state slid right into the Pacific."

I used to imagine the state cutting loose like a glacier, floating off into the ocean: a gargantuan party barge carrying the sinners to their doom or, possibly, their salvation. Brother Ray's sermons, which surely were intended to instill in us a reverence for our roots, an allegiance to our region above all others, and a fear of evil urban centers, had the opposite effect on me. His passionate warnings planted the seeds of my desire to head west.

"Don't leave," my sister pleaded eighteen years ago, on the last day of my last summer in Mississippi. She was twelve then, standing in the doorway of my bedroom, watching me dismantle it piece by piece. My bookshelves were bare, my closet empty. A studio apartment was waiting for me in San Francisco. When my admission letter to medical school had arrived six months before, with a promise of financial aid, I'd been convinced that my life was finally beginning.

"Christmas is just around the corner," I assured her.

"You won't come home for Christmas."

"Of course I will."

"Where will you get the money?" She flopped onto my bed, all arms and legs and chipped pink nail polish. Her legs were already longer than mine, stick thin and covered with soft light brown hair. Her height had always been a source of mystery, a secret clue to her paternity, one I could never quite decode. The only thing our mother would tell us about Heather's father was that he was a regular guy, a very decent person. "Don't worry, he's not doing time at Whitfield," she would say. "Tall and blond. Like the cute one in *The Dukes of Hazzard*."

Heather flipped through the folded clothes in the suitcase, messing up the order I had so carefully imposed on my meager belongings. "Can I have this?" she asked, pulling my favorite shirt from the bottom of the pile — a chambray button-down that had belonged to my own father, who died when I was five. He'd been sitting in the shade of an oak tree outside the bank where he worked, enjoying his pimento cheese sandwich, when a large limb fell from the tree. "It was instant," I'd been told at the time. "He didn't suffer." Only when I was older did I begin to doubt that his death was painless. The chambray shirt had been worn and washed so many times it felt as soft as an old sheet. I didn't want to give it to her, but I understood that this was a test. She was making a sacrifice, and she wanted me to make one, too.

"Yes," I said, as she unfolded the shirt and tied it around her waist. I felt so guilty for leaving, I'd have given her anything. My undergrad work had been at Mississippi State, only three hours from Laurel. Every other weekend for four years, I hitched a ride home with a girl from my dorm. I didn't always want to go, but each time I walked through the door of the house where I grew up, I was reminded once again how much my sister needed me: the piles of dirty laundry, the empty cupboards, the way Heather rushed into my arms, talking a mile a minute, while our mother remained behind the closed door of her bedroom, sleeping off the exhaustion of two full-time jobs and her lingering grief. I'd spent every holiday and summer in Laurel, out of obligation as much as lack of money, so that it felt, in many ways, as if I'd never left home. Now I was leaving for good.

"You wouldn't like San Francisco," I told Heather. "It's freezing in the summer, and you can't get fried catfish or proper hush puppies. Anyway, what would Mom do without you?"

"What will *I* do without *you?*"

4

12:52 p.m.

"You moved the furniture," he says. "New bookcases?"

Dennis Drummond. I'd recognize that voice anywhere.

"Ikea." I try to match his casual tone, aware that every word I say from here on out will have consequences.

The cellphone crackles, and I move to get a better signal.

"I looked and looked, but I can't find that book I gave you," he says.

"The Notebooks of Malte Laurids Brigge."

"You remember." He sounds pleased. "Do you still have it?"

"Of course."

I don't tell him that I came across the book not that long ago, when I was going through the shelves at home, deciding what to keep, what to give away. It was late at night, I was alone. I hadn't seen Dennis

Drummond in almost a year. It seemed, at last, he had forgotten me. I no longer looked over my shoulder at the hospital. I no longer stiffened when the phone rang.

"Can you believe it's been eighteen years since we met?"

"No," I say honestly. "I can't."

"Tell me what you remember," he urges. "From that day."

I take a deep breath. He wants to hear a story. So be it. This is nothing new. All those times we talked, he was always asking, in some form or another, for a story. More often than not, I would comply. Something about him made it easy to open up. By the time I realized that he was storing everything, filing it away in memory, I had already given him too many keys to my life.

"It was at Green Apple Books, on Clement Street," I say. "We were in the new fiction aisle, and we reached for the same book at the same time. There was only one copy."

"You wouldn't let go of the book." He's right about that. His fingers had lingered on the spine. So had mine. "What happened next?" he insists.

"I said you could have the book, but only if you took me out for dinner."

"I noticed your accent. I loved your accent, but you've lost it."

43

"I was fresh out of Mississippi. I haven't lived there in a long time."

He seems calm. That's good. I keep talking. Even when Heather sits up in bed, her face twisted in pain, I keep telling the story. "You said you'd do more than take me to dinner. You'd also buy me another book. We went upstairs, where they keep all the obscure paperbacks. You pulled out *The Notebooks of Malte Laurids Brigge.* You told me it was Rilke's only novel."

I think for a moment and am surprised to see it so clearly: Dennis, standing in the aisle, holding the book, his hair already slightly gray, even though he couldn't have been much older than I was. "When I asked what it was about, you said, 'Time and death.' "

"Time and death," Dennis repeats. "Funny, I don't remember that."

There is such tenderness in his voice, and yet I know that Eleanor is in the room with him, bruised and bloody. Less than an hour ago, he dragged her across the parking lot by her long, dark braid. Before that, he beat her. And that is not all — I know that Dennis also has Betty and Rajiv. I do not know how far he is willing to go.

Over dinner that night eighteen years ago, I learned that Dennis was from Woodside, a

44

small town thirty miles south of San Francisco favored by the equestrian set and wealthy Silicon Valley types. His father worked in tech; his mother was a near recluse who left the house only to be with her horses. Dennis had a business degree from Stanford, where he'd met his girlfriend, with whom he had recently broken up.

I knew hardly anyone in San Francisco. He was good-looking and funny. He told me he worked for his dad's start-up.

"What's a start-up?" I had asked.

I liked the fact that he wasn't in med school, the fact that we didn't know any of the same people. His recent breakup wasn't a red flag — far from it. In a way, it made him seem safe. I didn't want a boyfriend; I was busy.

"We had burritos at La Cumbre," I continue.

"Do you remember what happened after that?"

"We went back to your apartment in the Duboce Triangle."

"It was an amazing night."

How far to take this? What to say? I remember how he removed my socks so gently, one by one, before we made love on his narrow bed. I remember how he lifted

45

my shirt and kissed my breasts. I remember thinking that it was nice to be close to someone, in this strange city where I'd been feeling achingly alone. I remember that his apartment smelled like oranges. I remember the green pillowcases on his bed, and a white ceramic doorstop in the shape of a sheep's head. When I woke up in the morning, he was lying on his side, staring at me. Had I noticed, even then, that there was something vaguely frightening in his intensity? I can't remember.

Over the next few days, we talked on the phone a couple of times. He asked me out again, but I was swamped with med school. The following week, he called to say that he and the girlfriend had decided to make another go of it. We parted on friendly terms.

Four years later, when I was in my first year of residency at UCSF, on rotation at the VA hospital, I stepped into an examination room to see an attractive man sitting on the table, clad in a paper gown. His hair was longer, unkempt, and he had a beard. If it weren't for the name printed on the chart, I might have had a hard time believing it was Dennis.

"Whoa," he said.

I lowered the clipboard, stunned. "What

are you doing at the VA?"

"Didn't I tell you? I was National Guard."

I shook my head. "No, you didn't mention it. What about Woodside, Stanford, the silver spoon, and the start-up?"

"All true," he said. "But before the start-up, when I got out of Stanford with a business degree I never wanted in the first place, I figured the National Guard would be a safe form of rebellion."

It felt weird, standing there in front of him with my clipboard. He had every right to be here, of course. And yet, considering our personal history, it felt like an invasion of my professional space. "Was it?" I asked impulsively. "Safe, I mean?"

"Not so much. I eventually ended up in Desert Storm. It was supposed to be quick in, quick out, overnight victory. I wasn't prepared for the charred bodies lined up beside the road leading out of Kuwait City."

"I can't believe you didn't tell me."

"If I remember correctly, we didn't waste a lot of time on small talk." He looked me up and down. "The white coat looks good on you, Julie."

"Short white coat," I said. "I'm a resident." My beeper started vibrating on my hip. "Sorry. I wish I had time to catch up, but that's my attending physician. What

47

brings you in?"

He pointed to his heart. "It hurts," he said, "now that I've seen you in your short white coat."

"Really," I said.

"Okay, it's not my heart. Just a lowly pain in the gut."

I asked him the requisite questions, jotted things down on the chart, feeling utterly confused but not unhappy to see him. It was like finding an old ticket from a great concert in the pocket of a coat I hadn't worn in years.

"Lay back," I said finally. He did. I pressed my fingers to his abdomen. "Does this hurt?"

"No."

"This?"

He grimaced. "Yes."

I was a toucher then, and I still am today. I know doctors who prescribe a slew of tests the moment a patient walks through the door, but I prefer to listen first and use my hands.

Dennis squinted into the light and said, "This is a little weird."

"If I remember correctly, you have a thing for beer."

"Why, you want to go grab one?"

"How often do you drink?"

"Breakfast, lunch, and dinner."

"Seriously," I insisted.

His face reddened. "Yep."

"Headaches?"

He nodded.

"Do you feel sluggish in the morning after drinking beer the night before?"

"Check."

"Sit up, please."

I listened to his heart, felt his lymph nodes, unsettled by our unexpected intimacy. By then, I was with Tom; touching an old lover, even in this context, felt vaguely inappropriate.

"So," he said. "What's wrong with me, Doc?"

"It's possible that you've developed a gluten allergy. Go off the beer and bread for two weeks. No pasta, crackers, nothing with wheat."

"I'm allergic to wheat?" He sounded disappointed.

"Maybe, maybe not, but there's no harm in ruling it out."

He reached for his jeans. "Now that I've thoroughly embarrassed myself with my rather pedestrian illness, can I get dressed?"

I couldn't help smiling. "After I shut the door, you can do whatever you want." I took a step toward the door.

"Can I take you out to dinner?" he asked.

"Thanks, but I have a boyfriend."

"Bummer."

For a few moments we just looked at each other. Finally, I reached awkwardly to shake his hand. "It was good seeing you."

"You too, Julie." He didn't shake my hand so much as hold it. "See you around?"

"You know where I work."

Two weeks later, I ran into him in the cafeteria.

"You were right about that allergy," he told me. He had shaved his beard, and his face looked lean and tan. "I switched from beer and bread to wine and tequila, and now I'm fine."

"Then why are you here?"

"One of the counselors here runs a support group for veterans of the Gulf War. Turns out, a bunch of us are more fucked up than you'd expect."

"You don't seem fucked up."

"We're all fucked up. It's an anger-management group. Plus, I was kind of hoping to see you. How serious did you say that boyfriend of yours is?"

"Pretty serious," I answered, smiling.

After that, I'd sometimes see Dennis around, and we'd have coffee in the cafeteria. He always had a lot of questions, and I had no reason not to answer them. I trusted him, and over time, I came to consider him a friend. That year, Tom and I got married. A couple of years after that, I finished my residency and took a long-term position at the VA. Eventually Dennis got married and had a baby girl. His marriage didn't last. When I saw him, I never knew what to expect. If things were going well, he'd be on top of the world, in an ebullient mood, looking trim and handsome. But if things weren't working out, which seemed more often the case, he'd be gloomy and bloated, dressed sloppily. He had jobs and lost them, he fought with his parents, he wrangled with his ex over custody of their daughter. Every few months, he'd call me, and we'd have coffee, and I'd hear about his latest troubles and, occasionally, triumphs: a new relationship, a better job, a temporary truce with his parents. "What about you?" he'd say, and I'd look into his blue eyes, feel that slender thread still connecting us, and fall into the same old pattern of talking more than I should.

He'd listen intently, nod his head in all the right places, and at the end of our conversation I'd always feel a bit better. But then, invariably, everything would spiral out of control again. It was sad to see him losing hold. I wondered if these tendencies had been there all along; had time and circumstance simply intensified the person he'd already been? Or was it more complicated? Had the cumulative trauma of military service, divorce, unemployment, alcoholism, and the rest changed him at some fundamental level? Could this happen to anyone?

It wasn't until two years ago that Dennis really started getting weird. He'd completely lost custody of his daughter, and he seemed desperate for someone to talk to. He'd argued with the counselor who ran the PTSD group. When I suggested counseling with another colleague of mine, he became enraged. He'd run through a string of meds and decided none of them was right. I felt for him. At the VA, prescriptions are limited by government contracts. Off-label prescriptions aren't uncommon, simply because we have fewer choices than private hospitals. A patient who needs Zoloft might get Paxil instead; someone whose symptoms call for Lamictal might end up on Topamax. Off-label uses are particularly widespread among the psychotropic drugs, whose boundaries seem more fluid. A psychiatrist might end up prescribing a drug to treat one or more symptoms, without treating the root cause.

Eventually, Dennis became more demanding. Coffee once a month suddenly wasn't enough. He would insist that I meet him for lunch or help him fill out a job application. He started coming to the VA with made-up ailments, always insisting he see me. Last year, I worked out an arrangement with the staff to pass him on to someone else. Often, it was Rajiv. Dennis started calling me at home then, and hanging up. Finally, Tom and I had our phone number changed. Somehow, Dennis got hold of the new one. "I just want to talk to you," he'd say on the voice mail, over and over again.

One night, when Tom and I were at home watching a movie, a car started honking in front of the house. I recognized the old burgundy Mercedes with the dented hood.

"I'll take care of it," Tom told me. Before I could stop him, he was out the door.

Dennis's desperate voice drifted up from the street. "Just five minutes," I heard him tell Tom. "I just have to talk to her."

I turned off the light and watched through a slit in the curtain as Tom tried to calm him down. Tom was seven or eight inches taller than Dennis, a solid wall of strength. They talked quietly for a while, and I could no longer hear what they were saying.

Finally, Dennis got in his car and drove away. Tom came back inside, frowning.

"What did you say to him?"

"I reasoned with him. I told him that he can't be showing up at our house. I told him that you're very busy, and that his behavior is scaring you. He talked about his ex-wife, and then he talked about his daughter. I told him I was sorry that he's going through a difficult time."

"That's it?"

Tom pulled me close. "I also told him that if he ever comes back, I'm going to beat the shit out of him."

I stood back and looked up at Tom. "You said that?"

Tom tends to speak softly, perhaps to counteract his size. I'd never seen him threaten anyone before. But it seemed to have worked.

After that, to my enormous relief, Dennis simply disappeared. He stopped calling. He stopped coming by the hospital; he stopped sending anonymous letters in the mail.

By the time I found the Rilke book on my shelf, I no longer felt afraid to be alone in my house at night. Dennis had surely found a new girlfriend, a new job, a new person on whom to unload his burdens.

I sat down in the living room, turned on

the lamp, and began to read. I read the book cover to cover in one sitting. When I closed it, I remembered that there had, after all, been a reason I was drawn to Dennis Drummond: he had an interesting mind.

5

6:35 a.m.

All cities smell in summer.

On the opening page of Rilke's novel, a young writer named Malte watches a pregnant woman "pushing herself with difficulty along a high warm wall." He is comforted by the fact that the hospital is just beyond the wall, where the woman will be received, her baby delivered. And not far from that hospital is another one, Val-de-Grâce Hôpital Militaire. Everywhere, hospitals where the suffering can be saved. But the smell is terrible, Malte thinks, a smell of "iodoform, the grease of pommes-frites, fear."

Of all the beautiful lines in the book, one line stuck with me: "All cities smell in summer."

Today, the line comes to me again. There is a different smell in the air — something burning. Standing beside my vandalized Jeep, I scan the sky. In the distance, the black plume rises. I take a mental inventory of the spot, trying to map it in my mind, but I can't quite figure out where the smoke is coming from. My compass has always been off. I know every path in the human body, the organs and skeletal muscles, the passages that carry blood from one place to another, all that intricate geography as familiar to me as my own face in the mirror. When I was in medical school, I used to dream the human body in startling detail, much in the way one dreams the streets of a hometown one has left behind. But when it comes to the actual streets of my city, I often draw a mental blank.

I open the door to the Jeep and reach across the seats, careful to avoid the shattered glass. From the glove compartment, I take a laminated map of San Francisco, the surface mottled with coffee stains. The map is rendered in bright oranges and teals, sprinkled with X's placed there by Tom over the years. Many of the street names are obscured by his tiny, strangely neat handwriting, an ongoing diary of our life together in the city: *Luna Park, where you met my parents, 11/12/1999,* written near Valencia and Eighteenth, *bonfire, 7/5/2004,* penned across Ocean Beach. The last entry, *Graham Parker at the Great American Music Hall,* next to an X at Polk and O'Farrell, was dated March 5, four years ago. Is that when we stopped going to concerts together? Or is it simply when he stopped writing them down?

I reach under the driver's seat and pull out the emergency kit. I tear open the packet of Tylenol and swallow the pills. I have no water, and they scratch going down; the bitter taste lingers on my tongue. I remove the small red Bakelite, circa 1964, that I co-opted years ago from Tom's collection of vintage radios. Every couple of months, the local news stations will run a segment on earthquake preparedness, and they're always reminding residents to have a battery-operated radio handy.

Flicking the switch sends out a burst of static, and I adjust the dials until the tail end of Chris Isaak's song comes through . . . *It's you I'm dreaming of.*

I slide the map and the radio into my bag. The smoke in the distance seems to be growing higher, darker, every minute. The Marina, perhaps. I think of 1989, the Loma Prieta earthquake, all those houses fallen in upon themselves. It was before I arrived here, but I've heard that the city, then, smelled like a city on fire.

6

"Tomorrow's the big day for you, isn't it?" Dennis's question is muffled by cellphone static.

"I'm trying not to think about it."

"I remember when I turned forty," he says. "I was expecting some huge epiphany, but it turned out to be just an ordinary day."

"That's what I was hoping for."

All the echoes one hears by the age of forty. When you're young, everything seems new. In your mid-twenties, it begins to dawn on you that the world is full of surprise repetitions: a face recalls some other face, a novel some other novel, a song an entire summer or an old relationship. By your late thirties, it seems the world is made of these echoes. A patient in his late eighties once told me that old age is like living inside a déjà vu.

"Your sister's giving you quite the birthday present." Dennis laughs.

"How did you know?"

"There's a picture in the top drawer of your desk of a woman who looks a lot like you. Taller, brown hair, different nose, but she's definitely related. It has to be the sister you used to talk about. There's a date on the back. It was taken two months ago out at Sutro Baths, and she's very pregnant." There's a pause. "I saw the two of you going into the hotel together last week."

I feel a spike of panic. How long has he been watching me?

"She's in there with you now, isn't she?"

I glance over at Heather. She is lying with her eyes closed, the blanket draped over her knees, waiting. Greg Watts has left to find help. It's just the two of us now.

"Yes," I say.

"I heard her in there, you know, when I was with Eleanor. She was trying to be quiet, but I heard."

"Why Betty?" I ask quietly. "She's taken care of you a number of times. You always got along."

"An antidote to Eleanor," Dennis deadpans.

"And Rajiv?"

"Just be grateful I didn't grab your sister, too. I wanted to. I could have. You know — for what she did to you. But I didn't,

60

because I knew you'd be mad."

How much did I tell him? I can't remember. That time was so painful, and Tom became so distant. One thing I can say for Dennis: he was always there.

"You shot at me," I say, still not able to get my mind around it.

"I'm sitting here with my Sig and my MP5. If I wanted to hurt you, I would have."

"I have to set the phone down," I say.

"Leave it where I can hear you."

As I lift the blanket to examine Heather, I try to shut out the thought of Dennis at the other end of the line, armed and angry. "You're seven centimeters," I say.

"What does that mean?"

"It means I'm right on time." I palpate her abdomen. "The baby's ready — the head is right where it should be."

I wish I had a fetoscope to check the baby's heartbeat. I wish I had clean blankets, sterile instruments, good light, a trusted nurse. I wish I had something to give her for pain. All my training, everything medicine has to offer, and my sister will end up having her baby in a dark room in a ramshackle VA hotel.

"I'm glad you're here," Heather says. After three tours in Iraq and Afghanistan, she has about her a commanding sense of calm.

I think of Rilke's pregnant woman, making her way along the wall. What is it about a woman in labor that softens the hardest hearts? Maybe it has something to do with the idea that whoever she might be, and whatever she might have done in the past, she's now bringing into the world something new and entirely innocent. At that moment, all is forgiven; she has the chance to begin again.

7

Beyond the windows of the VA hospital cafeteria is a hill that slopes steeply down to the sea. And half a mile across the ocean the Marin Headlands rise up, brown hills dotted with white buildings. Rugged and wild, this is where the Pacific Ocean meets the San Francisco Bay. Without fail, standing in line each morning for my coffee, I am stunned by the beauty of it all. How strange to find the world's greatest view hidden behind a dirty window in a run-down VA cafeteria.

From the trailhead behind the hospital, you can see the foghorn atop the water like a maritime wedding cake. On foggy days, with its relentless moaning and the competing sounds of the ships calling to each other in their low, vibrating tones, it sounds gloomily apocalyptic, as if a herd of prehistoric beasts has descended upon the city from across the ocean. The day Heather returned was such a day, blue and windless. It was just past seven on a Wednesday morning in October, and I was following my usual routine — grabbing a cup of coffee in the cafeteria before my shift, ticking off the day's schedule in my mind.

She sat alone in a booth up against the wall, her back to the door. She could have been anyone — someone's girlfriend, someone's wife, a young veteran just home from the war. It wasn't until she turned her head to look out the window and I saw her in profile that I knew. I stopped in my tracks, caught my breath.

I had not laid eyes on her in more than four years, had not even spoken with her in that time. While I'd always assumed our reunion would be on neutral ground, Heather had deliberately chosen my space, with its constant low murmur of voices and the hum of machines, the aquamarine walls bearing cheaply framed prints of breaching whales, the aqua-and-pink booths with their aqua-and-pink tables, and the blue, everywhere blue, especially when you glanced out the long rows of windows, beyond the cheerful shabbiness of the cafeteria, to the rough Pacific. What did that mean? Or was I misreading the gesture? After all, she was the veteran here; I was only an employee.

She stared out the window and then continued drinking her coffee. A newspaper lay open on the table in front of her, but she didn't appear to be reading.

I had often wondered what I would say when we saw each other again. Each time I found myself thinking about our reunion, I would put it out of my mind. Running helped. So did movies. Mostly, there was work, and it filled my days. When I wasn't at the hospital, there were medical journals to read, lectures to give, seminars to attend, interns' phone calls to return.

I held my breath, scanning Heather for signs of injury.

She turned suddenly, as if reacting to a loud noise or to the sound of her name — although there was no noise, and I had not said a word. Later, I realized how difficult that moment must have been for her, how she had taken the excruciatingly awkward first step after so long a silence. There's a Nathaniel Hawthorne story I read in college in which a man walks out of his house one day, planning only a brief absence, but the more time passes the more impossible a reunion seems — so that decades go by before he finally returns home to his wife. I understand now how families become estranged, not by design but by embarrassment. You come to a point when so much time has passed that it seems impossible to make the first move.

She'd been twenty-five years old the last time I saw her, the day she turned our lives on end. Now she was twenty-nine. Her hair, which she'd worn long and bleached blond since high school, was cropped to her shoulders and had reverted to her natural brown. She wore almost no makeup, and her face was fuller, healthier-looking, the sharp cheekbones gone soft. She used to pride herself on her pallor, avoiding the sun with stubborn dedication, but now her complexion was sun-kissed, a spate of freckles splashed across her nose. I hadn't seen her with freckles since she was a child. She had always been beautiful; now that she'd stopped trying so hard, she was even more so.

"Heather?"

She smiled, activating tiny lines around her eyes. "Hi." Even her voice was in a lower key — the voice of a woman, not a girl. "Have a seat," she said.

"I can't," I said instinctively, even though my shift didn't start for another hour.

"Why not?"

Everything about the way she spoke to me, what she said, was so nonchalant, as if

66

the years of silence, and the event that had preceded them, had never happened.

Reluctantly, I slid into the booth across from her. "You look good," I said. "I like the bangs."

She ran a hand self-consciously over her hair. "Thanks. It's nice to be out of fatigues."

"It was four years ago that you enlisted. Are you free and clear?"

"Ha. Is anyone ever?" She laid her hands on the table in front of her — an old habit, acquired when her high school French teacher told her that the French always keep their hands in sight during meals. In those days, she'd dreamed of living in Paris. "I'm not reenlisting, but they have a way of dragging you back in. I had a platoon sergeant who was being processed for retirement when he got called back, thanks to Stop Loss."

Heather flicked her coffee cup with a fingernail. "You're staring."

"Sorry." I glanced away. It came as such a relief to simply look at her. Her face was more serious than before, her dimples already etched into permanent lines. She seemed young for that, but then, I'd seen soldiers in their twenties whose hair had turned white.

She sipped her coffee and frowned. "Ugh."

"Rule number one: never get your coffee from the cafeteria. There's a stand around the corner. It's just Starbucks, but it's fresh."

"Just Starbucks," she said, shaking her head. "Out in the desert, I'd have given my left arm for a Starbucks."

She looked down at her coffee, twirled the paper cup around. "It's good to see you, Julie."

I didn't respond. I thought of Ethan. I wasn't sure I was ready for her to walk back into my life.

A gardener moved slowly past the window, head down, the loud buzz of his weed trimmer cutting through the silence. The sound faded as he crossed the lawn, whacking away at the wildflowers. Bits of yellow and pink went flying. The cafeteria door was open, and a rich scent of grass wafted in, and something else — honeysuckle.

"Mmmm," Heather said, turning her head. "Smells like Mississippi."

I couldn't help smiling. "Remember Buddy? I wonder what ever happened to him."

She turned away from the window, angling the left side of her face toward me. "Sorry?"

"You're favoring your left ear," I said, and it dawned on me that she'd been doing it all along.

She frowned. "IED. My right ear is shot. The doctor called it sensorineural hearing loss."

"Didn't they give you a hearing aid?" I asked.

"Yes, but I hate it."

"Are you okay otherwise?"

"Ten fingers, ten toes," she said. "I'm okay. There are little things, of course. I've started getting headaches." She tapped the newspaper in front of her. "I have to read the same paragraph over and over. I can't remember the last time I made it through a novel."

I thought of her as a child, all those Nancy Drew mysteries and Judy Blume books and Chronicles of Narnia volumes stacked on the floor beside her night table, how she'd read them into the wee hours, so that I'd have to drag her out of bed in the morning and practically dress her for school myself.

"Besides the headaches," she continued, "I can't always control my temper. I get really mad about the dumbest things. The last VA doc I saw said the temper doesn't have anything to do with the explosion, that it's typical PTSD, but I'm not sure."

"If I were deaf in one ear, I'd be pissed, too," I said.

Heather grinned. "I see you haven't lost your winning bedside manner."

I didn't tell her that I see ravages of PTSD every day: drug addiction, alcoholism, domestic violence, depression. I didn't tell her about the kid who ended up in the ER every couple of months for repeated suicide attempts. The last one succeeded.

"What really gets me is that I can't remember the punch lines to my favorite jokes," she said. "I'll start telling one, and I'll get halfway through it before I realize I don't know how it ends." Jokes had always been Heather's way of saying hello, saying goodbye, flirting, even apologizing. As a kid, she would spend hours at the kitchen table, scribbling jokes in a bright red notebook.

"Anyway, here I sit, right? All in one piece. With a sexy war wound to boot." She brushed aside her bangs, and I repressed a gasp. There was a three-inch scar just above her left eyebrow.

"Jesus, who did that?" Someone had botched the stitching, leaving a jagged, raised line along her forehead.

"It wasn't the medic's fault. Our convoy was on patrol near the COB, driving down this rural road. It was deserted, or so we thought — nothing to see for miles around. It feels like something's crawling around in my helmet, so stupidly, I take it off, just for a second, and this kid, couldn't have been more than ten, eleven years old, steps out from behind a tree, grinning. He's covered in dust, because everything and everybody there is covered in dust, but even so you can tell he's a beautiful kid, big brown eyes, wavy hair, like he just stepped out of one of those old Benetton catalogs. He reaches into his pocket and lobs this big, sharp rock at me. It splits my skin right open. I'm bleeding like crazy, and then these older kids — fourteen, fifteen years old — start coming out of nowhere, only they don't have rocks, they have guns. Our guys return fire, the kids start dropping like flies, and the driver just floors it. In the chaos we couldn't find the medical kit, so somebody closed the wound up with superglue as we were barreling down the road. By the time I got to the field hospital, there wasn't much they could do, aesthetically speaking."

"I can't imagine what you've been through." The words were inadequate. I'd known it all along of course, in the abstract. But being with her, hearing her stories, seeing the scars, made it real.

"They were just kids," Heather said, shuddering. "Anyway, you were asking me about something?"

"Buddy," I said, feeling foolish. I'd confronted this feeling many times with my patients. The conversation would turn to serious matters, something terrible that had happened to them in the war; there would be a window of vulnerability, of honesty — and then it was as if a switch would flip, and we were supposed to go back to discussing mundane things. As a physician, I should have been able to make the transition, but in all my years of practicing medicine, I'd never gotten used to it.

"From Laurel," I added. "The kid who used to cut our grass for free because he had a crush on you."

She nodded, seemingly happy to change the subject. "I heard Buddy moved to Birmingham. He married a girl from New Jersey, and they own a Krystal franchise."

She gathered the sections of her paper into a neat pile and placed it carefully in the center of the table. Then she wiped the table with a napkin, which she folded and tucked into her coffee cup. "Do you have time to go for a walk?"

I glanced at my watch; it was still forty-five minutes before morning rounds. I'd been coming in early for months, avoiding the moment when Tom walked in the door from his night shift at the radio station. I didn't quite know how to face him anymore in the early hours, those hours that had once been so intimate. I used to stay in bed longer than I should, just to feel him curl up beside me, his skin layered with the smells of the station, his hair out of whack, his breath smelling of chocolate milk.

As I followed Heather out of the cafeteria, I wondered if she could sense how wary I was. Waiting to hear her latest angle, her newest troubles. Waiting to suss out the truth from the fiction. Ever since I'd left Mississippi, eighteen years before, Heather had never shown up on my doorstep without needing something. Each time she arrived, there were always lies, and something bad happened. I'd always managed to put it behind me, until the last time, with Ethan, her one mistake that was too big to forgive.

8

6:52 a.m.

I hobble up to the intersection of Front and California, my ankle throbbing. The brisk, briny smell of the bay mingles with the scent of chestnuts from a stall. A small crowd has already gathered at the cable car turn-around, in the shadow of the towering office building at 101 California. The building, with its distinctive pleated façade, has a tragic history: in 1993, a businessman named Gian Luigi Ferri entered the offices of the law firm Pettit & Martin and began firing with two handguns and a pistol. He roamed several floors, killing eight people, before shooting himself. In the aftermath, the California legislature passed some of the most stringent gun laws in the country. Later, Stephen Sposato, whose wife, Jody, died in the attack, would carry their infant daughter in a backpack while testifying before Congress. The man with the motherless baby in the backpack helped Barbara Boxer push the Federal Assault Weapons Ban through Congress. The expiration of the ban in 2004 is in the news every time there's a mass shooting, one more piece of emotionally charged evidence the secessionists use to point out the fundamental differences between California and the rest of the country.

Now another young man with a backpack stands at the end of the line, intently reading a worn copy of *Home-Grown Medicine: A Marijuana Primer.* There's a reason San Francisco has a reputation; half of what people say about this city happens to be true.

The backpack moves, a tiny hand pops out, and a baby appears.

My stomach does that weird looping thing it always does at the sight of a baby. I settle on the sidewalk to wait. My ankle is on fire. I turn on the Bakelite, hoping to distract myself from the pain. Tom's on the air, all control and good humor. You'd never know that he's been up all night, that his personal life is falling apart.

"Thanks for tuning in to KMOO on this highly unusual Tuesday morning," he says. I always thought the call letters were bizarre, a strangely rural reference for an urban station in a city teeming with vegans, until Tom explained to me that the guy who started the station in the fifties was from Montana, where he'd made his money on cattle.

"I'm looking out my window, and I can see a big ugly cloud of smoke out near the Marina. Call in if you know the scoop. Let's be calm, people. Let's be civilized. There's no need for this thing to be rancorous. Just ask lawyer Linda."

That last part's for me. I'll miss them, all those coded messages coming through the airwaves. I wish I'd written them down over the years, a secret history. After the divorce, how long will it take for him to replace me with someone else, to direct his mercurial comments to someone with whom he's building a new, perhaps better, history? And how long will it take for me to truly start over, to find my way in unfamiliar terrain? The problem with marriage is that it provides a false sense of security. When you have walked down the aisle, when you have spent years building a life together, when your finances and emotional interests are so intricately intertwined, it can seem as if an essential part of your existence on this planet has been mastered. With the matter of love taken care of, you think you can concentrate on other things. It's not that

76

love is forgotten, only that it seems set in stone. Until you realize it isn't.

My old mentor, Dr. Bariloche, comes to mind.

It was June, and I had just graduated from medical school. I should have been with the rest of my classmates, who were having a party to celebrate before everyone scattered to do residencies at hospitals around the country. There was a general feeling among us that one weight had been lifted, while another, more serious weight would soon be on our shoulders. The party promised to be a raucous affair, a fitting end to four hard years. Instead, I was at a funeral.

At sixty-five, Dr. Bariloche was still a substantial woman, tall and sturdy. She and her husband, a graphic designer nine years her junior, had planned to travel the world together as soon as she retired. That afternoon, as Dr. Bariloche and I stood on the damp lawn outside the church, she said to me, with tears in her eyes, "I picked him young so he wouldn't die on me. Honestly, if I'd known he would have a heart attack at fifty-six, I'm not so sure I would have married him. Is that wrong?"

"Not at all," I reassured her, though I was thinking that maybe it was.

I held her arm as we navigated to the

limousine and joined the procession of cars headed back to her house, where her niece had organized the mourners. At some point, several hours later, I noticed that Dr. Bariloche had disappeared. I found her sitting alone in the bedroom, drinking a glass of wine, examining the books on the shelf.

"Come in," she said, motioning for me to sit on the bed beside her. She reached out and ran her fingers over the books on the shelf, stopping on a worn blue spine. "I remember when this book came out," she said. "I'd just started my residency, my first day on the job. I was walking back to my apartment from the hospital, and there was a large display in the window of the bookstore, stacks and stacks of this book. I went in and bought it. A man had bled to death in front of me that day. He'd been stabbed, and the orderlies wheeled him in, and as the blood was pouring out of a wound in his side I froze for several crucial seconds. Afterward, I walked around in a daze. I bought the book because I needed something to distract me."

I sat there in silence, feeling the warmth of her body next to me on the bed. The room was cold and smelled of vanilla candles. Though she had never been easy on me, had at times, in fact, made my life miserable, it is fair to say that I loved her.

"The day I bought this book was the end of one life, the beginning of another," Dr. Bariloche said. "The day I met my husband was another beginning. The day he died, another ending. And here I am unfortunately, beginning again. The problem is, I have no idea where to start." A lock of dyed black hair escaped her bun and fell into her eyes. She tucked it behind her ear, with a gesture I had seen her make hundreds — no, thousands — of times. "We tend to see life as a continuum, Julie, but really, it's a series of phases, generating a series of different selves. You leave one life behind and start another. And each time, a different version of yourself emerges."

It was unlike Dr. Bariloche to speak in such symbolic terms. She had a scientific mind; there was a hardness about her that put some of the other students off but that I had come to respect.

"When you arrived here four years ago, you were a very nervous young woman with great grades, a scholarship, and no confidence. To be honest with you, Julie, the first time I heard you speak in class, I doubted you were cut out to be a doctor."

I squirmed uneasily. She'd never said as much, but I'd always suspected it.

"Now look at you." She allowed one finger to settle lightly, fleetingly, on my knee. "Top of your class, flying colors and all that, and off to your next phase, your new beginning. I have to admit, I'm a little jealous."

"I'm waiting for UCSF to tell me they made a mistake," I said. "It was startling enough when they accepted me for medical school. To do my residency here too — it's more than I hoped for."

"You earned your spot," she said.

I noticed then that her hands were trembling. I'd seen those hands intubate an infant, remove a bullet lodged centimeters from a man's spine, hold down a screaming woman on dialysis, comfort a thousand different patients. I'd never once seen them tremble. She looked up at me, and on her face was an expression I'd never seen there before. It took me a moment to identify it: fear.

"What will I do now?"

Of course, I didn't have an answer. Nor did I, at that moment, imagine I would one day be in her shoes: starting over, out of context, with no clear path ahead.

9

"I heard a rumor," Dennis says. His voice over the cellphone is oppressive, but I keep the volume up high, hoping to hear Betty or Rajiv, or Eleanor. I want to hear their voices, just to know they're okay.

"What's that, Dennis?"

"People say you're getting divorced. Is it true?"

"Unfortunately, yes."

"That should make me happy," Dennis says. "But actually, it's really fucking depressing. You and Tom looked like you had it all figured out, Doc. If you can't make it work, where does that leave the rest of us?"

Last night, I arrived at KMOO just past midnight, as I had done so many times in the past. Entering the building I felt a rush of warm nostalgia, along with a sense of regret — the feeling you get when you leave a city you've grown tired of, only to realize there were so many things you wanted to do but never got around to. I brought Marnee Thai in take-out boxes, Mitchell's ice cream for dessert. I tried to make the night last as long as possible. I ate slowly and talked slowly. Neither of us looked at the divorce papers on the table, which Tom only needed to sign. Odd, how easy it is to end a thing that took so long to create.

It was just past two in the morning when I told Tom I was going home. "You can barely keep your eyes open," he scolded. "Spend the night here."

He led me to the old leather couch in the staff lounge and put a blanket over me. The couch smells permanently of cigarettes and Kool-Aid. It is a historic couch. The list of musicians who have crashed there, over-dosed there, and fucked there is legendary. There's the story about Grace Slick and a young male intern that is retold every time they hire a new employee. There's the story about Skip Spence of Moby Grape. And of course there's the one about Norman Greenbaum and the night he wrote "Spirit in the Sky." To all those legendary drug binges and sex romps might be added my own history with Tom. Last night, as I was driving to the station, I promised myself that I wouldn't confuse matters by going down that old familiar road.

I don't know how long I'd been dozing when the song came on. I almost felt it more than heard it, that quiet crescendo, and when I opened my eyes Tom was standing in front of me, a sad smile on his face, a questioning look.

"Come here," I said. He lay down beside me, the old cushions sinking under his weight.

By the time the words broke quietly through the fog, we were halfway out of our clothes. The song — Dire Straits, "Telegraph Road" — had been a secret code between us ever since the first time he played it for me at the station, more than a decade before. "It's fourteen minutes long," he had said then, locking the door behind him. He'd played the song for me a dozen or more times since then, always when we were alone at the station in the middle of the night, and, every time, I had read it as a signal, an invitation.

But this time was different, because I knew it would be the last.

I touched his hair where it grazed his temple, traced a finger along his eyebrow. I love his eyebrows; they're wild, out of control, and seem to grow more unruly by the year. You could send him to a spa and a tailor and a personal shopper, and he'd still manage to look as if he'd just rolled out of bed. The clothes designers make these days, with some mythical metrosexual male in mind, never look right on Tom. He's too tall, for one thing, and too broad in the shoulders to fit into those skinny shirts. In high school he eschewed the obvious sport, basketball, and instead played baseball and ran cross-country. He still has a runner's shape from behind.

In photographs, side by side, we look comically mismatched. Even in my highest heels, I'm dwarfed by him. While he doesn't have the kind of looks that translate well in photos — there's something slightly off in the symmetry of his face, a vague and misleading suggestion of a history of fist-fights — I can still glance at him from across a room and feel all those familiar stirrings. Even at our worst, during those times when we seemed to be fighting all the time, I wanted to go to bed with him. Sex was easily the best and least complicated thing about our marriage; I can't imagine life without it.

Last night, it was just as good as always, maybe better. All that sadness, all that history, distilled into one final act. Maybe I could live without his companionship at movies. Maybe I could live without his familiar presence at the breakfast table, the constant, comforting refrain of us. But how can I live without this?

Tom's hands smelled like the soap they keep in the bathroom at the station, a concoction of lemongrass and sage that always makes me sneeze. At some point we knocked over a Coke someone had left on the table in front of the couch. It sank into the carpet, making soft fizzing sounds.

As the Dire Straits song was coming to an end, Tom got up, pulled on his pants, and hurried out of the room. He was too late. On the intercom I could hear the final notes of "Telegraph Road" as Tom was running down the hallway, and then I counted the seconds of silence — one thousand one, one thousand two, one thousand three, one thousand four — before his voice came on the air.

"That was four seconds of silence," he said. "Which is about how long you'd have to defend yourself from a bear who's charging at you from a hundred feet. So if you're headed to Yosemite this weekend, keep that in mind."

A minute later, Tom came back. "You're dressed," he told me.

"You're not." I tossed him his shirt.

He stood looking at me, the shirt in his

hand. Our bodies were aging. When did that happen? For so long, we'd been young, and then, quite suddenly, we weren't. A few of the hairs on his chest had turned gray; I'd never noticed it before. It made me feel a deep tenderness toward him.

"That was nice," he said.

"Better than nice."

He put his shirt on, buttoned it. I followed him into the studio and took my place in the chair against the wall. I had sat here so many times, watching him work. I wouldn't be doing this again, either. It's the reverse of falling in love, when everything is sweet and exciting, when everything is a first that raises the question, Will this happen again?

"Jules," he said, turning his chair to face me, "I love you."

"It's the oxytocin," I said, attempting a joke.

He didn't laugh.

"The biological love drug. When a woman has an orgasm, her body releases oxytocin, which creates a sense of bonding. She's lying there with the man inside her, and all of a sudden her body is flooded with this hormone that makes her feel close to him. Biologically speaking, it's probably there to ensure the woman's fidelity, or at least her ongoing affection, increasing the chances that the man will provide for her young. Funny thing is, when the male orgasms, his body releases only a fraction of what hers does."

"In that case," he retorted, "you should be the one saying you love *me,* because I'm pretty sure that was an orgasm you had at the end there." He was fiddling with the controls, and Admiral Radley came on, "I Heart California."

"There's a trick," I said.

"A trick?"

"When we were on the couch, in the middle of it, I was rubbing circles in the small of your back, remember?"

"Of course I remember. It's one of my favorite things that you do."

"Funny thing is, for men, being rubbed in the small of the back has the same hormonal effect an orgasm does for women. It releases a superdose of oxytocin."

He rolled his chair over to me, put his hands on my knees. "Did they teach you that in medical school?"

"No," I laughed, "I read it in *Glamour.*"

Even as he spoke, his fingers were tapping to the beat. Tom glanced at the ceiling, just for a second, and I knew from the look on his face that he was silently admiring the song. He had a talent for distractedness that had always driven me nuts. I'd be spilling my heart out, thinking he was right there with me, but then I'd realize his mind was miles away.

"You're just going to Norway," I said, shaking my head.

That got his attention. He stopped tapping his fingers, looked me in the eyes. "I swear I'm not."

Going to Norway — our code phrase for some dream Tom plans to pursue but doesn't follow through on. One of the things I loved about him when we met was his relentless energy, his endless dreaming. He was always coming up with some big plan, and it took me a while to realize that the more manic his enthusiasm was for a project, the less likely he was to implement it. "Let's go to Norway for our anniversary," he announced to me during our first year of marriage. "We'll spend two weeks. We'll see the fjords, we'll drink hot chocolate in Bergen." I loved the idea. I bought travel guides, researched plane fares and lodging, invested in thick down coats for both of us, began mapping out an itinerary. As my plans grew more concrete, Tom's enthusiasm waned. When it came time to confirm our reservations, he hedged. "Listen," he said, "I think we need to do something closer to home this year. Work is busier than I expected. Let's save Norway for next year." So we went to Mendocino. Instead of two weeks in Norway, we spent three nights in a bed-and-breakfast by the sea. I was hugely disappointed, but I figured we would go to Norway the following year. We didn't. When our third anniversary rolled around, those travel books were still on the bookshelf, and the big down coats, which we'd tried on only once, laughing at our Michelin Man physiques, had never left the closet.

Long after I'd come to understand that what my husband said wasn't necessarily what he did, I still admired the boldness of his ambitions — everything from buying a piece of land in Hopland (which he did) to starting his own radio station (which he didn't) to building a beautiful set of bookshelves by hand (which he did) to learning how to surf Kelly's Cove (which he didn't). I was the type to calculate all the obstacles in my way and, using those calculations, decide whether something was worth pursuing. I had always secretly liked the fact that for Tom, the next big possibility was always just around the corner.

Now he had it in his head that the next big possibility was, once again, us, but I saw the warning signs.

"Admit it," I said. "I always know when you're going to Norway."

He pulled my chair closer. "It's an art, not a science. You have been wrong."

"I've got to get some sleep. Wake me up before you leave."

"You can sleep anytime," he said, frowning. "I'll make some coffee. We can talk."

I'd heard it before. He stays up all night and sleeps during the day — a pattern he established long before he became the Voice of Midnight. A small percentage of the population is neurologically wired to be nocturnal; surely, Tom belongs to that subset. He would never admit it, but I know he views my work schedule suspiciously. In the beginning of our marriage, I made an effort to go to shows with him as often as possible. I was never cut out for it, though, even in my twenties: staying out until three in the morning listening to some band he insisted I'd be crazy to miss, then waking with a monster headache and pounding back coffee and aspirin before morning rounds. Eventually, I stopped going to the shows with him. One night several years ago, when I bowed out of backstage passes to an Ogres show at the Bottom of the Hill, Tom couldn't hide his disappointment.

"You're not as fun as you used to be," he complained.

"I'm doing a diagnostic lecture with seventy-five first-year residents tomorrow morning. I need to sleep."

"Right." He turned away. "I forgot what an important person I'm married to."

Later, he apologized, but his barb had struck the heart of a fundamental difference between us. He's the perpetual big kid, always up for fun; I'm the serious one. During the years with Ethan, we were more in sync than at any other time in our marriage. I'd finally found a way to let my guard down, experiencing the world through Ethan's eyes. I worked saner hours and learned to say no to unnecessary commitments — conference appearances, weekend volunteer work. For a while, I stopped publishing, surprised to discover that I didn't really miss it. Meanwhile, Tom became more settled. He took wholeheartedly to the role of father; when he wasn't working, he was home. He no longer felt the need to see every new act that came through town. We developed an affection for places that had held no interest for us before: the zoo, the Discovery museum, the old cannons of the Presidio, where Ethan loved to climb. To our astonishment, domesticity suited both of us.

And then we lost Ethan. If there was one defining rupture in our marriage, an unforeseen event that rearranged everything, it was this. A loss that neither of us was prepared to face. One that we failed to see each other through.

After that, the ground shifted so slowly, I'm not sure either of us noticed it for what it was. I retreated into my work, into the seriousness of my days, while Tom started going out more often, staying out later, hanging out with an increasingly rowdy crowd. He'd do things that were completely ordinary in his world: the occasional line of coke, a weekend here and there in Vegas, snowboarding trips to Tahoe with guys from the station on slopes way beyond his skill level, one of which ended in a broken collarbone. It was nothing extreme, really, but it was enough to make me wonder, sometimes, what we were doing together. When he watched me fall into bed at nine o'clock at night, exhausted from a day with patients, uninterested in the new Wilco album he wanted to play for me, he must have wondered the same thing.

"Sometimes I feel like I'm married to my college boyfriend," I'd said last year, after a long argument that had left us both drained and weary. "It's as though you think less of me for not doing the beer bong when I have finals in the morning."

"And sometimes I feel like I'm married to my college professor," he snapped. "Like you're evaluating every move I make, judging whether or not I measure up."

When your marriage breaks up, you look for easy answers. Not long ago, I was fooling around online when I came across an interesting study involving factory workers in Boston; it found that marriages in which one partner works the night shift and the other partner works the day shift are twice as likely to end in divorce. I forwarded the article to Tom, who sent back a one-word response, tongue-in-cheek: *bingo.*

Sometimes, a divorce is a series of failures piled one upon another, a laundry list of hurts and disappointments and missed communication, and other times, something big happens, some cataclysmic event that tests the foundations of your marriage. But how do you know, before it happens, whether or not you're prepared? San Francisco burned in 1906 because the city was built of wood, and the existing infrastructure was unequipped to deal with the flames that followed the quake. The Bay Bridge collapsed in 1989 because it hadn't been built properly to begin with. Californians are always waiting for the big one. In the hall closet, we have a large Rubbermaid box that serves as an emergency kit, containing water, canned food, first aid items, flashlights, important phone numbers, five hundred dollars in cash, and one of Tom's hand-crank radios. But there's no emergency kit for marriage. No neat plan you can turn to when the ground shifts beneath your feet.

10

"Last time I saw you," Dennis says, "you and your sister weren't exactly on speaking terms. What changed?"

"A lot," I say, turning down the volume on the phone.

" 'A lot'? That's all I get?"

Heather is sitting on the edge of the bed, holding her stomach, trying to breathe through the pain.

"What do you want from me, Dennis?"

There's a pause. "I've had a bad day. A really fucking bad day. I came to the hospital this morning to give you a birthday present, but when I got here, they gave me the runaround, like they always do. They told me you weren't here."

"I wasn't."

He doesn't seem to hear me. "They refused to page you. I went over to the hotel, but Eleanor said she hadn't seen you."

"She was telling the truth."

"That's the problem, Julie. I don't know who's telling the truth anymore. I can't even be sure you are. Everything's so fucked up."

"I wouldn't lie to you, Dennis. I've always been straight with you."

"Remember how you used to tell me stories?" he asks. From the sound of his voice, he might be crying.

"I remember."

"Tell me one now. Is that too much to ask? One last story before —"

"Before what?" I ask gently, and I'm scared.

But he doesn't answer. I can hear him breathing on the other end of the line. "Don't leave anything out," he insists.

I glance at Heather. She is silent, staring at the wall.

I go into the bathroom and shut the door behind me. "She came back eight months ago," I begin.

That morning at the VA, as Heather and I made our way down the trail behind the cafeteria, she stopped and turned to me.

"You asked why I'm here," she said. "It's this." She placed a hand on her stomach.

"Jesus," I said.

"Ha," she quipped. "No immaculate conception here. Just your garden-variety mortal baby."

"Congratulations." I was struggling to wrap my mind around the idea.

"Thanks, but I'm not so sure congratulations are in order."

"How far along?"

"Five weeks, give or take."

"You've been to a doctor?"

"Does this count?"

"You're taking your prenatal vitamins? Folic acid?" In my mind, I sorted through a litany of concerns. "You're not drinking, I hope. A glass of red wine every now and then is fine, but you can't be too careful —"

"Not so fast," she interrupted. "I'm not sure I'm going to keep it."

"But you have to keep it."

Where had those words come from? I was a physician, not a Sunday school teacher. The more rational side of me chimed in to say she most certainly did not have to keep it; after all, her past actions in no way indicated that she would be a good or responsible mother.

"Julie," she said. "Put your own history aside."

My own history. Years of infertility and failed longing summed up so succinctly, like a gaping hole in a résumé. All those years I'd tried to have a baby after we lost Ethan. All the consultations with fertility specialists, all the pills and shots and calendars. All the planning and plotting and praying, the endless strain on my marriage, the arguments, the feeling that I had turned into a person I didn't even recognize. All of it for nothing. And here she was, my little sister, pregnant. And not necessarily in a position to be grateful for what, to me, would have been a miracle.

I said the most rational thing I could think to say, the same thing I would say to a patient in these circumstances: "Have you talked with the baby's father?" Old-fashioned, maybe, but Heather, of all people, knew what it felt like to grow up without one.

She resumed her brisk pace. The path was narrow, but instead of following behind I fell in step to her left, so that she could hear me with her better ear. "That's where things get tricky," she said.

"Don't tell me you don't know who it is." I regretted it as soon as I'd said it.

"Give me a little credit."

"I'm sorry. What is it, then?"

"Use your imagination."

"He's married?"

Her silence confirmed my guess. "I see."

"Jeesh — you don't have to say it like that."

"Like what?"

"Like you could have seen it coming. Like, of course Heather went and got knocked up by a married man."

"I was just thinking it's going to be complicated, that's all."

"He's separated," she said. "He lives out here, and his wife is on the East Coast. They don't have kids. It's not like I'm a home wrecker."

"If they've been apart so long, why don't they just get divorced?"

"It's not that easy."

"No, I guess it never is."

By now we'd reached the bottom of the trail. We'd been together for no more than half an hour, and already the tension was bubbling beneath our words. There was a bench at the bottom of the path. I sat down and patted the seat beside me. "Sit."

"I'm not five years old. You can't boss me around."

"I'm a doctor, and you're overexerting."

"According to week five in *What to Expect When You're Expecting,* I can pretty much do anything I want right now short of shooting heroin."

"And stinky cheese," I said. "Seriously."

She held her hand up, Girl Scout–style, and said solemnly, "I swear I will not shoot heroin or eat stinky cheese."

I took a deep breath. I could tell her my life stood still after we lost Ethan. Four years, two months, I could tell her, and not a day went by that I didn't think of him. I could tell her what it had done to my marriage, and I could tell her that I still hadn't figured out a way to forgive her. But if I told her these things, I feared I might never see her again.

She glanced at me and pulled a hard candy out of her pocket. "Butterscotch?"

"No, thanks."

She sat down beside me and stared out at the ocean, working the candy between her teeth.

"What a view," she said. "Can you believe you get to work here? Do you ever pinch yourself? It's about as far as you can get from Laurel."

"Strange words from a woman who just returned from a war zone."

"Granted." She tilted her head, looking at me with an expression I couldn't read. "You've lost your accent, you know."

"It wasn't intentional," I said, somewhat defensively, but that wasn't entirely true. "What was it like over there?" I asked, changing the subject.

"You don't want to know."

100

"Actually, I do. I kept waiting for an email, just something to say you were still alive. I recorded *News Hour* every night, I never missed it." I didn't tell her that I held my breath each time the television's sound went mute and the names of the soldiers lost in action began to scroll across the screen. That the roll call of the dead always gutted me. *It could have been her,* I thought, every time.

"If anything had happened to me, you would have heard it from Mom. Anyway, I made it out, didn't I?" She shook her head. "Three tours. When I joined, I had no clue what I was in for. Then I get to basic training and I'm in with all these kids, these boys, eighteen, nineteen years old, full of themselves and all gung ho to go to war and start blowing people's heads off. I was only twenty-five, but they made me feel old."

"I was stunned when you signed up. I guess I never thought of you as patriotic in that way."

"It wasn't about that. By the time I joined, September eleventh was a distant memory. One of the guys who'd been there for a few years said what all of us were probably thinking. He said, 'You don't walk into a tent in Suwayrah and think of planes hitting the World Trade Center. You walk in and think, "Where did all these fucking flies come from?" ' "

"So all that God-and-country stuff. None of it applied to you?"

"My reasons were more selfish. The army was an escape."

"Hawaii is an escape. Paris, maybe. The Middle East, not so much."

She laughed. "In a lot of ways, being home is harder than it was over there. At least there I had a purpose. Each day I woke up and had a job to do. Sometimes it was the most menial, tedious task you can imagine, but I knew what was expected of me."

"What was your job, exactly? Mom mentioned you did some writing."

"I guess somebody figured out I could string sentences together, so they put me in the press office. It was new for me, having something I was good at. And it was interesting, meeting people, shaking hands with senators. Then I come home, and when someone finds out I've been over there — civilians, I mean — they get this look, almost as if they're embarrassed for me."

"I'm not embarrassed for you," I said. "I'm proud."

Heather stretched her arms in front of her, elbows locked, and cracked her knuckles two at a time — that old familiar gesture.

She was herself, but different. She'd always been strong-willed, but now she seemed capable, composed. It was difficult to see in her the girl who had needed so much for so long, the difficult girl who had always been a crooked counterpoint to my straight and narrow.

"Why here?" I asked. "Why didn't you go home?"

She smiled wryly and sang a line from that Steve Forbert song about Laurel — "*It's a dirty stinking town, yeah. . . .* Anyway, it's not my home now any more than it is yours."

"There's Mom," I pointed out.

"The last thing Mom needs is more of my problems." She picked up a pinecone from the ground beside her foot and began to pluck away the seeds. "I saw a lot, you know, terrible stuff. The day the kid hit me with the rock was by no means the worst. But for some reason that's what I remember most vividly from all three tours of duty. I saw him step out from behind the tree, and I knew instantly that something was wrong, but he was a boy. A little boy. I was trying to get my helmet back on when the rock hit me, and for several seconds I didn't know it was just a rock. I thought I'd been shot in the head. I really don't even know how to describe it — you feel certain that you're dead, and then you realize that you're alive. And at that moment, do you know who I thought of?" She didn't wait for my response. "I thought of you."

I didn't know what to say. Why was she here? What did she want from me? It felt tremendously manipulative, her sudden reappearance in my life, her unspoken demand that I allow her back in, forgive and forget. As relieved as I was to see her, I was also angry.

We sat for a couple of minutes in silence. Finally, I ventured another question. "Really, who's the father?"

She didn't look at me when she said, "You won't believe me if I tell you."

In the past, I'd discovered that if my sister preceded a statement with "You won't believe me," there was a pretty good chance she was right. But some nugget of truth was always buried in the fiction. The challenge was in figuring out where the lies ended and the truth began.

"That wasn't so bad, was it?" Dennis says, jerking me back into the present.

"No."

"Just like old times. Didn't it feel good to get it off your chest?"

"Yes," I lie. I open the bathroom door and

go to Heather. She's still sitting on the edge of the bed, her face pinched with pain.

"You know what I miss?" Dennis says.

"What?"

"You used to need me. When we talked, it was like you could relax and really be yourself. You said it was the best therapy. I bet Tom didn't know, did he?"

"Know what?"

"How close we were, Julie. How much you revealed in our little heart-to-hearts."

11

7:04 a.m.

The gripman releases the brake, and we begin to move. The businesses are closed, but the sidewalks are already bustling. There is a man selling bear-shaped balloons, a scantily clad woman on stilts dressed like a sexy Uncle Sam, waving a banner that says, DIVIDED WE FALL on one side and HAPPY HOUR ALL DAY AT EDINBURGH CASTLE on the other.

The line on the sidewalk beneath the cable car sign has grown. The wind has picked up, a wet, stinging, San Francisco cold. The man with the baby stuffs his book into his messenger bag and retrieves a red fleece blanket, which he pulls over the backpack, concealing the baby's head completely. The baby bobs around under there, laughing.

As the cable car screeches to a stop in front of us, the conductor opens the latticework gate, shouts "All aboard!" and steps back to let the passengers file on. The inner compartment fills up fast. When I was a kid in Mississippi, I used to watch movies on TV — *The Birds, I Love a Soldier* — and dream of being Tippi Hedren in a tailored suit or Paulette Goddard in overalls, making my way up and down the steep hills of this city by cable car. In my childhood daydreams I held on to a strap, balancing elegantly on the sideboard, but in reality I edge my way into an open seat on the outer bench, relieved to take the pressure off my ankle. I lift my foot so that it is suspended a couple of inches above the floor. Passengers are still finding their seats when the conductor grabs the rope and jerks it back and forth with a whipping movement of his wrist.

I frantically text Heather. *You OK?*

12

"I'm sitting in your chair, Doc," Dennis says. "I'm looking at your calendar. You're a really busy woman."

I cringe at the thought of him touching my things.

Years ago, I underwent an intensive one-week training seminar in dealing with patients who became belligerent or threatening. The training had been mandated following an ugly scene at the Denver VA hospital that left three staffers and a patient dead. Two days of the seminar had been devoted to dealing with hostage situations. We used to have a one-day refresher course each year, but the course went the way of comprehensive psychiatric services and our full-time crisis counselor: it was lost to budget cuts.

One thing I do remember is the importance of establishing rapport with the hostage taker. But in this case, our rapport is the root of the problem. If we hadn't been friends all those years ago, if I hadn't climbed into his bed when I was twenty-two and lonely, if I hadn't spilled everything to him after we lost Ethan, then he wouldn't be in my office right now, holding three people I cared about at gunpoint.

"You let them get too close," Betty warned me, years ago, when Dennis started getting weird. "This isn't the first time."

Betty was right. I don't always maintain the proper boundaries. Maybe it's some lingering remnant of Mississippi; back home, everybody talks to everybody about everything. In Laurel, you can't walk into the Piggly Wiggly without walking out with someone's life story. Sometimes, I miss that. Despite San Francisco's reputation as a free-for-all, it is, for the most part, a cordial city. Personal space ranks right up there with personal freedoms.

When patients come in the door of the VA, we ask so much of them. Taking a personal history is a necessarily invasive process, designed to get the most information in the shortest amount of time. When I began working here, I discovered that if I shared a little bit of myself, patients were much more willing to open up to me. Even though every patient walks in with a basic desire to know what is wrong with him, it's also natural for him to hold back on some of the details that might cast him in an unfavorable or an embarrassing light. A good physician gets past that reluctance quickly. The sooner everything is on the table, the sooner I can make a proper diagnosis. If that means mentioning a TV show I like or talking a bit about where I came from, so be it. But Betty was right: sometimes, I go too far.

"Dennis," I say, "is Eleanor okay?"

"Not really. She's not breathing too well."

"Listen, Dennis. I need you to put Rajiv on."

"I can't do that."

"How's Rajiv doing?"

"Oh, he's fine. Very even-keeled, that one."

"And Betty?"

"Pretty good. She's not hurt, if that's what you mean."

"Good," I say. "Listen, why don't you let Eleanor go?"

"This isn't about Eleanor."

"What is it about?"

"It's about me and you."

"You're talking to me, Dennis. I'm here. If it isn't about Eleanor, if it isn't about Betty and Rajiv, why not just let them walk out of there?"

Dennis laughs softly. "Why would I do that?"

"Why wouldn't you?"

"Because as long as they're here with me, you're talking to me, and no one's going to storm the room and shoot me."

"No one's storming anything, Dennis. No one wants to hurt you. Greg didn't hurt you."

"I bet Greg didn't tell you he knocked on the door after I'd brought the others in here and volunteered to take someone's place."

It doesn't surprise me. "No, he didn't."

"That's how I knew he wouldn't mind walking across the parking lot to give you the phone. He's a stand-up guy. I've always liked him."

"You could have just called the room," I say.

"Yes, but then they could tap the line."

"They who?"

"The people who are leading the coup."

"There's no coup, Dennis."

"You really believe that? Can't you see this goes all the way to the top?"

"There's no conspiracy theory. It's just a vote."

"You think I'm paranoid." His voice is growing agitated. "That's what they want you to think, Julie. You are so naïve some-times."

Something else we learned in the crisis management class: it's easier to deal with someone who has demands. Bank robbers who want money, hijackers who want asylum, ex-convicts who want a friend released from prison. The worst kind of hostage taker is one who has no set demands, one who already feels his life is worth nothing, someone with nothing to lose.

13

7:16 a.m.

I turn up the volume on the Bakelite, surprised to still hear Tom's voice. The morning guy must be running late. "You know, when you think about it," Tom says, "seceding is a lot like breaking up. You think you can't live without each other. All of your interests are intertwined, your history's all mixed up together. But then, all of a sudden, you're separate entities, on your own. It's downright scary. So here's a classic breakup song, and I'm sending it out to the girl in the sky."

With that, Billy Idol's voice breaks through the static, singing "Sweet Sixteen."

The girl in the sky. That, of course, would be me: fifteen years ago, the Fillmore, the annual KMOO concert. Billy Idol was on the bill, another attempt at a comeback, along with the Goo Goo Dolls, Yah-Yah Littleman, and a few other acts. I'd just finished the third year of medical school. For months, I'd been in constant motion, with little sleep and no social life. As much time as I spent surrounded by colleagues, I'd begun to feel isolated from normal life. This was a rare celebratory night, and I planned to make the most of it. I'd had a lot to drink, and to top it off, when I stepped outside for air, someone offered me a joint. The pot had quickly gone to my head. What strikes me now is how young I'd been then but how old I'd felt, needing to escape already — all those hours playing doctor until, at some point, it became who I was.

When "Dancing with Myself" began to play, someone dragged me into the mosh pit. I closed my eyes and lost myself in the music. It felt ridiculous and strange, wonderful, like going back to high school to relive a youth I'd never had. As the crowd pressed forward, I was pushed farther and farther toward the stage, the bodies packed around me so tightly that my feet actually lifted off the ground. I kept going higher, higher, until I was on top of the mass of bodies, cradled horizontally by hundreds of unfamiliar hands. Someone's finger caught my hair, pulling my head back at a painful angle; someone's sharp ring grazed my cheek, a hand grabbed at the crotch of my jeans. The ceiling seemed impossibly far away, the lights of the stage blinding, and I began to panic. The song stopped, and Billy Idol started singing "Sweet Sixteen," a cappella and achingly slow. Suddenly, two powerful hands wrapped around my waist. I felt myself being lifted, floating through space. My feet landed on the other side of the barricade, inches from the stage. My knees buckled; someone held me up. Moments later I was backstage, sitting in a folding chair next to a large man, who was pressing a cold bottle of water to my lips. It was hard to believe he was real, that the dizzying flight above the rowdy crowd had actually happened to me.

"You okay?"

"You're so. Big," I managed.

He laughed. "Thanks. I guess."

His eyes were dark, nearly black. His hair was shaggy and wild. For a moment I wondered if I'd inadvertently smoked something stronger than pot. I shook my head, trying to clear out the cobwebs.

"Where did you come from?"

"Backstage. It looked like you were in trouble, just floating through the sky out there."

I leaned against him, still woozy from the

pot and the heat, and together we watched the rest of the Billy Idol set. It all seemed miles and miles from the normal context of my life.

"I've never dated a bouncer before," I mumbled.

I closed my eyes and let the music wash over me.

The crowd cheered as Billy Idol left the stage. He walked right toward us, bringing with him a scent of musk and sweat. His hair, up close, was even more blond than it was on TV, like some punk rock halo. We all seemed to be swimming in a weird, watery blue.

"Be right back," the giant said to me. He shook Billy Idol's hand. "Great set, man." Then he walked onstage. "I'm supposed to say a few words here, but how can I follow that?" he bellowed into the microphone. "We'll be back in fifteen with Sister Hazel."

After a quick wave to the roaring crowd, he returned to sit beside me.

"You're not the bouncer," I said.

"Nope."

An awkward silence followed. I was relieved when the next band arrived. The giant whispered something to the lead singer just as they were going onstage. "We'd like to dedicate this one to the girl in the sky!"

Ken Block shouted, and with that, the band launched into "All for You."

I elbowed the giant, unbelieving. "Did you do that?"

He shrugged.

"You did that," I said, stunned.

"I'm Tom," he said.

"Julie."

After the last band had played, Tom made some promotional announcements and, much to my relief, came back to me.

"Do you need a ride home?" he asked.

When we pulled up in front of my apartment building, he got out of the car to open the passenger-side door. "Thanks for rescuing me," I blurted out.

"Sure," he replied, cuffing me on the shoulder a little too hard. A thought raced through my head, a thrilling notion of what it would be like to make love to him, like going a practice round in the ring with someone who didn't know his own strength. I must have been smiling, because he demanded, "What's funny?"

"Do you want to come in?"

Upstairs, in my apartment, he wandered around as if he belonged there, checking out my books and CDs, complimenting the view. He picked up a photo of me and Heather taken when I was ten years old and she was an infant; I held her in my arms, beaming. "It's you," he said. "You look just like yourself. Who's the baby?"

"My sister, Heather."

"Where is she now?"

"Mississippi. She hasn't had an easy time of it, really."

"Why's that?"

I sensed he wanted to hear the whole story, not just a stripped-down, small-talk version of it. So I grabbed a couple of beers from the fridge, and we sat down on the bed that doubled as a sofa. I told him about Heather's missing father, and about my dead one. I told him about shopping for school clothes at the Salvation Army; about sitting in the muted light of my childhood church, feeling horribly out of place, while the preacher lectured furiously to a rapt congregation; about finding my mother alone in her room, sobbing, staring at photos of my father, years after he had died. I told him how desperately I'd wanted to get away, to start a new life where no one knew me.

"I suppose I wanted to reinvent myself."

"And you did." He pulled my feet into his lap and began rubbing them. "You live in the most beautiful city in the world. You're putting yourself through school. You're on your way to becoming a doctor."

"All true." My mouth felt cottony; my whole body had gone limp and warm. "But the thing about reinvention is, no matter how much you change everything on the outside, you still know where you came from. You've still got all that stuff from middle school clanging around in your system. It's almost like you're living a double life, just waiting to be caught. Waiting for someone to walk up to you and say, 'I know who you are. Enough with the charade.' "

"It's not a charade," Tom said. "It's your life. You made it."

"You make it sound so simple." I glanced at the clock, yawning.

"Too early for breakfast?" he asked hopefully.

I reluctantly pulled my feet out of his grasp. "Come on, I'll make you my special drop biscuits with cheese."

The following night, I tuned in to KMOO. Around midnight, Tom dedicated a song to me: Al Green's "Here I Am (Come and Take Me)."

I turned up the volume on my crappy radio, and I did something I hadn't done in a very long time. I danced alone in my apartment.

There's so much about that time of my life that I've forgotten; the whole phase feels like a blur of sleepless nights soaked in coffee, a whirlwind of patients and procedures and emergencies, one seminar blending into the next, ambulatory care conferences and frantic days in the acute care clinic, endless presentations by the faculty in which I took notes furiously and felt my head would burst with information, depressing shifts at the community clinic. But I remember with tremendous clarity that night at the Fillmore — the throb of the music, the heat, the bodies pressed against me, the unwilling horizontal flight over the crowd. I remember the hands around my waist, the feeling of floating in space — and Tom. We had two weeks to get to know each other before I started my summer rotation with the National Health Service Corps in Oakland, two short but densely packed weeks during which I fell completely, unquestionably, in love with him.

The best thing about my relationship with Tom from there on out was that we had no messiness between us, no drama. After that night, I never dated anyone else. There were no ugly breakups and subsequent makeups, no questions of exclusivity. Our relationship felt like something I'd fallen into by some divine kind of luck.

Years later, driving home from the VA hospital late on a summer night, I was startled to hear Tom telling the story of how we met on air. He played my pot-infused crowd-surfing for laughs, but when it came to his own role in the story, he didn't whitewash a thing. "I thought I was getting a one-night stand," he told his listeners. "Instead, I got a life."

14

Tom and I were in bed when I told him about Heather's return. He was leaning against the pillows, reading *Q Magazine.* I sat beside him, rubbing lotion into my hands. It was a cool night, but the window was open anyway, the sea air drifting in through the screen. The foghorns were bellowing. I could see the neighbors' yappy dog relieving itself in their purple hydrangeas. "Buster boy," the neighbor called in his thick Cantonese accent, "come here, Buster boy." It was part of the nighttime litany of our life, the sound of the neighbor calling in the dog, and I imagined that if I lived anywhere else I'd have a hard time falling to sleep without it.

Our house sits on a hill thirteen blocks from the Pacific Ocean, sandwiched between two similar houses, attached on both sides, the long narrow properties separated by wooden fences. Our bedroom — my bedroom now — is on the second floor, with a view to the backyard, and the neighbors' yards, and beyond the yards the streets and houses sloping down to the long sands of Ocean Beach. The room is dominated by a very tall, long sleigh bed that we'd picked up at an estate sale in Berkeley during the first year of our marriage. At nighttime, especially with the foghorns going and the moonlight shining on the yards down below, the bed feels something like a ship, adrift on the edge of the city. Back then, it was the only place I knew we could talk with no distractions, the only place quiet enough, and intimate enough, for me to share the startling news.

Years before, when Heather had left to join the army, Tom had said he didn't want to see her again. He'd meant it.

"She's back," I said. There was no good way to tell him what had happened, no way to ease into the subject.

"Who's back?" he mumbled, still absorbed in his magazine.

"She's finished her active duty."

He put the magazine in his lap and stared at me, confused.

"She came to the VA today," I said.

"She just showed up?"

Down in the yard, Buster ran across the

grass. Mr. Yiu stood by the fence in his sweatpants and T-shirt, waiting for the dog. Mr. and Mrs. Yiu had children and grandchildren in Fremont who came over on weekends, and they had brothers and sisters and parents and friends who joined them every Saturday night for mah-jongg. The room where they played was next to our bedroom; late into the night we'd hear the tiles slapping the table, the loud, happy voices, the Chinese opera they played on a very old tape deck.

I often envied the liveliness of that house. Ours had once been lively, too — when we had Ethan. The sweet, incessant chatter, the playdates, the songs. In those days, the stereo was always on; Tom and I both wanted Ethan to grow up in a house filled with music.

For years, Mrs. Yiu had been urging me to have a child. First, she wanted me to have one for Ethan. "He needs little brother," she would insist. And then, she wanted me to have one for myself. "You are too sad. A baby makes everyone happy." And for years, I had been assuring her that I was trying.

"I walked into the cafeteria," I told Tom, "and she was there."

He lifted his knees, dragging the covers with him, leaving me exposed. "The nerve of her, showing up like that."

I tugged the covers back. "She seemed different."

"Don't tell me you're giving her the benefit of the doubt," he shot back.

"You haven't even heard the story," I said, irritated. These days, we were so much quicker to set each other off. Even I didn't entirely understand why I suddenly felt the need to defend my sister. Was it the baby? Did the fact that she was carrying my niece or nephew change everything?

"Anyway, she's pregnant."

He shook his head, scowling. "Perfect. The poster child for maternal instincts. Is she married?"

"No."

"So what's she here for? Money?"

"She hasn't asked for anything," I said defensively. "Think what you will about her, she was never like that."

When Heather left, it had been easy to draw the lines of loyalty — to side with my husband instead of the sister whose recklessness had cost us so much. But in the intervening years, the ties between Tom and me had begun to fray. We were both quicker to anger, more prone to argue over small things. Between his work and mine, we spent less time together. For both of us, losing Ethan — the child who came to us so unexpectedly — had been devastating. Afterward, when we tried and failed, again and again, to have a child, I felt a drowning sense of hopelessness. Tom weathered my infertility much better than I did. Over the years, his attempts to console me — "We're fine just the two of us," he would say, or "A baby wouldn't replace Ethan" — had only made me feel that he didn't understand the depth of my desire.

"Listen, Jules, your sister wants something. Otherwise she wouldn't be here. You can't let her into our life. She'll just fuck things up. That's Heather's talent. It's what she does."

He pulled me toward him and started kissing me. On the radio, Tom could talk and talk. But at home, when it came to the stuff we really needed to discuss, he had a habit of stopping conversations before they really started. And I was an easy target. It was too easy to retreat into the familiar comfort of sex, too easy to save the argument for some later date.

If I'd been more honest with him, I might have said, "It was all fucked up already. Before she came back, we'd already fucked it up." I might have asked, "Are we going to make it?" But I didn't, because we were on

126

our ship. This was where we were good together, the best. This was where we never faltered. It was a good place to pretend.

But the following night, I turned on the radio at the usual time, just to hear Tom's voice. "Here's the Mendoza Line," he said, "with 'Love on Parole.' " The lyrics were sadly fitting, and I couldn't help but feel that this was his way of telling me something he wouldn't say outright:

And for all your talk of ending the fray,
There's not a part of your heart that would
    have it that way.
Oh, ya couldn't make a cup of tea
Without a battle strategy.

Four months later, I came home from work one night to find Tom sitting on the end of our bed, one sock on, one sock off, his suitcase already packed.

"What's this?" I asked, thinking he had a business trip I'd forgotten about.

I'd stripped off my work clothes and was searching in my dresser drawer for sweat-pants, debating whether to cook or to order pizza, when he said, "I can't do it anymore."

I turned to him, half-dressed, certain I'd heard him wrong. "What?"

"I found a place to stay," he said.

Things hadn't been good between us; that was no secret. Things, in fact, had been very difficult. Heather's arrival had only made things worse. But in all our endless arguments, we'd never talked about this. Not really.

"It's a six-month lease," he said. "I think we both need some time to figure out what we're doing here."

"What we're doing here?" I repeated, incredulous. "This is how you talk about the last fifteen years of our lives — what we're *doing* here?"

He lay back on the bed and stared at the ceiling.

I went over to the bed, knelt beside him, and shook him as hard as I could by the shoulders. He closed his eyes as if to completely block me out of his sight. "Look at me!" I said.

"Getting angry isn't going to help matters," he said, so calmly I wanted to scream.

I let go of his shoulders and collapsed on the bed beside him. I was stunned. "That's it? No discussion? You just go out and find yourself a new place. You just make this decision for the both of us."

"I'm sorry." He was; I could see it on his face. He was sorry and he was scared, and yet, he had already decided to do it — to make a trial run of life without me.

"You can't do that." I felt the tears running down my face, and I was ashamed to be falling apart in front of him when, instead, I should have been making my case in a calm, rational way. I'd never been a crier. In fact, it was one thing Tom had liked about me in the beginning, the fact that, with me, there was no emotional roller coaster, everything an even keel. It came with the profession. I considered it a good quality.

He seemed confused by my tears. He reached out and patted my hand, as if he were consoling a casual acquaintance. It was too much. I started pounding on his chest with my fists. He grabbed my wrists and held them so easily, like a parent restraining an angry child.

"I'm sorry, Jules," he repeated. "I really am. But you can't pin this all on me. I'm just the one who pulled the trigger. If you think about it, you'll realize that someone had to. Something had to give."

I stopped fighting and pulled my wrists away. In my bra and underwear, I suddenly felt naked. I got up from the bed and reached for the first thing I could find to cover myself — the sweatshirt he'd been wearing that day, which lay crumpled on the floor. Downstairs in the kitchen, I opened the refrigerator, closed it. Pizza, I decided. I'll call Victoria's. I couldn't think any further than that. There were plenty of questions I wanted to ask my husband, but, deep down, I already knew the answers.

It wasn't working out; on this point, Tom was right. But when it came to his physical absence from my life, it turned out I was totally unprepared. The morning after he moved out, I made coffee and sat in bed, listening for the neighbor calling in his dog. The door opened, the dog's leash clinked, a few minutes passed. "Buster boy," Mr. Yiu finally cried. "Buster boy." I closed my eyes and let the sound wash over me, relieved to still have this.

I missed Tom far more than I'd expected. The simplest things were the most difficult to let go of: the sound of his boots on the stairs when he came home in the morning, the fact that he always knew which movies were playing and what new albums I might want to hear, the musky-sweet smell of his skin, the great, easy sex. The one thing I didn't miss was the fighting.

"God, Julie," Heather said when I told her he was gone. "I'm sorry. I hope it didn't have anything to do with me."

"We've been moving in this direction for a

long time." What I didn't say was that her sudden presence in our lives had exacerbated an already impossible situation.

"Well, looks like you're losing a hot hunk of a husband and gaining a big fat barn of a sister."

She meant it as a joke, but she was more right than she could know. It wasn't supposed to go this way. With Tom, I'd made a vow. Heather was the one who'd taken Ethan away from us, and Tom was the one who'd seen me through that loss. He was my partner, the one I had chosen, the one who had chosen me. Heather and I were born to each other, the way you're born to a country: an imposed allegiance. Between a marriage one chooses and a blood relation one doesn't, shouldn't marriage be the more powerful bond?

15

"Tell me something," Dennis says. "If California secedes, where will you go?"

"I won't go anywhere. California is home."

"You can't stay at the VA hospital if there's no VA in California."

"I'll find another hospital."

His voice grows angry. "Then how will I see you?"

Heather is lying on the bed. She rises up, her face contorted, her skin alarmingly pale. She bears the contraction silently. I rub her shoulder the same way I did when she was little; I wish there was more I could do for her.

"I'm not that hard to find," I tell Dennis.

"We used to be such good friends."

Heather drops back on the pillow, trembling. "We're still friends," I say impatiently.

"Then why do you avoid me? Why don't you return my calls?" There's something frightening in his tone.

"I'm sorry, Dennis. I'll try to do better. I promise."

For several seconds, he says nothing.

"Just let Eleanor go," I say. "Let her get medical attention. You don't need an injured person on your hands."

He's silent. I resist the urge to fill the silence.

"You're right," he says brokenly. "I really don't."

For a moment, it seems as though I might be getting through to him.

"Anyway, Eleanor is a pain in the ass," he says. "She's always been a pain in the ass. Wouldn't you agree?"

How do I respond? The truth is, he's right. Eleanor seems to thrive on making life difficult for others. If you ask her a simple question, you never get a straight answer. She's unkind to patients, surly with staff. She makes fun of the doctors in front of the residents and tattles on the residents to the doctors. And she's not just unpleasant; she's downright incompetent. It's the catch-22 of government work. No matter how bad an employee is, you can't get rid of them. You just keep shuffling them around. The only reason she was working the hotel desk this morning was that having her in the hospital lobby was too demoralizing; a few weeks ago, having rotated her through practically every department of the hospital, HR finally found the place where they thought she would see the fewest people and, therefore, do the least damage.

"In fact," Dennis says, "it's not unreasonable to assume that the world would be better off without Eleanor."

There's a thud in the background. Then a woman shrieks and begins sobbing.

"What's happening, Dennis?" I ask, frightened.

"Eleanor is always yapping; now I'm giving her a reason to."

I hear Rajiv's voice. "Please put the gun down," he says calmly.

"You haven't hurt anyone yet," I say desperately. "Dennis — we can still resolve this."

"I know we can. Me and you. Eleanor's just getting in the way. It's almost like you care more about her than you care about me."

"That's not true. I care about you very much."

"Then you won't mind what I'm about to do. This will be a favor for you — remember what a pain in your ass Eleanor used to be when you were both working the second floor?"

A chill goes through me.

"Dennis, wait —"

"No!" It's Betty's voice.

A deafening sound comes through the line, so loud I instinctively jerk the phone away from my ear.

"There," Dennis says. "No more talk about Eleanor. She has wasted enough of our time."

16

After that Wednesday in October when Heather walked back into my life, we didn't see each other for several days. She'd been vague about where she was staying, but she promised to meet me in the cafeteria again the following Wednesday.

Meanwhile, I braced myself for the possibility that she wouldn't be back. I couldn't stop thinking about the baby. I fantasized about holding it, rocking it to sleep, feeding it bottles, carrying it through the city in a sling, its warm body snug against me. It was a leap, I knew, one that assumed so many things: that Heather would decide to have the baby, that she would remain nearby, and that she would allow me to be involved.

So when I walked into the VA cafeteria on the scheduled day and saw her sitting there, fifteen minutes early, I sighed with relief.

I slid into the booth across from her. "Since when are you a morning person?"

She folded up her paper. "There's a lot you wouldn't recognize about me. On the forward operating base in Kandahar, we had to be up at five. It's amazing what you can accomplish in a day if you get up with the sunrise."

The army. Of course. It was the same answer she would give over the next few weeks for so many fundamental changes: her disciplined exercise routine, her orderly finances, her complete sobriety. I'd heard different variations on the same theme from my patients. Aimless or troubled kids who went into the army because it was their last option and found peace and purpose in the intense drills, the set-in-stone hierarchy of command, the unrelenting requirements for the maintenance of one's uniform, work station, and living quarters. During the years of her aimlessness, I'd thought what Heather needed was a college education, a career path, and a steady relationship. It turned out that what she needed was more drastic and far more simple: orders to follow, a clear path set by someone else, a purpose beyond herself.

"It's weird," she said. "Growing up, I imagined a totally different life. When everything happened, I had to get away, I had to do something extreme. I remember walking down Sloat trying to figure out what to do. I looked up and saw the army recruiting office. I didn't even think. I just went inside. It seemed like a sign."

By "everything," I knew she really meant one thing. She meant Ethan. Of all the conversations I wanted to have with my sister, I wasn't ready to have that one. Not yet. After all these years, the pain still felt too raw.

"I've got a few minutes," I said instead. "Want to walk?"

When she stood up, my gaze instinctively went to her stomach.

"You're real subtle." She patted her belly. "Yes, the creature is still in here."

"Does Mom know?"

"Lord, no. She'd have her whole church praying for me."

I opened the back door of the cafeteria, and the salt air hit our faces, cool and sweet. I thought of the baby, growing day by day, a tiny collection of supercharged cells that might one day be my niece or nephew.

When I looked at Heather, if I pushed the scrim of my anger aside, I still saw the infant girl in my arms, the toddler stepping out into the street half a second before I reached forward and pulled her back, the eighth grader weeping about a boy who'd kissed her at the Fourth of July fireworks and then ignored her, the teenager who called me to bail her out of jail after she got caught with marijuana, the college student who flunked out freshman year and was too scared to tell our mother, the young woman who always had some ill-advised boyfriend who didn't treat her well and some crappy job that didn't pay enough. The years of too much drinking and too many drugs. Things had never gone right for her; she had never been happy. Now maybe she could be.

Heather and I took the Battle of the Bulge trail again, through the blackberry vines and over the footbridge, down and down until we reached the wider Lands End path, with its grand views out toward the sea. She told me about a Christina Aguilera concert she'd attended on the base, and in the same breath, she told me about the terrible aftermath of a roadside bombing. "All of it runs together," she said. "It's hard to remember what came first." She told me about a friend who had died when he jumped off the back of a truck and broke his femur. "His femur," she said, incredulous. "A perfectly healthy twenty-five-year-old with a wife and baby at home. The break sent an embolism to his heart." She shook her head. "I spent seven months sitting in

139

Suwayrah playing Xbox and reading novels and practically peeing in my pants every time I heard an explosion. The place was a magnet for incoming rocket fire. The one bright spot was the food. We had Pakistani civilians cooking for us. They were amazing. I talked this one guy into giving me his recipe for Lahori beef karahi. You'll have to come over one of these days so I can cook it for you."

"Come over?"

"I've decided to stick around. A friend of mine is letting me borrow his place in the Mission while he's back East." She glanced up to gauge my reaction. "You don't look too thrilled."

"I'm glad you're safe," I said. "I really am. But you can't expect everything to just magically go back to how it was."

"Fair enough." She broke a twig from an overhead branch. "But maybe you should let me know just how long you plan to keep punishing me."

"I'm not punishing you."

She tossed the broken halves of the twig into the underbrush. "It sure feels like it."

Was she right? Was I was measuring out some sort of long overdue punishment for the hell she'd put us through? I just didn't know how to be with her, how to act. Every time I looked at her, I thought of Ethan, and the anger came rushing back.

We walked in silence. Finally, I asked, "Have you thought more about what you're going to do?"

"Of course — I think about nothing else." She turned to me. "One day I want to have the baby, the next day I don't. Here's the thing: if it was five years ago, it would be easy. Back then, I would have just ended it. But I'm twenty-nine, more than old enough to take care of a child. At some point along the line somebody decided that you have to go out and live this whole productive life, make a ton of money, satisfy all your desires, travel the world, and sell your start-up before you can have a kid. But think about it: Mom was twelve years younger than I am now when she had you."

"How does the father feel?"

"He's hard to read. When I first told him, he was ecstatic. Now I'm not so sure. But his wife never wanted children, and that's been very difficult for him. He loves kids."

"How do you know his wife didn't want children? You can't exactly trust a man you're having an affair with on the subject of his marriage."

"Julie, I'm not naïve. And technically, it's not an affair."

"You're sure he's being straight with you? If it's really over between them, why aren't they divorced?"

Heather brushed my words aside with a wave of her hand. "He's spent a long time getting to where he is. If the story got out about an extramarital affair, with a love child to boot, it would completely derail his career."

"That sounds like a convenient excuse," I persisted. "People get divorced all the time."

"This is different."

"How?"

"He isn't —" She paused, searching for the right words. "He isn't normal."

"What does that mean? You make it sound like you were impregnated by an Oompa-Loompa, or Edward Scissorhands."

"Funny. What I mean is, he's kind of a public figure."

"Seriously? How public?"

"Very."

"Really," I said. I wanted to give her an out, a chance to tell me that she was kidding, to stop this train before it ran off the tracks.

"Yes, really," she insisted, a defensive note in her voice. "It's a weird situation. That's why I want to have the baby at the VA, with you. It will be just you and me and the

142

father, maybe a nurse. No cameras, no crowds, no one who might keep a reporter on speed dial."

I'd been convinced that she had changed, that she had gone into the army and come out a new person. And in so many ways, she had. But clearly, she hadn't lost her ability to lie with a straight face, to tell a story completely out of step with reality and then all but dare me to call her on it.

"Okay," I said. "I'll play along. He's famous. He's beyond famous. He's the fucking king of England."

"I hate it when you get like this."

"Like what?"

"Like you know everything about everything."

As we walked, the wheels in my brain were turning, producing a mental slide show of all the lies she had told in the past, big and small, years and years of lies. Heather and I had reached the cliffs. The Golden Gate Bridge, in the distance, was almost entirely obscured by fog, only the tops of the two orange towers visible. But the water directly below the cliffs was bathed in sunlight. We sat on a bench to rest, and for a couple of minutes we said nothing, just staring out at the view.

"So you've come back because you want

me to talk you into something," I said finally. "Or maybe talk you out of it. But you've got the wrong person. I can't claim to be the voice of reason. I can't claim to be impartial. I'll tell you straight up that I really hope you'll have this baby. If you do, I'll be there for you every step of the way. I'll babysit whenever you need me. I'll help you pay for child care if you want to go to work, and if you want to stay home with the baby for a while, that's fine, too. I'd help you find a good place to live."

I was practicing the same method with her that I use with my patients. Once a diagnosis is made, there are generally any number of variations on a course of treatment, multiple paths one might pursue. Sometimes the choice is so obvious, you need present only one scenario. Often, however, the case is less clear. As a physician, I have my preferences and prejudices, treatments that I believe, for reasons beyond mere scientific data, to be the wiser choice. In such instances, I may present more than one option, but I weigh my words in such a way as to make the decision, for the patient, seem almost clear-cut. It is a subtle deception practiced by every physician I know. Most of us rationalize these deceptions with the knowledge that our words are geared toward providing the best possible outcome: the ends justify the means. With Heather, though, my motives were far from pure. But she'd always been too good at reading me.

"I don't get it. If you're still so mad at me, why are you willing to help me?"

I could tell her that she was my sister, my responsibility. I could spin off some lie about how I was ready to put the past to rest. But that wasn't it; she must have known it as well as I did.

"After we lost Ethan, I completely lost hope for a while. I worked nonstop and tried to push him out of my mind, but he was pretty much all I thought about. I told myself that I could move on, that I could really get past it, if only I could have a baby. The baby was going to be my answer, my magic potion. But I've faced the fact that I'm never going to have a baby; my body just won't cooperate. Tom is dead set against adoption. After what happened —"

Heather looked away.

"For him, it has to be our biological child or no child. I'm never going to be a mother, but I'd make a damn good aunt."

"Unlike me, you mean."

Yes, I thought viciously, *unlike you.*

Had I gone too far, said too much? She'd lived with her guilt for more than four years.

145

It wasn't something we talked about, but we both knew it was guilt that had driven her halfway across the world, to a war zone where people were dying horrible, violent deaths daily. Now a hope for reconciliation had driven her here, to me. And yet, instead of telling her that everything was even, instead of welcoming her with open arms, no conditions, no questions asked, I was asking more of her. Demanding further payment on that old debt.

17

"Dennis." I'm having trouble catching my breath, understanding what just happened. "What have you done?"

"Something I should have done a long time ago: put Eleanor out of her misery."

"What?"

"You heard me."

It can't be true. Not this. "I know you," I say, still not wanting to believe it. "You wouldn't."

"Oh, you're wrong about that, Doc. Just ask Rajiv. I'm putting him on the phone."

"It's me," Rajiv says, his voice unsteady.

"Did he really —"

"Yes. She's dead."

I fight the urge to vomit. "Are you okay?" I whisper, but before he can answer, Dennis comes back on the line.

"Satisfied?" he demands.

How did it get this far? Everything has changed. I never realized Dennis was capable of this.

"You were on crutches," he says. "Why?"

It takes me a moment to register his question. How can he go on so calmly, after what he has done?

"I hurt my ankle," I say quietly.

"Are you okay?"

"Yes."

"You have to watch where you're going." He says this without a trace of irony, as if he has totally forgotten that, less than an hour ago, he shot at me. "You'll never guess who I've been listening to."

There's some shuffling on the other end of the line, and then my husband's voice comes through. "There's a protest on the Golden Gate Bridge, but before you join the throngs, you might want to consider the morning of May 24, 1987, the fiftieth anniversary of the opening of the bridge, when three hundred thousand souls surged onto the span, flattening the upper bow." Dennis must have turned on the radio on my desk. It's a red Panasonic Toot-a-Loop, a gift to Tom from one of his fans. I picture it in Dennis's hands; I picture Eleanor's lifeless body.

"The whole thing might have collapsed," Tom continues, "but somebody had the good sense to see what was happening and

148

usher the crowds back to dry land. I'm just saying, the water's cold. And very far down."

"I always liked Tom," Dennis tells me. "Weird, huh, considering he has something I've always wanted? Did I ever tell you I'm a big fan of *Anything Is Possible*? I listen every week. But when you met him, if I recall, he was still just the Voice of Midnight over at KMOO, wasn't he?"

"Yes, Dennis."

"He sure has come a long way. Every time I listen to him, I just keep thinking the same damn thing."

"What's that?" It's an effort to keep my voice even. They never taught us what to say after a hostage has been killed, where you're supposed to go from there. I picture Rajiv and Betty in my cramped office with Eleanor's bloody body. They would have tried to find something to cover her with. Rajiv probably used his white coat as a shroud; it must be soaked with blood.

"I just keep thinking that if I'd been the one you chose, instead of Tom, maybe I'd be the one who got rich and famous, and Tom would still be some fly-by-night DJ."

"Maybe so, Dennis."

Of course, I know he is wrong. Tom always had the talent for bigger things; he just needed a little nudging. It was eleven years ago that his star really started to rise. He'd been popular as the Voice of Midnight for several years when he came up with an idea for a show called *Anything Is Possible,* wherein he invited experts on the air to discuss everything from the colonization of Mars to the invention of a forgetting pill to the eradication of world hunger. The point of the show was that things that seem completely out of reach might actually not be so far-fetched.

I remember the night he came up with the show. We were at a party in Mill Valley when a guy walked up and threw his arms around Tom. He was thin and enigmatic, wearing a long wool coat too warm for the weather, looking more like a secret agent than the software designer he claimed to be. Tom introduced him to me as Wiggins, an old friend from Serra High. They talked about old times, the good-looking nun who taught them American lit, their days on the baseball team, a girl they'd both dated briefly. There were other names I'd heard before — Mike Potter, Tom Dugoni, whom I knew from UCSF, the multitalented Walt Bankovitch, and, of course, Barry Bonds. "He wasn't even the best guy on the team," Wiggins said, which is what guys from Tom's class at Serra always said, though I

150

never really believed it.

That night I leaned in close, feeling the buzz of Wiggins's nervous energy. Amid the noise of the party I strained to hear bits and pieces of his raucous stories, in which my husband appeared at seventeen, skinny and out of context, downing a six-pack every night, "and no luck at all with women," Wiggins claimed. He pulled me close, as if we, too, were the oldest of friends, and confided in my ear, "Clearly, *that* has changed."

Wiggins seemed on the top of the world. At some point he corralled us both and said, "Don't tell anyone, but last month I won three point five in the lottery." Tom thought he was fooling around, so to prove that it was real, Wiggins took us outside to see his car. It was an orange Avanti in pristine condition. "You remember how badly I always wanted one of these?" he said. The three of us went for a ride, speeding over the Golden Gate Bridge into the fog, then winding past the bay, through the Presidio, into North Beach. We ended up on Vermont Street, and as we took the twists and turns I felt an odd sense of elation. Wiggins's joy was contagious.

That night in bed, Tom nudged me awake, eager to share his new idea. "We become so accustomed to the patterns we create for ourselves," he said, his voice full of excitement. "We become so used to the way things are — scientifically, cosmically, personally — that we can't imagine things being any other way. But there's always another way. Common wisdom is, don't buy a lottery ticket, because no one wins the lottery. But here's the thing: someone always does win the lottery. Common wisdom is, get a real job, but there's Barry Bonds, just a regular guy from my high school, breaking Hank Aaron's record."

"And you," I reminded him. "Spinning records for a living."

"That, too," he said. "I want to do a new show, a show entirely devoted to the idea that what we think is out of reach is actually attainable."

I put my arms around him and buried my face in his neck. "I can tell you something that is extremely attainable at this very moment."

"Hmm?"

"Guess," I said, climbing on top of him.

"I know what I'm going to call the show." He unbuttoned the old shirt I'd worn to bed. "*Anything Is Possible.*"

The show quickly caught on locally, and that was good enough for Tom. After the first season, he was ready to call it quits and go back to doing nothing more than his late-night DJ spot, which he could practically do in his sleep, and which allowed him plenty of free time to spend on his land in Hopland, near the Russian River. I was the one who pushed him to pursue a second season. The second season was even better than the first, netting a slew of awards. The third season topped the previous two. I convinced him to hire a publicist, who helped him create a marketing kit and DVD. Before long, his show was in syndication. By the fourth year, Tom's voice could be heard on dozens of stations across the country.

One thing led to another, and he began doing voice-overs on the side for national television commercials. As a result, he has one of those maddeningly recognizable voices. I can't count how many times we've been at a restaurant or a party and the waiter or some new acquaintance has turned to Tom and said, "Do I know you?" Sometimes I'll be flipping channels and find myself strangely drawn to a car or a vacation destination or some brand of toothpaste, and then I'll realize that it's my husband's voice I'm hearing. Every time it happens, I feel a flush of pride.

I used to think Tom was proud of it, too.

"You know, I was happy just being the Voice of Midnight," Tom said out of the blue a few weeks before he moved out. It was a beautiful, cloudless day, and we were walking in Golden Gate Park. It was the third time in as many weeks that he'd suggested we go for a walk, and each time, he brought up some new grievance. In hindsight, I understood that those walks were a prelude to his leaving. Maybe he was trying to fix us, or maybe he was just trying to confirm for himself that we were unfixable.

"What?" I said, confused. "Your fans love *Anything Is Possible.* It's what made you famous."

"Did it ever occur to you that maybe I didn't need to be famous?"

"You were on the radio when I met you. You already had a following. Can you honestly say that you didn't want a bigger one?"

"Yes."

"I don't believe you. You were ambitious."

"No," he said emphatically. "You had enough ambition for the both of us."

"What's wrong with ambition?"

"Nothing, as long as it's your own. Your drive got you out of Mississippi — I understand that. All those certificates on your walls, the honorary dinners, the accolades

154

— you thrive on that stuff. It's like you need it to feel valid somehow. You've always had something to prove."

Was he right? I still felt the sting of the accusation I'd found scrawled across my Trapper Keeper in fourth grade: *poor white trash.* I'd tried to use nail polish remover to erase the insult, but it only smeared the ink.

"But I never had anything to prove," Tom continued. "I had you. I had my audience. I had my land, my music. I was happy where I was."

"You're happy now," I protested weakly, but obviously, he wasn't. He shook his head. "When Ethan was with us, I'd see you taking him to these music classes and Chinese lessons and Soccer and Smiles —"

"He loved Soccer and Smiles."

"Yes, but I couldn't help wondering what it would be like when he got older, where it would end. I always felt that wherever Ethan went to college and whatever he decided to do would be fine, as long as he was happy. But I knew it wouldn't be good enough for you. He'd have to go to Stanford, he'd have to be a doctor or a composer or the next Bill Gates for you to feel that you'd succeeded."

I felt sick to my stomach. "That's not fair."

"Isn't it?"

18

7:31 a.m.

The cable car is cresting Montgomery
Street when Josh Rouse's "Sweetie" begins
to play. *We'll sleep on rooftops, we'll ride on
bicycles,* Rouse sings. A man in a Giants
jersey stands on the running board, one foot
dangling over the street. I stifle an urge to
caution him. Every now and then a tourist
breaks a leg, or worse, mistaking our city's
most famous form of public transportation
for an amusement park ride.

I want to call Tom and say, "Don't do
this." I want to remind him that we had
figured it all out. We're going our own ways;
case closed. We've come too far to turn back
now.

"You should come by the loft," Tom suggested a few weeks ago, over lunch at Hog
Island Oysters. We sat outside, watching the
ferries in the bay. A tray of beautiful oysters
on the half shell gleamed between us. The

beer was so cold, the day so warm, it reminded me of the South.

"I'll make you dinner," he said. "I'll open an outrageously expensive bottle of wine."

"I can't," I said. "It would be too weird, visiting you at your place."

"It doesn't have to be my place," he said, dripping sauce onto an oyster with a tiny spoon. "It could be yours, too — your pied-à-terre, your home away from home."

"I like the home we have." I realized what I'd said. I also realized that I was verging on drunk and flirting with my soon-to-be ex-husband. "The one we had," I corrected myself. "Damn this beer. One of these days I'll become accustomed to you in the past tense."

He reached over and folded my hand in his. "I don't want to be past tense."

This was new. Unexpected.

"Isn't it a little late to be telling me that now?"

"It all seems too permanent, Jules. It doesn't feel right. This isn't what I intended."

In the old days it might have softened me — the way he held my hand, the way he looked at me, his dark eyes with their unsettling tractor beam effect. This was a man who knew how to pull me in. He always

157

had. But when he'd walked out, he had broken the marriage, and I knew it couldn't be repaired.

"What did you intend?" I asked, firmly pulling my hand away.

"I don't know. Maybe I wanted to shake us up, to make you see what you'd be missing without me."

He'd gotten it all wrong. I wasn't wired that way. How could he not know that about me, after all these years?

The first weeks after he left, we barely talked. Two months into the separation, he called my cell from out of the blue, late at night, his voice slow and loose; he'd been drinking. "I'm confused, Jules. I thought I wanted a fresh start, but now I'm not so sure."

It was so like him, to think he could control the conversation, that the ball would always be in his court. "You sound as if you think it's all up to you," I said.

"What are you saying?" he asked, startled.

"You turned my life upside down. I'm still mad as hell at you, and maybe now I'm the one who wants a fresh start. Did that ever occur to you?"

"Are you saying you don't want to talk to me?"

"I do and I don't," I said.

"As long as you're on the fence, I'm going to keep calling you," he said.

His tone was so casual, so infuriatingly confident. I hit End Call. Then I dialed Heather.

"So now he wants you back," she said.

"I don't think he knows what he wants."

Soon, we were talking several times a week, but our conversations weren't bringing us closer. I began to feel more like his therapist than his estranged wife. One minute he wanted to move back in; the next minute he wasn't sure. He was like a child trying to choose between the comforting stuffed animal he's loved for years and the shiny new toy. A month ago, when I finally filed for divorce, Tom suddenly knew exactly what he wanted. But by then, it was too late.

Now, as the cable car rocks past the clots of protestors shouting slogans, I strain to hear the music from the Bakelite. *Crooked couple standing side by side,* Rouse croons. *Is that me? Is that you?*

There's something willfully blind about Tom's song selections today. As if all that old charm will pull me back in, as if a night in his bed — or, rather, on his couch — will erase everything. As if we can go back in time.

19

"When I was deployed," Dennis says, "every time someone got shot or blown up, there'd be some dumb fuck who insisted that it happened 'for a reason.' That always pissed me off. Like everything was supposed to be okay, because there was a reason behind every shit thing that happened."

He's sobbing now. Is it remorse, or is it fear?

"But I'm sitting here looking at Eleanor, and there's blood all over the floor, and even though I can't stand her, I'll be damned if I can think of any divine purpose."

I don't know what to say, what will set him off, so I remain silent.

"I bet you never say that to the family after someone dies," Dennis moans, sniffling. "I bet you never feed them that load of crap about how it happened for a reason."

"You're right," I say cautiously. "I don't."

"I swear to God, I didn't plan to do it. So

here's my question: What if I didn't have a choice? What if it's written in the laws of the universe?"

"Do you believe that?" I ask softly.

"Nice try," he says snidely. "I asked you."

What I believe is this: there is no divine flow chart, no elegant spiritual mathematics through which our lives are processed. Events occur, we respond to them, we make choices, and our lives are shaped accordingly. But what is the right answer for Dennis at this moment? For the sake of Betty and Rajiv, I must tread carefully.

"I believe in cause and effect," I say.

"Okay, that's fair," Dennis says. It's quiet, and I can tell he's thinking. "Let's say you had to choose a day in your life that changed everything. What would it be?"

I don't even have to think about it. "August nineteenth, seven years ago."

It was ten o'clock on a cold Sunday night.

Tom was at work, and I was alone, decompressing with an old episode of *The X-Files,* when the doorbell rang. Who could be visiting at this hour? I looked through the peephole and, to my astonishment, there stood Danielle, one of my patients from the free clinic in the Tenderloin where I volunteered twice a month.

I opened the door. Danielle wore a dirty

yellow sweatshirt and jeans that sagged off her bony frame. Her lipstick was bright pink, garish against her pallid skin. Seeing her on my doorstep, so out of context, was startling.

"How did you find me?" I asked.

"You were in the book. Over at the Shell station."

The phone book. Who used that anymore?

I immediately thought of her twenty-one-month-old son and had a terrible feeling. "Where's Ethan?"

"In the car." She pointed to a beat-up Toyota parked haphazardly by the curb.

"Is he okay?" I asked, but I didn't wait for an answer. I moved past her, down the steps to the street, and opened the back door. There was no car seat. Ethan was propped between two pillows, swaddled in blankets. A seat belt was crossed over his small body, a diaper bag on the seat beside him. I unbuckled him and lifted him out. He didn't stir. His skin was clammy, and through the blankets I could feel that his diaper was soggy. Instinctively, I put my ear to his mouth to make sure he was breathing. He was. I grabbed the bag, carried him up the steps and into the house.

"Come in. It's freezing."

"I can't," Danielle mumbled. "My shoes

are dirty."

"It's okay. Come inside."

Ethan's head rested on my shoulder, surprisingly heavy. A child so small, so light — and then this good, solid weight against my shoulder. I breathed him in; his hair smelled like peaches. My sleeve was soaked through where his small body rested against my arm. I looked at his face in the light, relieved to discover that his color was fine, his breathing normal.

Danielle kicked her shoes off and stepped across the threshold. Her feet were pale and filthy, but her toenails, like her lips, were painted a happy shade of pink.

I jostled Ethan gently. He startled but didn't wake. "Did you give him something?" I demanded.

She looked at me, confused.

"Medication," I clarified. "Benadryl? Cough medicine?"

"No." She shook her head emphatically.

"Does he always sleep this hard?"

"He's just tired. We were out at Union Square today, working."

"Working?"

She held out her hand and pantomimed asking for money.

"You took him with you to panhandle?"

She shrugged. "Tourists love him."

"He shouldn't be out there, Danielle. He's just a baby."

Her face turned red, and I realized I'd been close to shouting.

"Who's gonna take care of him? The fairy godmother?" She scratched nervously at her neck. "I shouldn't have come here."

I lowered my voice. "We've been through this, Danielle. You're eligible for day care. Your child and family services worker can arrange it for you."

In the two years I'd been volunteering in the Tenderloin, I had tried hard to follow the advice of Dr. Bariloche, who had introduced me to clinic work back in medical school. "There are a lot of sad stories, mountains of need," she cautioned. "It will break your heart, but you have to keep your distance." For the most part, I'd been able to do just that. It probably would have been the same with Danielle, were it not for Ethan.

A couple of weeks before, she had brought him in with a fever, screaming in pain. It was a nasty ear infection. I wrote a prescription for antibiotics and called downstairs to have it filled. Danielle and Ethan weren't in our records, so I gave Ethan a plastic dump truck to play with while I went through the standard questionnaire with Danielle, filling

164

out the details of their medical histories. She seemed desperate for someone to talk to. She opened up to me about her drug addiction, which she'd been battling for years. "I quit cold turkey the day I found out I was pregnant," she said. "It was the hardest thing I've ever done."

Shortly after giving birth, she confided, she'd fallen back in with the people she used to know, and things had spiraled out of control. "But I'm done with all that now," she vowed. "I'm going clean. Every time I look at him, I know I don't have a choice. I have to get better." She told me about Ethan's father, who was serving time for armed robbery. "The best thing that ever happened to me was when he got locked up. I finally feel safe." As she talked, she kept adjusting her headband, a pretty wooden one engraved with an intricate pattern.

It was plain to see that, for all her terrible choices, Danielle was trying hard to be a good mother. Ethan's clothes were a bit dirty, but he seemed well taken care of, with no bruises, no burn marks, none of the heartbreaking signs of abuse that one so often encounters in the children of addicts. He easily climbed into his mother's lap and put his arms around her neck, to which she responded with kisses and chatter. There was an obvious bond between them.

At one point he toddled across the floor, patted my knees with his dimpled hands, laid his head down on my lap, and started sucking his thumb. My heart turned over; I was instantly disarmed. I put my hand on his head, then his cheek, which was red and warm from fever. His unruly curls were as soft as air, his skin impossibly smooth. I gave Danielle a paper bag containing a bottle of bubble-gum-flavored antibiotics, a bottle of grape-flavored Tylenol, and two medicine droppers. I gave Ethan his first dose and carefully explained the instructions to Danielle, extracting a promise that they would visit in a couple of weeks for a complete checkup. When I left the clinic half an hour later, I was startled to see her standing at the bus stop across the street in the driving rain, clutching a squirming, crying Ethan to her chest.

"It's miserable out," I said. "Let me give you a ride home."

"Thank you," she said, on the verge of tears.

Her apartment was in the Outer Sunset, a block from Ocean Beach, on the ground floor of a shabby building. By the time we got there, the rain had vanished, and the sun was shining over the Pacific. The living room was cheerfully crowded with baby books, teething rings, and toys. The kitchen door led onto a small, enclosed patio. Danielle had hung a hammock from two hooks on the patio's ceiling. She plopped Ethan into the hammock, and he laughed as she swung him back and forth.

"Hey, want to stay for dinner?" she asked. "We could eat out here. With those trees, it's totally private. No one can see in. Not bad for the projects, huh?"

I was caught off guard, with no ready-made excuse, and so I ended up staying. Over hot dogs and Diet Cokes, Danielle peppered me with questions about my job, my husband, my family. "Do you want kids?" she blurted at one point.

"One day," I said, "probably."

I was still relatively young at the time, thirty-three, so wrapped up in my work that it didn't seem like a good time to start a family. Tom wasn't ready yet, either. And besides, unlike most marriages, ours had not begun with the assumption that there would eventually be children. We had never definitively agreed that we wanted to have them. Still, in the back of my mind thirty-five loomed large, the age when the biological clock strikes some gloomy midnight hour and conception suddenly becomes more difficult. I knew that if we did want to be parents, we would need to start sooner rather than later.

As we were clearing up the dishes, she looked at me shyly and remarked, "I don't know many people like you."

"Like me?"

"Educated, married, a good job. All your nice clothes. I bet you live in a really nice house."

There was no accusation in her voice, but I suddenly felt pierced by guilt. How easy my life must seem, from her perspective. "I've been lucky," I said.

I couldn't escape the feeling that I had already crossed some invisible boundary. The fact that, two weeks later, she was standing in my house at ten o'clock on a Sunday night only confirmed that I had gone too far.

"Sit down," I told her. "I'm going to change him."

I carried Ethan into my bedroom and laid him on top of the covers. I put my hand on his tummy and jostled him gently, trying to rouse him. He screwed his face up, his eyes flew open, and he let out a loud cry. Overcome with relief, I scooped him up, swaying back and forth. "It's okay," I crooned.

"You're okay." Soon he stopped crying. I sat him on the bed and opened the diaper bag. The powdery smell of the disposable diapers, the comforting orderliness of them, stacked flat and white at the bottom of the bag, and the sound of the plastic tabs sticking into place took me straight back home to Mississippi. I'd been so proud, in those days, to play the dutiful big sister, the mom-in-training.

"Good as new," I exulted, lifting Ethan high in the air, and he laughed as if we'd discovered some brilliant new game. In the diaper bag, I found a soft blue T-shirt and pants, a tiny pair of white socks with trains stitched across the elastic. The anger I felt toward Danielle eased, seeing the care she had taken in arranging his things. I dressed Ethan and carried him back to the living room, where Danielle was walking in circles around the coffee table, biting her nails.

I sat down on the couch, cradling Ethan in my lap.

"What's going on?" I asked.

"I'm trying," she said. "I'm trying so hard."

"You have to try harder. If you keep up like this, you're going to lose him."

She looked at me as though I were the most naïve person on the planet. "It's not that easy," she said. "This thing, addiction, it's with you every minute, every second of every day. And when you have a kid, it's a thousand times worse. Every time I look at him, I can't help thinking he'd be better off without me."

Later, I would realize I should have offered some words of reassurance at that moment. "That's not true," I should have insisted. "Ethan needs you." But I didn't say it; deep down, maybe I agreed.

Ethan was squirming on my lap, so I set him down on the floor. He was instantly off and moving, touching everything he could get his small, fat hands on. I walked around behind him, nervous that he would hurt himself. I kept taking things out of his fingers, steadying him when he looked like he would topple. Eventually, he plopped down on the rug by my feet and became engrossed with a loose thread.

"So, are you going to tell me why you're here?" I said, trying to make eye contact with Danielle, but she wouldn't look at me. She kept pacing, chewing her nails.

"I'm in a little trouble."

"What kind of trouble?"

"I got caught with some stuff."

"Stuff?"

"Meth," she said, not meeting my eyes.

"My lawyer says I have to check into rehab this week. If I don't, the judge is going to put me in jail." She sat down on the couch and put her head in her hands. "Everything's falling apart. I was thinking maybe you could take care of Ethan, just for a little while."

"What?" I said, startled.

"My lawyer says I'll be out of rehab in thirty days."

"Don't you have family?"

"A sister in Glendale, but she won't take him. She hates me. Anyway, I don't want her anywhere near him. She's not a nice person."

Ethan had lost interest in the rug and wandered back over to me. He held out his arms, and I picked him up. His soft curls brushed against my chin. *Keep your distance,* I scolded myself. "It's impossible," I said, as much to myself as to her. I had a life, a career, a husband. I had responsibilities. Tom would never go for it.

Danielle gave me a pleading look. "You like Ethan, I know it. Don't you? You light up when you hold him."

Just then, Ethan reached up and patted my face, babbling, "Mama." I was aware, of course, that toddlers just learning to talk tend to call all women "mama" and all men

171

"dada." Even so, I melted. The wheels started turning in my brain. Just a month. It was nothing. I had some vacation time coming, and anyway, Tom and I could afford to hire someone to help out. *Say no,* my brain was telling me. But I didn't want to say no.

"I can't promise you anything," I said, "but I will at least talk to my husband." I was surprised by the words as they came out of my mouth.

"Thank you," she said, beaming. "Oh, God, thank you." She wiped her eyes with her sleeve, smearing mascara across her face. "Ethan will love it here," she said, as if it were a done deal, as if I'd given her a definite yes instead of a lukewarm maybe. "His caseworker's card is in the diaper bag. Her name is Terry. Anything you need to know, she can tell you. I packed Ethan's favorite blanket and binky. He can't sleep without them. He likes to have music on the radio when he goes down for a nap. Country music works best, for some reason. I can't stand it, but he likes it, so . . ."

Her voice trailed off. She came over, lifted Ethan out of my lap, and pressed her mouth to his hair. "I'll miss you, little man," she whispered.

"It's only maybe," I reminded her. I kept

waiting for her to leave, but she didn't. "The heat is off at my place," she ventured finally. A question, a nudging.

I looked at the clock. It was late, and it was so cold out, I'd had the heater running all day. Danielle's place by the beach must have been freezing. "You can stay in the guest bedroom tonight. I'll talk to Tom in the morning, when he gets home from work." What was I doing? I wasn't sure. Nothing in medical school had prepared me for this.

After making up the guest bed with fresh sheets, I stood in the doorway of the living room, watching Danielle. She had showered and changed into flannel pajamas I'd lent her. She'd even consented to eat a few bites of a grilled cheese sandwich. Clean and fed, she was now calm, quiet, and totally oblivious to me. Ethan had fallen asleep in her lap, and she was cradling him, crying softly.

That night as I drifted off to sleep, I felt strangely comforted by the knowledge that Ethan was asleep down the hall, warm and safe.

When I woke up early Monday morning, Danielle wasn't there. A note lay on the kitchen table, and on top of the note a key. She'd scrawled a message on the back of an envelope. *I'm sorry for not saying goodbye,* the note read. *Here's a key to the apartment so you can pick up Ethan's things. Please don't bring Ethan. If he comes home he will want to stay.*

That was it — no phone number, no further explanation. I read the note over and over again, feeling a strange mix of nervousness and happiness. When I saw Ethan curled in the guest bed, mouth open, breathing loudly, I felt oddly at peace. I lay down beside him. There was a smudge of bright pink lipstick on his ear.

When Tom came home from work, I was still watching Ethan sleep.

"What's going on?" he asked, standing over us, thoroughly baffled.

"We need to talk."

Tom made a pot of coffee, and I explained everything, then laid out my case: it would only be a few weeks. We could hire a sitter for the daytime while I was at work. I'd take some vacation days. "Wouldn't it be fun to have a child around?" I said, desperately hoping that he felt the same. "Sort of like a trial run."

Tom pulled me toward him, wrapped me up in his arms, smiling. "Uh-oh," he said. "Are you getting baby stars in your eyes?"

"Maybe."

He wandered into the bedroom where

Ethan was sleeping. We stood by the bed, watching him. "He's a cute kid," Tom said finally.

"Insanely cute."

"Thirty days?" he asked.

"Thirty days."

He wrapped his arms around me again. "Why not?"

At that moment, I loved him more than ever.

"Will you two be okay while I'm at work this morning?"

"Don't worry about us," he said. "We'll kick back with some *Sesame Street* and Cream of Wheat."

And I didn't worry. That was one of the best things about Tom: he was always up for anything.

20

7:40 a.m.

I glance over at the baby in the backpack, who has fallen asleep, his head bobbing against his father's neck. The father is on his cellphone, texting. I long ago got past feeling envious at the sight of parents of babies and young children, parents whose very nonchalance is evidence of their good fortune. Instead, I feel a tug of desire.

This morning, more than usual, the city feels so raw. Every corner holds some memory I can't escape. The cable car lurches forward again, and the sudden motion sends a shooting pain up my leg. We don't get far. Up ahead on California Street, a crowd has gathered. The driver keeps pushing uphill, but our progress is glacial. Several passengers decide not to wait, jumping off the cable car in the middle of the street. A few policemen are trying unsuccessfully to disperse the crowd.

I can't stop checking my watch, thinking of Heather. It takes nineteen minutes to travel a single block.

21

"I have to set the phone down again," I say.

"Don't hang up." Dennis's voice sharpens.

"I need to check on my sister. I'm not hanging up. I promise."

"You better not."

I think of Rajiv and Betty. Are they sitting? Standing? Where are they in relation to Eleanor's body? Rajiv never enjoyed treating Dennis, who was always a bit belligerent with him. But he did it anyway, as a favor to me. How much time do I have before Dennis hurts someone else?

I set the phone down and lift the blanket. Heather is dilated about eight centimeters. "You're doing great," I say. "It won't be long."

"Go," she says, pointing at the phone.

I pick the phone up. "I'm back."

"I don't like it when you do that."

"Listen, Dennis, my sister's going to give birth any minute."

His voice softens. "I remember when my Isabel was born. They had to do an emergency C-section. We weren't sure she was going to make it."

I contemplate my next words carefully. "You know, Betty worked neonatal at Mills before she came to the VA. I could really use her help right now."

There's silence on the other end. I close my eyes.

"Betty," Dennis says.

"Yes?" Betty's voice, soft and calm.

"Julie tells me you used to help out with the babies. Is that true?"

"Yes."

"She asked for you, but you know what?"

I hold my breath.

"I like you, Betty. I feel better having you here with me." He laughs softly, and I remember how he used to do this, laugh at the most inappropriate times. "Did you hear that, Julie? Betty's not coming."

"Okay, Dennis." I realize I'm trembling. "That's fine."

"You only told me the happy part of the story," Dennis says. "I want to hear the rest."

I close my eyes. "Not now, please."

"Yes, now."

22

That morning on grand rounds at the hospital, my mind kept drifting to Ethan. I asked someone to cover my afternoon shift and drove over to Danielle's apartment to pick up his things. As I turned the key in the lock, I felt, once again, an uneasy sense of boundaries crossed. What was I doing? How would I explain this to my colleagues at the clinic? I decided I wouldn't explain it at all. A month would come and go very quickly.

I was relieved to find the apartment quiet, clean. Danielle must have already checked into rehab. The thought crossed my mind that she might have run, that I might have been played for a fool. But no, it wasn't possible. She would never leave Ethan behind.

The place smelled like the beach, a good, salty smell, but the wet cold coming off the Pacific cut through the apartment. The cold was especially intense near the windows, where the wind whistled through. A light bumping sound was coming from out back, or maybe from a neighbor's apartment; I couldn't tell.

In the bedroom, I found a small suitcase packed with Ethan's clothes. Beside the suitcase was a cardboard box filled with toys and books. There was something so tender in the arrangement of the toys, and in the clothes folded neatly in rows — shirts, pants, pajamas. What must it be like for Danielle to love him so much and yet be unable to be the kind of mother he needed?

The kitchen was tidy, a note taped to the coffeemaker: *All set, just turn it on.* I opened the lid and saw that Danielle had filled the tank with water and put ground coffee in the filter basket. A white mug stood on the counter, and beside the mug a few wrinkled packets of sugar, a carton of nondairy creamer, and a spoon. I was touched by the gesture — so ordinary, so polite — and for an instant I glimpsed a different kind of life, the life Danielle might have had. I flipped the red switch on the coffeemaker, and it began to gurgle.

A neighbor's door opened, closed. There were loud voices in the hallway — teenagers, cursing. The voices died down, and the mysterious bumping sound continued. A door led from the kitchen onto the back patio. I glanced through the small, square window, but I could see only a corner of the patio — a potted plant on a low table. I walked through the apartment once again, making sure the lights were off, the appliances unplugged.

I wandered into the living room, where an old futon covered with a yellow quilt faced a small television perched on a milk crate. Beside it was another crate, this one filled with books — *The Very Hungry Caterpillar* and *Mister Seahorse* mixed in with *Breaking the Cycle of Addiction* and *A Beginner's Guide to Résumés*. I picked up a Bible with a red leather cover, Danielle's name embossed in gold. Inside the Bible, a bookplate said, "A Gift of Glide Memorial Church." A satin ribbon marked a page in Isaiah, where Danielle, or someone, had underlined chapter 1, verse 18: "Though your sins be as scarlet, they shall be as white as snow; though they be red like crimson, they shall be as wool." I remembered the verse from childhood, how the words had frightened and thrilled me. And then I recalled something else: that I had once won a Bible drill with that very verse. Every Sunday morning, I would stand at attention with the other children in front of the congregation,

Bible in hand, listening to the preacher call out a book, chapter, and verse number, my finger itching to find the page. I rarely won, but it didn't matter, because the reward was usually a letdown anyway: a crocheted bookmark or a little gold lapel pin in the shape of praying hands. But once, upon being the first to find Isaiah 1:18, I'd won a Chinese finger trap, which I'd kept in my treasure box for years, even after the red paper had lost its weave.

How strange it was to come upon these words now, in another place and time, so far removed from the context in which I remembered them. I wondered about the Chinese finger trap, if I might still find it in some dusty corner of my mother's house in Laurel. Occasionally, she would send me notes in the mail, quoting Bible verses or Baptist catchphrases she feared I had forgotten. "Once saved, always saved," she might write — an admonishment to me and also, I imagined, a balm to herself, for my abandonment of the church had confused and saddened her. When I visited home, there would be pink envelopes addressed to me from the church I'd attended as a child, with my name typed across the front, a blank place where I was supposed to write in my tithe. I hadn't tithed in more than twenty years, and still, they wasted these envelopes on me. Sometimes she would forward me emails from radical political campaigns, claiming our country was being punished for taking God out of the schools. My mother's voice, her face, her mannerisms, had changed little since I'd left home — and yet we had, it seemed, become strangers to each other. I sometimes wondered if that was inevitable, when a child grew up and moved away — or could it have been avoided? Had I failed her in some fundamental way? After Heather joined the army, I tried to call more often and visit a couple of times a year, but I was always uncomfortably aware of my mother back in Laurel, alone in the shabby duplex in an increasingly dodgy neighborhood she refused to leave. "This is home," she would insist.

Back in the kitchen, I poured the coffee, black, and sat down at the rickety table, which bore tiny handprints in green paint. As I sipped the coffee, I had a strange feeling of having sat down to another life. Why had my life turned out one way and Danielle's another? What determined the paths we took? Danielle had been raised by her grandparents. She, too, had a sister, one who was apparently doing fine. Nature versus nurture — that baffling old question. What had led to Danielle's unraveling? Was it something neurological, an ingrained predisposition to addiction? Or was it something else, simply a matter of one bad choice leading to another?

The bumping continued. Probably some issue the landlord needed to fix. Didn't it drive Danielle crazy at night? How did she sleep?

I stood to look at the photographs on her refrigerator. All of them were of Ethan, mostly snapshots but also one of those studio portraits from Olan Mills, with Ethan propped awkwardly against a fake plastic fence in front of a background of painted trees, even the requisite windmill. A calendar thumbtacked to the wall was still on the previous month. I took it down and flipped backward through the months, forming a picture of Danielle's life — home visits from the child services worker, visits to the clinic, hastily scribbled phone numbers beside the names of a dozen or more men: Eduardo, Rick, Dwayne. Were they suppliers? Worse? I was ashamed to realize I was making all the obvious assumptions, wondering how Danielle paid the bills.

Outside, the wind grew stronger, the bumping louder. Now I felt certain that the sound was coming from the back patio. I finished my coffee, rinsed the cup in the sink, and went outside to investigate.

My gaze fell first on the potted plant. But then I looked left, toward the section of the patio not visible from the kitchen window. I reached out to steady myself against the door frame. I must have cried out, I don't remember. The rope was fastened to a large metal hook that had been drilled into the underside of the roof. The hammock that used to be suspended from the hook lay crumpled in the corner. She hung there, the rope digging into her skin. There was blood where the rope had cut into her neck. The stool she must have stood on, which she must have knocked over in a moment of brutal determination, lay on its side a couple of feet from her. Instinctively, I reached up and felt for her pulse.

I had seen so many dead bodies before — hundreds of dead bodies. As a physician, it was a thing you were supposed to get over, and, to a great extent, I had. They take care of that in medical school. One is trained, on the dissection table, to see not a person but a cadaver. "A body is not a soul," Dr. Bariloche pointed out to me on the occasion of my first dissection, when I turned pale and couldn't keep my hands from shaking. "A body is a matter of study, of science. Bone and tissue, organs and arteries: no longer a person."

And she had been right. Over time, dead bodies ceased to be a source of discomfort for me. This was due, in part, to the fact that I worked at the VA and my patients were all adults, often elderly. I thought it must be more difficult for my colleagues in other fields — oncology, pediatrics. For the most part, I felt a kind of detached affection for the human body, the same way a mechanic might feel about a car that comes through his shop. There is the desire to understand the object, to make sense of it. One sees a dead body and understands that there is a history behind it — but as a physician, it is not the personal history that intrigues me so much as the physiological one: the body as a record of a physical life, the body as map.

Despite this, I had seen very few dead bodies of people who were not my patients. There had been my father, all those years before, at the funeral — so disturbing in his casket, with his over-bright cheeks and too-smooth hair. There had been a friend whose body affected me deeply, because he was only in his thirties, and because when I saw him I remembered building houses out of hay with him in the pasture behind his house when we were children. And then there had been a handful of patients with whom I'd become close. But for the most part, a lifeless human body was a matter of professional duty, a matter of course. While it might elicit a degree of sadness, it did not often cause outright grief.

When I saw Danielle, all those years of training melted away for one horrifying minute. Her eyes were open, her face terribly swollen. There were other things; she must have been hanging there for a long time, several hours. She must have clawed at her neck, desperate to loosen the noose.

I fought back tears.

I should have known, should have managed to stop her. I must not have been listening. It must have been in her eyes or her voice, or in the words she spoke to me, but I had failed to see or hear it. I had just been so tired, so angry with her for putting Ethan in harm's way. When she'd said that Ethan would be better off without her, I had barely protested.

As I turned to walk inside, something on the ground caught my eye — a beautiful wooden headband, the one she had been wearing on the day I met her. I picked it up. For some reason, I felt that it shouldn't be trampled on.

Back in the kitchen, the coffeemaker was still ticking. One of Danielle's final acts, apparently, had been to prepare the coffee for me. Just moments ago I had sat there drinking it, like it was no big deal. I picked up the phone and dialed 911.

The day moved with glacial slowness. While waiting for the police, I searched for a suicide note but found nothing. I called Tom and told him what had happened. "Are you okay?" he asked. And then: "My God, poor Ethan!"

The first police officers on the scene introduced themselves quietly, relieved to discover that I was not related to the victim. Over the next two hours, a slew of people shuttled through the apartment, taking photographs and collecting evidence. They left as dispassionately as they had come. The officers used a kitchen knife to cut Danielle down. She was so thin, but the tough-looking cops still struggled under her weight. I helped them cover her with a blanket I found in the bedroom. It didn't quite reach her feet, and I turned away from the sight of her blue socks peeking out below the blanket. It took an eternity for the coroner to arrive. When she did, she was talking on her cellphone, eating a package of Little Debbies.

It was late afternoon by the time I got in the car and drove home. Tom and Ethan were in the living room, racing Hot Wheels across the coffee table.

Tom came over to me, and I collapsed into his arms.

"Mama! Dada!" Ethan squealed, waddling over to us.

Tom went into the kitchen and returned with a postcard. "This was in the mailbox."

It was one of those cards you can get for ten cents at Fisherman's Wharf, with a blurry photo of Golden Gate Bridge on the front and a banner of white text: "Greetings from the City by the Bay." On the reverse side was a note, written in smudged blue ink: *I've gotten everything wrong, but I'm determined to get this right!!! I know you will take good care of Ethan. Please don't let anyone take him from you! You will be a great mother!!! Danielle.*

I stared at the note, hands trembling. It had been postmarked Saturday afternoon. She must have known, when she came to see me on Sunday night, that she was going to end her life. No one had ever asked me for anything so big, so monumental. People trusted me every day with their lives. But this was different.

Again and again during the following weeks, I imagined Danielle's last moments with Ethan, the way she must have pressed her cheek against his hair, breathing him in, the way she must have kissed him. How long did she look at him before she pulled the covers over his sleeping body and left? I hated myself for not hearing her, for not waking up when she left my house to set her terrible plan in motion. I thought of all those people who leapt to their deaths from the Golden Gate Bridge each year; statistics showed that if someone intervened and the first attempt at suicide failed, the person had a high likelihood of surviving the next few years. So often, it takes just one person to say, "Don't do it." I should have been that person for Danielle. I should have seen the warning signs. "He'd be better off without me," Danielle had said. She had uttered these words in my own house, and I had said nothing.

The funeral was held two days later at a church on Geary. There were only five people in attendance. The grandparents who had raised Danielle were dead, she'd been estranged from her sister, and she had apparently had few friends. In an unsettling turn of events, the priest asked me to speak. I had been introduced to him by the social worker, Terry, as "Danielle's friend" and Ethan's temporary guardian, so he must have assumed I knew her better than I did. I stood in front of the cluster of strangers, feeling entirely out of place, and said something about what a loving mother Danielle had been, and how much she would be missed.

The next day, Tom and I hired a family services lawyer, who filed a petition to the court for emergency custody. The judge granted it, for a period of three months. "If no next of kin comes forward," our lawyer explained, "you can begin proceedings for a more long-term arrangement."

"What do you mean, 'long-term'?" I asked.

"Well, there are several options we might pursue under these circumstances. You'll have to go through the foster care system. The father's paternal rights have been terminated, as he will be incarcerated for at least three more years. What do you know about the next of kin?"

"There's an aunt, but she didn't even come to the funeral. Danielle wouldn't have wanted her to have anything to do with Ethan." I pulled the postcard out of my purse and placed it on the desk. "Danielle sent me this before she committed suicide."

The lawyer glanced briefly at the note. "Unfortunately, this is hardly a legally binding document. The state is unlikely to take the deceased mother's wishes into consideration under the circumstances." He slid the postcard back across the desk to me. "But you never know," he continued. "Maybe the aunt isn't interested. Before we go any further, let me ask you — is adoption something you two might want to pursue?"

"Adoption?"

I looked at Tom. He squeezed my hand. In his eyes I saw fear but also possibility. This was the man who so fervently believed that anything was possible, the man who made a living debating the skeptics. "We become so used to the way things are," he had said on the night we took the ride with his old friend Wiggins in the orange Avanti, "we can't imagine things being any other way. But there's always another way."

Sitting in the attorney's office, I took a nervous breath. The whole thing felt surreal. Just days before, our lives had seemed so neatly arranged; we had each other, we had our work, and one day, when and if the time was right, we would make the decision to have our child.

Then, with a knock on the door, everything had changed.

23

8:02 a.m.

We're taking on more passengers at Kearney when John Lennon's voice comes through the radio, singing "Beautiful Boy."

How can Tom play this now? He used to play it for Ethan, and sometimes, at night, he'd sing it to him. I'd stand in the hallway outside Ethan's room and listen. Tom's voice was too deep to hit the notes properly, but that only made the song sweeter somehow.

Beautiful boy. It is how I think of him now. It is how I thought of him during the time he was with us, which, by any accounting, was far too short.

I would cup my hands around his small round face and stare at him for as long as he would allow it — never more than a few seconds. "A whirling dervish," Tom used to call him, "our little Tasmanian devil," referring to Ethan's relentless energy, the fact that he was incessantly in motion. Sometimes Tom would pick him up and look under his shirt, sending him into a spasm of giggles. "Where's the Pause button?" Tom would tease, pressing his belly button. "Is this it?"

I'll admit there were many times, in the first few weeks, when I panicked, wondering whether Tom and I had made a mistake. But Ethan always won out over any doubts. Just a few months into his time with us, I was startled to realize I couldn't imagine life without him. A dangerous attachment, I knew. At any moment, a relative might step forward out of the woodwork, a judge might sign a paper, and our world would come crashing down.

We quickly settled into our new routine. I would leave for work each morning at seven-thirty, and Tom, just home from the night shift, would spend a couple of hours with Ethan, feeding him and playing before the babysitter arrived. Tom, as usual, would spend the day sleeping, except on Thursdays, when he recorded *Anything Is Possible*. For years, the station had been trying to get him to take the morning rush-hour shift — more listeners, higher pay — but the odd hours suited him, and he couldn't imagine relinquishing his role as the Voice of Midnight. He'd wake up in the afternoon to relieve the babysitter. Home from work, I'd find Tom and Ethan sprawled on the living room floor amid a minefield of Tonka trucks and Duplo blocks. Our evening meals changed to accommodate Ethan. Instead of take-out burritos or Thai food, our table would be laid with plain buttered pasta, sliced carrots with brown sugar, vanilla yogurt. In the evening, Tom and I took turns reading to Ethan before tucking him into bed, and after he fell asleep — it was a lengthy process, getting him down — the two of us would spend a few hours together before Tom left for work. Both of us were utterly exhausted. My job had always been demanding, but caring for a small child was tiring on a whole different level, a kind of emotional and physical shock to the system. How had my mother done this, alone, with my sister and me?

And yet, the little joys Ethan brought into our life were so constant and so utterly new to me, I wondered how I'd lived without them. The first time we took him to the beach, pointed to the ocean, and said "Waves," his eyes lit up with understanding, and he began to wave. "He waved at the waves!" I told my mother over the phone, finally feeling that I had something I could share with her, a subject on which we could relate.

After the first month, we enrolled him at the child-care center at the VA campus. I would visit him during my lunch break, and at the end of the day we would walk through Lincoln Park to the Legion of Honor, where he liked to look at the iron statues of men on horses towering over the front lawn. There was such a sweetness to that time, the feel of his small fingers curled around mine, the way his eyes grew wide as he gazed up at the statue, his shrieks of pure delight when he touched the water in the fountain in front of the museum.

It amazed me how quickly Ethan began to feel like an essential part of our lives. I had fallen in love with him. It was happening to Tom, too. Often, in the middle of the night, Ethan would cry out, and I would bring him into the big bed to sleep with me. When Tom got home from work in the morning he would crawl in bed beside us, and we would hold hands over Ethan's sleeping body. "He smells like bread," Tom would say, burying his face in Ethan's hair.

While we didn't share a name or a genetic code, I came to think of Ethan as our son. He called me "Mommy," and he called Tom "Daddy." We were, in every way that really mattered, a family.

After several home visits from our case-worker, Terry, miles of paperwork, and a slew of required classes, our emergency custody was turned into long-term foster care. Meanwhile, our adoption attorney worked to get the glacially slow process moving.

For almost two years, we negotiated the limbo state of foster parenting. "Where did he get those beautiful curls?" other mothers would say in public, glancing from Ethan to me. My hair is straight as a board, a dirty shade of blond, while his was dark and lustrous, with curls so beautiful I couldn't bear to cut them. Long after we lost him I'd still find curly strands of his hair on the sofa cushions, in the fibers of the carpet.

I had to work sometimes not to become envious of the parents whose children were theirs to keep. At a play group, a party, an Easter egg hunt — wherever — I would find myself standing beside another mother, who would point to a child and say, "That one's mine." Such a simple declaration. Almost always uttered with a naked sense of pride. I came up with my own phrase for these occasions. I would smile and point at Ethan and say, "I'm with him" or "This is Ethan" — leaving out the crucial word, "son."

By carefully omitting the words that didn't belong to me, or to us, I felt as if I was betraying him. But as much as I wanted to, I could not promise him that I would be his mother for the long term.

The problem was Danielle's sister, Allison. She had never expressed even the most rudimentary interest in Ethan before Danielle's death. Then, seven months after Danielle's suicide, Terry told us that Allison wanted to meet her nephew. I was seized with fear. Why, after all this time, would she take an interest in him? Tom and I decided that the best thing we could do was to try to get along with her, to make her like us. If she saw how happy Ethan was with us, surely she wouldn't interfere. On the day of her visit, I cleaned the house from top to bottom, made coffee, and set out cheese, fruit, and pastries.

At four in the afternoon, an hour after the scheduled time, the doorbell rang. The cheese was sweating on the plate, the edges of the cut pears had begun to brown, and the coffee had turned bitter. Ethan's little blue pants and striped T-shirt were wrinkled and smeared with yogurt. I opened the door to find a woman of average height with a razor-sharp blond bob, dressed in a beige suit and pointy heels, clutching a cellphone.

"Sorry I'm late" were her first words of greeting. "Bridge traffic."

I looked for some resemblance to Danielle, and it was there, around the eyes, the mouth. "Allison Rhodes," she said, thrusting her hand toward me.

I invited her inside. When Tom offered to take her purse, she declined, holding it close to her side. Ethan was running around the living room in circles, dragging a stuffed snake behind him. He paused briefly to point at her and demand, "What's *that*?"

"This must be Ethan," Allison said. She walked over to him and patted his shoulder stiffly. "He's dark. What's the ethnicity of the father?"

"Greek," I said, taken aback. Did she fail to notice how beautiful he was? I looked at him and saw a sweetness so complete it was impossible not to fall in love with him; how could she be immune to his charms? "Is this the first time you've met Ethan?" I ventured.

She shook her head, and the bob remained in place. It was the kind of hairdo that could survive a tornado. "Danielle and I were estranged years ago, before he was born, but I visited when he was a few weeks old. I'm surprised she had him, to be honest. Before him, there were abortions, you know. A few."

I didn't know. There was really so little I knew about Danielle. I had thought some of those answers might come from Allison, but I realized now that anything she had to tell me about her sister would be ugly, filtered through years of disdain, even hatred. I didn't want to go down that road. One day I would have to tell Ethan what I knew about his mother. In my mind, I already had part of the script: *I met your mother at a clinic. She was troubled. She loved you very much. She wanted the best for you.*

"The flapping." Allison perched on the arm of the sofa. "Is he autistic?"

"No," I said. "He just flaps his arms when he's excited." I'd had experience with children on the autistic spectrum; Ethan didn't fit the diagnosis. Out of an abundance of caution, I'd done a good bit of research, and we'd had him evaluated by a specialist at Stanford's Lucille Packard Children's Hospital, who'd given us a name for his condition.

"Complex motor stereotypy," I explained to Allison. "CMS. The pediatric neurologist thinks there's nothing to worry about."

"What causes it?" she asked, frowning.

"No one really knows," I said. "It's still a relatively new diagnosis."

"He needs to get control of that," she said, "before the other kids start making fun of him."

"He's two and a half years old," Tom said. "The other kids don't notice."

At that moment Ethan popped his thumb into his mouth and started sucking enthusiastically. Allison got up and went toward him, and I thought she was finally going to play with him, but instead she reached down and jerked his thumb away from his mouth. "No!" she said, slapping his hand.

Ethan stared at her, as stunned as Tom and I were, and then he started to cry. I rushed to him and picked him up. "We don't hit him," I said coldly.

Ethan pointed at Allison. "Bad," he said. Then, more loudly: "Bad lady go time *out*!"

Allison continued to stare at Ethan, as if observing a stranger's unruly dog instead of her own nephew. "He's rambunctious," she said. "Like his mother."

"He's a little boy," I said. "He has a lot of energy."

"I have two boys and a girl. They all know how to sit still."

I exchanged glances with Tom.

My heart clenched at the thought of Ethan living with this joyless woman. She was there for forty minutes, and she never

202

did hug Ethan. She didn't even smile at him. "I'll be in touch," she said as we escorted her to the door. It sounded more like a threat than a promise.

For weeks after that, the sound of the phone ringing tied my stomach in knots. Every time, I was terrified it would be her. But the phone call never came, and, gradually, I began to relax. After that visit, we didn't hear from her for more than a year, and I began to believe that she wanted nothing more to do with Ethan.

"It must be so hard to think about giving him up," people would say when they learned of our situation. "I could never do it."

And I would think, *I can't do it either. If it ever comes to that, I won't be able to.*

On the radio, the song comes to a close, John Lennon singing softly about his beautiful boy.

And then Tom is on the air, saying, "I know a girl who thinks I've forgotten. That was my mistake. But here's the thing: I never forgot."

24

"So you and your sister have reconciled?" Dennis asks.

"Something like that."

"Then why is she staying at the VA hotel? Why isn't she staying with you?"

"She thought it would be easier this way."

"Right."

I don't like the way he says it — like he's judging me, judging us.

When the guy whose apartment Heather was borrowing returned home a few days ago, I invited her to stay at my place, but she refused. "It would be weird," she said.

"Weird how?"

But as soon as I said it, I realized she was probably remembering the last time she spent the night, when everything went to hell.

"The VA hotel is clean and cheap," she said. "Anyway, I like being around the other vets. I feel at home there."

It's not what I would have chosen, Heather having the baby with me at the VA, but she insisted.

"I haven't delivered a baby in ages," I'd pointed out months ago, when she'd first made the request.

"But you *have* done it," she said. "It was part of your training, right?"

I nodded. "One month on the maternity ward at San Francisco General."

"It freaked you out the first time," she reminded me. "Placenta all over the floor, shit on your surgical gloves."

"Right," I said, remembering it as clearly as if it had been yesterday. "They came in too late for an epidural, and the father was screaming at me to do something about his wife's pain. I think his exact words were 'Can't you do something to put her out of her goddamn misery?' "

"The baby was fine," Heather reminded me. "The mom was fine. The dad hugged you at the end and gave you a coupon for a free salad bar at Fresh Choice. By the time your month in the ward was up, you told me you could have delivered babies in your sleep."

"It was a very long time ago."

"You'll be great, Julie. Like riding a bicycle."

"The VA doesn't even have a maternity ward."

"I don't need the bells and whistles," Heather said. "Women have babies at home in the bathtub every day. Need I remind you of the lowly circumstances of your own birth?"

She was talking about a supermarket in Jones County, Mississippi, where my mother had been hiding out from a tornado when she went into labor with me. The very thought of my seventeen-year-old mother on her back in the storage room, being coached through her contractions by a middle-aged store manager named Ryan Ranahan, who kept repeating, "There's nothing to it, honey," made me queasy. Our mother used to say that I'd summoned the weather. "All drama from the word go," she'd say. "Not Heather. Heather came along quiet as a feather." Which was true. My sister made her entrance following two hours of labor in a near-empty maternity ward, took one blurry look at my mother, and fell asleep.

"Heather was the sleepy one," our mother used to say. "You were the hungry one." Moments after my entrance into the world, while the storm ripped the roof off the store and the manager fumbled around in the dark for a pair of scissors to cut the cord, I'd climbed my mother's slick belly and latched onto her breast with a ferocity that astounded her. Tree limbs plowed through the windows, produce flew like ammunition, and I drank.

"That was a different time and place," I told Heather. "Mom did what she had to do. There's no reason for you to have anything but the very best care."

"You're my sister," she countered. "Who's going to take care of me better than you?"

"Think of the red tape," I said. "There's paperwork, there's protocol."

"Are you telling me that if a woman walked into your hospital in labor — a veteran, no less — you'd turn her away?"

"No, but —"

She reached over and grabbed my hands. "Listen," she pleaded, and I knew there was more she wasn't saying. "This is really, really important to me."

Her eyes were wet, her expression so hopeful. I saw the jagged scar on her forehead, the way she turned her left ear toward me. I thought of all the time she'd spent in the army, trying to atone.

"I'll think about it."

"Okay," she said, grinning in that way she used to as a kid, when she knew she'd gotten her way.

"If you're honest," Dennis says, "there's a little part of you that wishes someone else was delivering the baby. Am I right, Doc?"

I glance over at Heather, who is standing beside the bed, leaning on the mattress for support. "No, I don't think so."

"And a little part of you," he says, "that wants to take the baby and run."

25

After Heather's return, she met me every Wednesday at the VA. She would be waiting in the cafeteria when I arrived before my morning shift, the day's *Chronicle* spread on the table in front of her. The paper would be covered with pen marks; she insisted on reading, despite the headaches, and had worked out a system of summarizing each paragraph in the margin before moving on to the next.

"I'm trying to teach myself how to remember again," she told me.

Beside the newspaper would be a plate of eggs and bacon, hash browns smothered in ketchup, an empty milk carton. In the past, she'd been a stingy eater, preferring cigarettes to meals. It pleased me to see her enjoying her food, filling up for the baby's sake. While she finished her breakfast I'd order two coffees from the Starbucks — regular for me, decaf for her — and we would walk the rocky path down to the cliffs. We settled into the routine as if by accident, without any discussion, and I began looking forward to our weekly walks, during which my sister and I slowly got to know each other again.

For me, it was a process of discovery more than one of reacquaintance. Heather had changed in so many ways, it was difficult to recognize in her the young woman who had walked out of my life more than four years before. The one thing that mercifully had not changed was her accent. Heather could still draw a two-syllable word out to kingdom come. When we were together, I found my own accent creeping back.

There was much we could say to each other, and much that, still, we could not. On the subject of our childhood, and of our mother, of the father who died and the one we never knew, as well as the subject of the town that we had both left behind, we talked extensively. Sometimes, caught off guard, she might talk about the army.

"What I remember most from my first tour is the darkness," she said once. "At night, it was pitch-black. There was no outside lighting at the base, and there was nothing nearby to provide even a smidgen of light. Some guy had brought *The Dark*

Side of the Moon with him, and he'd play that song "Brain Damage" over and over again in the middle of the night, and we'd all be lying there in our cots in the blackest black you can imagine, complete darkness, complete silence except for Pink Floyd, and the words would get inside my head — you know the song." And Heather sang a few lines.

I tried to imagine her lying there on a cot in the dark, but all I could conjure was an image of Heather at six, climbing into my bed in the middle of the night, too scared to sleep alone.

As for the matter of what happened to drive us apart, we were less vocal, as if we had made some silent agreement never to discuss it. While Ethan was clearly there between us — an accusation and an apology — it was as if we both feared that, by saying his name aloud, we might destroy our fragile newfound peace.

We instead settled into a gentler parody of our old selves — batting soft insults back and forth, allowing affection to seep in through the cracks instead of expressing it outright. It worked for us, felt more natural than the emotionally direct conversations sisters always have in movies, tears flowing without embarrassment. I couldn't imagine talking to Heather that way. We both inherited this sense of emotional distance from our mother, who hugged us quickly each night before bed and saved her I-love-yous for birthdays and special occasions. It always caught me slightly by surprise on Christmas morning, when the meager presents had been opened and the floor lay strewn with wrapping paper, and our mother, seeming truly happy, would look at each of us in turn and say, "I love you, Julie. I love you, Heather."

Gradually, Heather began stopping by the hospital unannounced. In the early evening, after my shift had ended, I would find her sitting on the bench near the entrance, and I would take her to dinner, or we would go see a movie at the Balboa. A couple of times, I went over to her place in the Mission and she made the Lahori beef, which was just as good as she'd promised. At first, I told Tom every time I saw her. But gradually, as his disapproval grew, I stopped mentioning our meetings.

Eventually, my lies of omission led to more outright dishonesty. One Saturday, when Heather called to ask if I wanted to meet her for lunch, I told Tom that I had to go in to work. I was surprised by how easily the lie rolled off my tongue.

One Sunday three months after Heather's reappearance, she asked, "What do I have to do to get invited over?"

"Come over this weekend," I said impulsively.

"Really?" she said, her eyes lighting up.

When I told Tom, he was furious. "I told you back then that I never wanted her to step foot in this house again, Julie. I haven't changed my mind."

He stood at the kitchen counter, stirring sugar into his coffee.

"Let's go out then," I persisted.

"No thanks."

"Where does that leave me?" I asked, setting my cup on the counter so hard coffee sloshed over the edge. "She's my sister. She's part of my life."

"That's a choice you've made," he replied, "but I don't have to be involved."

"If you had a sibling, you'd understand. It was four years ago! She went to war, for God's sake."

"You didn't make her go."

"Maybe not, but she went *because* of me, and now that she's back, it just feels right, having her around. She's my family!"

"*I'm* your family."

"That's different. Heather is my blood." What I didn't say was that the thing he and

213

I had together didn't feel much like family anymore.

"What about Ethan?" he said. "No blood ties, but we were a family."

"Don't bring him into this," I spat, furious.

"Isn't this all about him, when it comes down to it? When we lost Ethan, I lost you, too."

"I'm still here."

"No, you're not! And do you know what really kills me? You've got it in your head that this terrible thing happened to you, but it happened to *us*, Julie. I loved that little boy every bit as much as you did." He was shaking with anger. "All these years, I've tried to move on, for us, because before Ethan, we were good together. We were so in love. Don't you remember?"

"Of course I remember," I said, taking a step toward him.

Tom backed away, putting his hands up to block me. "But after we lost him, you shut down on our marriage. It's been *years*, and I keep waiting for you to come around. I've been so goddamned patient. But you never come around, Julie. You brought this child into our lives, and even though I wasn't ready to be a dad yet, I said yes, because you wanted it so much. I put everything into being a father to that little boy — *everything.* And it's like it never occurred to you that I have every right to be really furious with you, because it was *your* sister who fucked everything up for us. You knew her better than anyone."

He lowered his voice to almost a whisper and delivered the final blow: "All this time, you've never taken any goddamned responsibility for what she did." He flung his spoon into the sink, and it clattered against the stainless steel.

Now I was the one who was shaking. I collapsed into the kitchen chair. Something dawned on me with a slow and terrifying force. "You blame me. All this time, you've blamed *me.*"

He was silent.

Outside, there was the sound of empty cans rattling; someone was going through our recycling. Because there were no windows in our kitchen, just a skylight, the room was subject to the whims of fog and clouds; it suddenly grew dark.

"What about when the baby comes?" I asked finally. "What if she wants to bring the baby over here? Are you going to forbid that, too?"

"What the fuck, Julie!" He walked to the table and stood towering over me. He grabbed my chin and turned my face toward him. "Look at me!"

His face was glowing with anger. He'd never touched me like that before, so rough, so implacable. I was too stunned — too scared — to pull away. "She destroyed us once," he said, his voice so cold it gave me chills. "Now you're letting her do it again."

26

That weekend, Heather did come over. Tom cleared out before she got there. When she arrived, I was still cleaning, rearranging. She thrust a spider plant into my hands. "I never know what to get for a hostess gift."

"It's perfect. I'll try not to kill it."

She slipped off her jacket — soft blue suede, big pearly buttons.

"This is gorgeous," I said, sneaking a peek at the label as I hung the jacket in the hall closet. Vera Wang. "Where did you get it?"

"A gift," she said.

"At least we know he has good taste."

She wandered into the living room, stopped to take it all in. "It's different," she remarked.

"We painted, moved the furniture around."

She walked over to the sofa, put one arm out behind her, one arm on her stomach, and eased herself down. Even though she wasn't very big yet, she already moved differently, aware of her growing belly. She'd always been a naturally graceful person, and it was strange to see her so awkward. She ran her hand over the leather grain of the sofa. "It's softer than it looks."

I wondered if she remembered that it was the same couch on which the social worker had sat that afternoon, side by side with Ethan.

"Is Tom working?" she asked. "Or is he just avoiding me?"

"He doesn't like this. Me, you. He thinks I should cut you off completely."

"I don't blame him." Heather was fidgeting with her ring. "If you need me to leave —"

I shook my head. "He'll come around," I said, although I was having a harder and harder time believing that. "Do you still like pot roast?"

"Love it."

"Good, it's got a while to go. But meanwhile, we have the first season of *The Bionic Woman* on Netflix."

Heather squealed with delight. When we were kids, we watched the show religiously. I settled on the couch and turned the TV on, and Lindsay Wagner's golden hair floated across the screen in slow motion.

"Jimmy knows her," Heather said offhandedly. "She dated his cousin or something."

"Jimmy?" I said. "Is that —"

She nodded. The father was still a touchy subject, one she rarely brought up. I had stopped asking, for fear of starting an argument. This was the first time she had mentioned a name.

"You've seen him?" I asked.

"He was in town last night for a big fundraiser at some swank home in Los Altos Hills. I met him afterward at his hotel."

"That's weird. I was supposed to go to a fund-raiser in Los Altos Hills last night too, but I ended up working late. Some health-care-reform thing with the governor."

"At the Bertram estate," she said.

"Yes," I said, confused. "How did you know?"

She glanced at me slyly, the corners of her mouth turning up. "Jimmy always sees the guest list ahead of time."

"Stop messing around."

Heather didn't say anything.

"You don't mean to imply —" I couldn't finish my sentence. Jimmy. *James.*

She raised her eyebrows.

"James Dupree," I said.

She nodded, cracking ice between her teeth.

"*The* James Dupree," I said, incredulous. This was too much, even for Heather.

"I knew you wouldn't believe me," she said matter-of-factly. Her eyes were shining.

"You're right."

"Suit yourself. But don't you even want to know how I met him?"

"Sure," I said, shaking my head. "This ought to be good."

27

8:20 a.m.

The cable car comes to a stop between the two towering pagodas. Here is Chinatown proper, the length of Grant Avenue canopied with hanging lanterns. As the driver brakes, sharp pains shoot up my leg.

One block over is the office I visited more than a year ago in search of some miracle cure. I found myself one afternoon climbing the rickety stairs of a three-story building, clutching the name and address that had been given to me by my neighbor Mrs. Yiu. At the top of the stairs was a red door, and tacked to the door was a sign I couldn't read, black calligraphy on cream-colored paper. Beneath the sign was a framed eight-by-ten, which appeared to have been taken from a magazine, of a smiling young Chinese woman holding an infant in her arms.

I rang the buzzer and waited. There was a rustling sound behind the door. Seconds later, it opened to reveal a man in a white oxford shirt and white pants. He was younger and taller than I'd thought he'd be. The voice on the telephone had led me to expect someone elderly.

"I'm looking for Dr. Alex Wu," I said uncertainly.

"I am Dr. Wu. Please come in." The door closed softly behind me. On the wall was a diploma in biology from San Francisco State, a master's in science from U.C. Davis, a certificate in traditional Chinese medicine from the Academy of Chinese Culture and Health Sciences, and, below that, Dr. Wu's NCCAOM certification. He smiled kindly as I glanced over the diplomas. "You're in good hands," he proclaimed. At this he held up his hands, palms forward, as if I might want to inspect them.

"Yes," I said. "You come highly recommended by my neighbor Alice Yiu."

"Alice was my piano teacher many years ago. She was once a great pianist, you know. As a child in Beijing, she was famous, a prodigy."

"Oh," I said, surprised. "I had no idea." I'd never once heard piano music coming through the thin walls that separated our two houses. Sometimes, she and I would talk, standing on either side of our shared

222

wooden fence. I used to lift Ethan over the fence to Alice so he could pet the dog. "You're a strong boy," she would say, and Ethan, beaming, would push against the wobbly wooden fence with all his might and proclaim, "I super strong."

Alice had never been shy with her questions, which is how she came to know the intimate fact of my failure to conceive. I, too, had asked questions, but she had somehow managed to avoid most of them. I knew very little about her. What, I wondered, could have made her give up the piano? I thought of what Dr. Bariloche said all those years ago: life is a series of beginnings and endings. You leave one self behind and move on to another.

Dr. Wu led me to a large rectangular room. Opposite the desk was a red leather sofa, flanked on either side by small tables, on which rested identical potted plants. The place smelled earthy and vaguely herbal.

"Let's begin with your personal history," he said, taking a seat behind the desk and gesturing toward the sofa. I sank into the cushions, embarrassed to observe my own knees jutting so high in the air. It felt unseemly, like some strange prelude to the pelvic exam.

From his desk drawer, Dr. Wu removed a

black notebook with red trim, still wrapped in cellophane. He meticulously unwrapped the notebook and opened it to the first page. "How long have you been trying to conceive?" he asked, pen poised above the page.

"Forever," I said.

Dr. Wu frowned, and I felt my face redden. I never liked it when patients talked in codes that only they could understand. The best patients were the ones who identified their symptoms and the attending time lines precisely, factually. From this, I could construct a patient's story and begin the path to diagnosis. "Forever" was not a quantity; it was merely a statement of emotion, of fatigue, of thwarted desire.

"Almost three years."

He smiled and jotted something down in his notebook. "Very good." I wasn't sure what pleased him more: the fact that I was cooperating or the promise of a professional challenge. "And could you describe your fertility regimen?"

"I just finished my second round of IVF," I said. Then I rattled off a list of drugs and shots and hormones, timetables and temperatures. There was the IUI; the Clomid, which made me crazy; the Follistim, which made me puke, and the Novarel, which made me gain weight so fast that I looked like I really was pregnant. My past read like a laundry list of all the traditional methods, which made up in thoroughness what they lacked in romance. "Nothing works." It seemed like the only thing we hadn't tried was surrogacy, which both Tom and I had agreed was not for us. "Too many hands in the pie," as he put it.

"And your husband?" Dr. Wu asked delicately. "You're certain this isn't his problem?"

"Yes."

It wasn't until we lost Ethan that we began trying to conceive. While we knew that having a baby wouldn't replace Ethan, losing him sparked an urgency that consumed me. Six months in, Tom got tested, and we discovered that the problem was entirely mine. My eggs simply were not vital. Again and again, I awoke sweating from nightmares in which my eggs took ugly forms: hard gray pebbles, black ashes, tiny metal spikes that rebuffed anything that tried to touch them. Each month, I felt the sense of failure anew. As a physician, I understood that the human body does not necessarily bow to one's bidding, yet I was startled to realize how much of my identity turned out to be tied up with that most basic biological skill: the ability to conceive. No amount of work or persistence could get me what I suddenly wanted most: a baby.

Of course, I said none of this to Dr. Wu. Instead, I asked, "Can you help me?"

He prescribed twice-weekly massage therapy and weekly acupuncture, in addition to a bitter concoction of red clover, raspberry leaf, lady's mantle, and something called false unicorn root, "to restore hormonal balance and encourage ovulation," he said. I choked down the concoction twice a day for several months, all the while keeping close tabs on the calendar, my temperature, and the rest. This, like everything, led nowhere.

28

"Did I ever tell you what my parents said when I joined the National Guard?" Dennis asks.

His voice sounds tired.

"They said the military wasn't right for you."

"Their exact words were 'The military isn't for people like us.' Meaning, it's the poor people's job to go fight the wars. That's part of why I joined; I knew that wasn't fair. I'd gotten everything I wanted all my life, but my friend Jeremy, this kid who worked at the stables where my mom kept her horses, joined the National Guard to pay for school. He does great, top of his class, but he gets pulled out of college senior year and sent to Dhahran. He's a week from coming home when he gets killed by fucking friendly fire. Friendly fire! What asshole came up with that term?"

"I'm really sorry," I say.

"They had it right in Vietnam. Not the war itself, but the draft. A draft makes everybody equal. You had guys like Elvis going to war. That would never happen now. Can you imagine Justin Timberlake stuck in a bunker in Afghanistan? Every time I see one of those fucking CALIFORNIA IS MY COUNTRY bumper stickers, I think of Jeremy. And all these guys who came back from Iraq and Afghanistan missing legs and arms, or worse. All that sacrifice amounts to shit if any state can just say, Guess what, we don't want to be Americans anymore."

I can hear him breathing heavily on the other end of the line. "Hell, I don't have to tell you any of this. I'm sure you've already heard it from your sister."

"Yes," I say. I understand why he's so angry. Most of my patients feel the same way. Not Heather. She's always been starry-eyed about California.

I don't tell him about the sweatpants she gave me a few weeks ago, bearing the slogan REPUBLIC OF CALIFORNIA right across the derriere. I've yet to wear them, but I've been tempted. It's startling, really, how enamored the good citizens of California have suddenly become with the symbolism of our tottering statehood.

Children in schools across the state, from

Eureka to Riverside, have begun saluting the California state flag. I'd be willing to bet that, until recently, most Californians didn't know what has, in recent weeks, become common knowledge: the flag was first raised in Sonoma in 1846, by a group of thirty-three American settlers revolting against Mexican rule. In coming years, the handmade burlap flag would be the subject of much derision, on account of the fact that the beast in the center of it looked more like a hog than a bear. The commander of the short-lived California Republic was William B. Ide, a farmer and sometime teacher from Massachusetts who had arrived on the scene less than a year before. When U.S. Army captain John C. Frémont showed up and claimed the area for the United States just twenty-five days after the revolt began, Ide enlisted in the U.S. Army. A historic state park in Red Bluff still bears his name.

Revolt. Protest. That's something San Franciscans are good at, for better or worse. You can't walk past the Federal Building without running into a group of activists decrying global warming, animal cruelty, the World Trade Organization, the government in general. It makes sense that the flag grew out of an impulse for independence, a thrusting of the middle finger at the powers that be.

A few days ago, the evening news played footage of boys and girls standing at attention, hands over their hearts, gazing up at that lunky, half-grinning grizzly bear heavy-footing it across a white background, a single red star in the sky to the west of his head, a red band across the bottom. CALIFORNIA REPUBLIC, it declares, as if we'd joined the Union reluctantly in the first place, as if that grizzly bear always had one foot out the door.

Earlier this week on Channel 4, I saw a classroom full of third-grade children singing the state song, a rather odd little tune called "I Love You, California":

It is here nature gives of her rarest.
It is Home Sweet Home to me,
And I know when I die I shall breathe my
    last sigh
For my sunny California.

A radio station in Sacramento is running a contest for the best state pledge, because we don't have one. Apparently, only six states do. It's news to me. This whole process has been a crash course in civics. As it turns out, most states require public school students to recite the Pledge of Allegiance to the American flag; California doesn't. The California constitution does, however, require that public schools provide "patriotic exercises" on a daily basis. The phrasing smacks of a different era. I picture rosy children in red, white, and blue doing calisthenics on a golden lawn — a bit of Communist-style group exercise for the democracy set.

Growing up, we had to recite two pledges each morning in school, one to the American flag, the other to the Christian flag — white, with a blue square in the upper left corner and, in the square, a red cross. Although it was a public school, no one took the separation of church and state seriously. I recited both pledges with passion. It did not occur to me that allegiances could shift, that the things I believed in as absolutes would fade. The things I learned in Sunday school now seem absurd to me — multiplying loaves of bread, tongues of fire, Jonah in the belly of the whale, a day when believers will be whisked up into the sky. Back then, it was not necessary to think about these outlandish stories, to analyze them. They simply *were*, just as America simply *is* my country. I did nothing to earn my citizenship. I was born into it, the laziest form of patriotism.

If the ballot initiative passes, a million things we take for granted will suddenly be turned on end. When the San Francisco Giants play at AT&T Park, will the fans stand and hold their hands over their hearts while someone sings the new California anthem? And who will get to write it? Tom tells me that invitations have already gone out from the secessionist faction of the state legislature to several California-based acts, from Oakland's own Green Day and Counting Crows to Don Henley and Glenn Frey.

On a more personal level, will everyone at the VA be out of a job? The VA has been my home for my entire medical career. The staff and residents and patients are my extended family. It's impossible to imagine packing up and moving to a different hospital, navigating the unfamiliar corridors and labyrinthine politics of a new facility.

And of course, the biggest question: Which flag will we salute? Last night, I did a test, just to see what it would feel like to say it: "I pledge allegiance to the flag of the Republic of California . . ." It sort of sounded right. It sort of didn't.

My first allegiance: my mother. In the foyer of the church on the day of my father's funeral, I am standing at her side, so close I can feel the soft fabric of her dress brushing against my face. She's wearing dark plum instead of black, my father's favorite dress. The eyelet hem hits high above her knees. Into the slots of her penny loafers — she is flat-footed and can't abide heels — she has tucked two shiny nickels to match her silver necklace, earrings, and bracelets. People are coming in, saying things to her in hushed voices, looking down at me as though I'm a poor lost puppy. They touch my hair, and their voices shake when they tell me what a sweet girl I am, how much they adored my father. Enormous Myrtle May says, "Girl, I remember when you brought the weather. Your daddy couldn't have been prouder."

I am five years old, and I don't understand why we're putting my father in a box deep in the ground. I've been told this is a funeral, "to say goodbye to Daddy," but I don't know where he's going, or how long he'll be gone.

"That old oak out in front of First Federal," whispers a lady from the church, fanning herself with an ugly pocketbook. "That branch just fell clean off like an act of God. Bless Tudy's heart, she'll be bankrupt come Sunday."

I don't know what "bankrupt" means, but hearing my mother's name, I feel fiercely protective.

The cemetery is next to a pasture, and it has been raining all week. The air smells of hay, manure, rainwater, and trees — a sweet, familiar smell. As we're walking to the grave site, our shoes stick in the mud. Mine are white with kitten heels, my first "big girl" shoes, bought special for Easter Sunday, and I'm upset that they're getting ruined. My mother and I sit in folding chairs right in front of the casket, so close, I think, I could reach out, open it, and climb in next to Daddy. He always lies in bed with me until I fall asleep, but last night he wasn't there. The pastor talks and talks; my mother cries and grips my hand, then pulls me into her plum-colored dress so close I can hardly breathe. At last the pastor says, "And herein we conclude this service." At precisely that moment a cow in the pasture lets out a long, solitary moo. I laugh out loud, certain it is my daddy, come to wish us well.

"Hush up," my mother says gently.

Then we're walking back to the car. Our shoes make soft sucking sounds in the mud.

"What's 'bankrupt'?" I say, too loud.

My mother squeezes my hand and looks down at me, so serious, and she says just as loudly, for the whole world to hear, "Don't you worry. I have two hands and a brain. I can work. No one in this family is going bankrupt."

In the car, she pulls me close to her and buries her face in my hair, all her bravery gone. I can feel her tears on my scalp. "Don't you ever leave me," she says.

Neither of us could have known that, only ten years later, I would be plotting a permanent escape.

Of course, we still talk every other Sunday, in the afternoon, after she gets home from church. I haven't told her about my divorce, and am at a loss as to how to go about it. What would she make of the notion that a marriage can simply be discarded, so essential an allegiance betrayed? This is a woman who still wears her wedding ring, thirty-five years after her husband died. I imagine she'd advise me to make things right, to take Tom back, to do whatever's necessary to hold the family together. She would likely say something about the whole being greater than the sum of its parts. But this is where the domestic equation breaks down: Without a child, are we even a family?

29

8:57 a.m.

The cable car moves slowly but steadily for a few blocks, then screeches to a stop. A crowd has gathered at the intersection of California and Hyde. It's not the usual swarm of people in a hurry, heading to work. The helicopter circles overhead, its white bundles of propaganda falling like snow. There's that sense of restlessness, as if, at any moment, this whole thing might erupt.

Teenagers in school uniforms are chanting, "Let us *go!*" Several middle-aged women with pro-union signs have gathered around the students. A confrontation appears to be imminent.

"Let them go" has become the rallying cry of a particularly virulent right-wing movement that views California as an affront to the values of the country. Their disciples, who camp out at public parks and

236

churches and even schools, shouting angry insults, point gleefully to the fact that California is on the verge of bankruptcy.

The governor has used this slogan to his benefit. "We grow more than half of their fruits and vegetables, and yet they say, 'Let them go,' " he wrote in his most recent open letter to California voters. "We send hundreds of billions of dollars to the federal government each year, and the welfare states receive our gifts without complaint, and yet they say, 'Let them go.' We've sent more than fifty thousand soldiers to fight their wars, and yet they say, 'Let them go.' We create the technology that builds their computers and their smartphones, and they say, 'Let them go.' The finest medical minds in the world are at work in our institutions of higher learning, developing biotechnology that will save their children's lives, and they say, 'Let them go.' Well, we agree. *Let us go!*"

The conductor clangs the bell and shouts into the crowd, trying to clear a path, but it's obvious they're not going anywhere. From here I can see the tower of St. Francis hospital three blocks away. Three long blocks, but still.

I push my way off the cable car, down into the crowd. Leaning against a newspaper kiosk, I send a text to my old med school friend Kim, who's a general internist at St. Francis. *Are you at the hospital? Need help.*

I'm counting steps to keep my mind off the pain — one and two and three and four. My ankle is on fire. Halfway there, a man thrusts a pink pamphlet toward me. As I dodge him, he calls out, "Dr. Walker?"

I search his face, trying to find the connection.

"You don't remember me, do you?"

Blue eyes, dark hair, mid-thirties. Medium height. Denim jacket. I've seen thousands of patients over the years. He could be any one of them — except, of course, he can really only be one of them. When he turns his head, I see the scar on his neck. A long, red welt, stretching from just below his right ear nearly to his Adam's apple. I was twenty-six years old and just out of medical school, doing my first year of residency, on rotation at San Francisco General, when he stumbled into the ER at three A.M., bleeding all over the floor.

The sight of the scar makes me uncomfortable, guilty. I remember how petrified I felt as I punctured his skin with the needle and pulled the thread. I remember worrying that he would bleed to death on my watch.

Gradually, the details come into focus. It

was the girlfriend who did it, with a serrated kitchen knife. When they came into the ER, he was calm, but she was screaming and hysterical. Only when security took her out of the room did the man say under his breath, "Crazy bitch. I'm not taking her back, I don't care if the bitch begs on her knees."

Half an hour later, she returned with vanilla ice cream from the cafeteria, touching his cheek and sobbing that she was sorry. He smiled at her through the haze of the anesthesia and said, "I love you, baby." Watching him eat the ice cream with the tiny wooden spoon, it occurred to me that there was so much I didn't know, so much I had to learn.

"Right," I say. "You had the girlfriend with the knife skills."

"Bingo," he says, running his fingers along the scar. "Your hands were shaking. When the stitches came out and I saw what was left, I cried like a baby. What can I say? I was young and vain. Want to touch it?"

"What?" I say, startled. I glance impatiently at my phone. No text from Kim.

"Your handiwork here." He points at the scar.

I'm not sure what compels me to reach out and run my fingers over the jagged

239

edges. The skin is slick and tight. "I'm sorry."

"Don't be. It's my good-luck charm. I'll be sitting in a bar, minding my own business, and some woman comes up and asks me what happened to my neck. They think I've been inside." He smiles. "One thing leads to another."

"Whatever happened to the girlfriend?"

He laughs. "I married her. Didn't last."

My phone buzzes, a text from Kim. *I'm here.*

"Where you headed?" he asks. "Looks like you're in pain."

"Down to St. Francis. I tore up my ankle this morning. I need to get it wrapped so I can go deliver a baby. Long story."

He stuffs his stack of pamphlets into his messenger bag. "Let me help."

"Really?"

"That's what I'm all about these days!" His enthusiasm feels oddly off, as if he's following a script.

I drape my arm around his shoulder. He puts an arm around my waist, I lift my bad ankle off the ground, and like this we proceed down the sidewalk.

"No offense, but maybe you ought to watch where you're going next time."

"And maybe you ought not marry girls

who try to kill you."

"Right, Doctor Lady."

At the hospital, he insists on escorting me into the ER waiting room. "You ever find yourself in need of anything, call me," he says. He pulls a pamphlet out of his messenger bag, scribbles his phone number on the bottom, and presses it into my palm.

It's always the same. I see someone out in public, someone who appears to know me. They look at me as though our relations have been intimate, as though there is some secret in our past tying us together. Even after all these years, it takes me a few moments to realize that it's not someone I know, really, just a former patient. But the strange thing is that I do eventually remember. Not names, but faces. I have an uncanny ability to put a face with an ailment or injury, to remember where I saw the patient and what I treated him or her for. It's a strange way to go through the world, knowing so much about other people's lives when they know so little about mine. Yet the imbalance has always suited me — always better to be the observer, not the observed.

As he turns to leave, I read the bold print on the pamphlet, surprised to discover that it has nothing to do with the vote. *So, why can't you achieve your goals? You can!* Below that exhortation, the image of a fleshy, balding man stares back at me. Under that, in a smaller font, is the message: *Dianetics reveals the source of all your unhappiness and self-doubt, and shows you how to get rid of it.*

I toss the flyer into the trash and try, for the umpteenth time, to get through to Heather.

30

"I met him in Kabul," Heather said that night at my house while the pot roast simmered in the oven. All this time, I'd been waiting for her to identify the father, and now that she had done so, it was even more outrageous than I'd expected. She was smiling mischievously — as if to admit, almost, that she was pulling my leg.

"My unit was stationed at an FOB just outside of town, doing security for a reconstruction team and training the local police, when my commanding officer told me that we were going to have a visit from a very important person."

The potted plant that she had brought as a hostess gift sat on the table between us. I sipped my wine. I didn't believe her, but I was still intrigued by the story, eager to see how she would get herself out of the hole she had dug. "I see."

"You can look it up," she said, defiantly

spearing a broccoli floret from the appetizer tray. "I'm sure there must have been articles in the paper about his trip."

How long had she been working on this fairy tale? Had she rehearsed it again and again, gearing up for the day when she would present it to me, or was she making it up on the spot? Had she told it to others, or was I getting the first draft? I thought of the stories she'd told me in the past. For as long as I remembered, she had lived in a fantasy world, populated by improbable meetings with celebrities and hairbreadth escapes from death. When she was small, it had been charming: she could tell you with a straight face that she had met Jimmy Carter at the K&B, or that a lion had crossed her path when she was walking home from school. Each tale came with vivid details. When she was small, her stories delighted me, and I, like our mother, took them as a sign of budding talent. "You'll be a writer one day," I used to say, but she'd never taken an interest in writing her stories down. I think it was the immediate reaction she enjoyed — the look on someone's face when she told her lies, the challenge of convincing a person that what she said was true.

As she got older, the stories became

milder, as if they had been calculated to be both dramatic and credible. The kind of stories that *could* have been true, if a person was inclined to believe her. I once heard her tell a new boyfriend about the time she was walking down the street and saw a group of workmen installing a plate-glass window several stories above, and in the next instant the big pane was suddenly in freefall. According to her story, the big pane shattered on the ground just inches behind her, spraying the street with shards but leaving her completely unharmed. "A split-second difference in my pace," she had told the mesmerized boyfriend, "a moment of hesitation as I walked, and the glass would have taken off my head." There was also the one about how she met Kevin Bacon while stopped at a red light in Oxford, Mississippi, and he took her out for a burger and fries. "He was the nicest guy in the world."

Heather lived in a dramatic world of her own making. The most frustrating thing about her stories was that, while I didn't believe them, there was no way to disprove them. Whenever I expressed doubt, she acted greatly wounded. "What, you don't think Kevin Bacon would find me interesting?"

I had no more reason to believe her story

about the governor than I had to believe any of the others. I knew that if I looked it up, I would probably discover that the governor had visited Kabul on the date she specified. Maybe she had met him, and I could see how, in her professional capacity, she might have had a conversation with him, in which case it was even quite plausible that he had flirted with her. But to create a version of her life in which they were in love and having a baby together — it was just too much. Why had I thought she had changed?

"Anyway," she continued, "I was assigned to show the governor around camp."

"So, what was he like?" My psychiatry course in medical school had included a unit on chronic lying. While it's not considered a mental illness in its own right, it is often grouped as a symptom with those of other mental illnesses — narcissism, delusional thinking. But there are also cases in which otherwise normal individuals leading productive personal and professional lives lie compulsively, with no apparent reason. In some situations, a frontal lobe injury is to blame. I'd read a fascinating study about chronic lying in veterans who had suffered just such injuries. Which might make sense with Heather, were it not for the fact that she'd been lying practically since she could talk.

"He was completely charming," she said. "But a little nervous. We had politicians coming through all the time. It was a photo op for most of them, and you could tell that while you were talking to them, their mind was somewhere else. With him, it was different. He was really listening. When I walked him around the base, his questions were genuine. He had an assistant, of course, a driver, the usual bodyguards, but he was personally taking notes. The other thing was that he didn't bring a photographer or camera crew. He had his own little point-and-shoot, but that was it. He was the first politician I've seen, and I've seen a lot, who didn't want official pictures of himself at the base."

"But how did you —"

"End up in the sack together?"

"Well, yes. It's one thing to show him around the base, but logistically speaking, the other seems almost impossible."

She looked away, and I realized she hadn't thought that far ahead in her story. Maybe this was the point where she'd confess that it was all an elaborate lie. But she kept talking.

"He was in the region for ten days. The

first day, after I showed him around, he took me aside and asked if he could have dinner with me that night. It didn't occur to me that he might be asking out of a personal interest. I thought he had some questions he wanted to ask off the record, which, quite frankly, would have put me in a very awkward position. He wrangled permission from my commanding officer for me to leave the base, and I went with his entourage to the Green Zone, riding side by side with him in the Humvee. There were contract soldiers in the front, and vehicles ahead of us and behind us, but in the backseat, it was just the governor and me. We kept bumping into each other as the Humvee plowed over the terrible road. He asked where I was from. I was nervous, so I was just sort of babbling on and on about Mississippi, and when I stopped to take a breath I realized that he was looking at me in a funny way, and it was so odd, it just sort of stopped me in my tracks, and I said, 'What?'

"He said, 'You're really beautiful,' and I was just sitting there, sort of confused. I mean, guys say shit all the time to get you in bed, it's what guys *do,* but this was the governor. It was different."

"Mmm-hmm," I said, playing along.

"So we had dinner in his quarters. I have

no idea what we ate — it was all so surreal. He told me that he had a project he needed help on. He wanted to draft a document to bring back to the state legislature and to a meeting of governors. Everything he'd seen had confirmed in his mind the need for a surge, and he wanted a solid report to take back to California. I got the feeling he was expecting a lot of political fallout and he wanted some ammunition. I'd written plenty of reports for the PR office, so it really didn't seem that strange. Of course, I assumed I would be working with one of his aides.

"I spent the night in a room that had been arranged for me in the Rasheed Hotel in the Green Zone. I still remember the shower — it was amazing, having my own shower, all to myself, with plenty of hot water. Anyway, the next day, I was escorted up to a room in his quarters. There was a desk, a few elaborate chairs, an oddly ornate sofa, a chandelier, and a gilded coffee table, which had apparently once belonged to a high-ranking minister. But there was no aide waiting there for me. It was just the governor, in jeans and a University of San Francisco T-shirt. We spent the day together, with a laptop computer and endless cups of coffee, working on this report. He kept asking questions, really wanting my opinion, asking me how I would phrase this or that, whether a paragraph struck the right tone. What impressed me most about him was his intelligence — which is an understatement, really. The guy is brilliant.

"There was a strange energy in the room. Every time our hands brushed against each other I got all flustered, like I was in junior high. But I just kept thinking, (A) it's the governor, there's no way a man like that would be interested in me, and (B) even if he is interested, it would be a very bad idea on my part, because he doesn't have the best track record."

As Heather talked, I found myself getting wrapped up in the story — leaning forward, listening intently, wanting to know what happened next. And then I had to remind myself that I'd fallen through this rabbit hole before — that I'd become completely invested in something she was telling me, only to realize, because of some inconsistency, some blip in the screen of her story, that she'd made it all up. I noticed that, as she was speaking, she rarely met my eyes.

"So it goes for three days. Me and the governor alone in this hotel room, with Blackwater standing guard outside. We're occasionally interrupted by a member of his staff or by someone bringing us food and coffee, but for the most part, it's just the two of us. And on the fourth day, we're forty-six single-spaced pages into this monster of a report we're writing, and he leans over and kisses me. And that's that. We didn't get any work done for the rest of the day, or the day after that, but I kept coming back to his quarters on the pretense of writing the report, which we did eventually get back to. We ended up talking about a lot of other stuff too — our childhoods, his career, his separation from his wife, all the ways I'd fucked up. I didn't leave anything out, and neither did he. He laid everything on the table, and I knew I had to do the same. By the time he left the country, it was a full-blown thing. I felt that I knew him better than I'd ever known anyone. It may sound melodramatic, Jules, but it's true. Part of it, I think, is that you're over there, isolated from everything you know. It makes emotions much more intense.

"A large part of me expected to never see him again," she continued. "Despite this amazing connection we had, I couldn't quite believe that any of it was real for him. Maybe, as soon as he got home, he'd forget me. But he didn't forget me. A few months later, just weeks before I'm due for dis-

251

charge, he's back in the Green Zone, and once again, he sends a vehicle to bring me to his quarters."

She brushed her hair out of her eyes, and I again saw the scar above her eyebrow, where the kid had hit her with a rock.

"I can't believe Mom was able to keep all of this a secret," I said.

Heather took a sip of her sparkling water. "Oh, I didn't tell Mom. She'd be livid. He's a Democrat *and* a Catholic."

"And married."

"I wasn't on the pill because it makes me look like a whale and feel like crap, moody as hell. And besides, before he showed up I wasn't seeing anyone. The truth is, I've never been the most responsible person in that department, and nothing had ever happened, and then there's you." She glanced at me apologetically. "Sorry, but Mom told me you were having a hard time getting pregnant, so I thought maybe it's something genetic, like maybe my eggs weren't firing on all cylinders. Anyway, I'd timed it, and I told him we were safe. Lo and behold, three weeks later, I'm peeing onto a pregnancy strip a friend of mine filched from the medical tent, thinking, *This* really *cannot be happening.*"

She leaned back, looking at me intently,

252

smiling slightly. Daring me to believe her.

"That's a great story," I said finally.

She frowned. "What's that supposed to mean?"

"It's just, with you, sometimes I don't know how much is —" I fumbled for the word. "Real, I guess."

"God, Julie," she said. "You're unbelievable."

"*I'm* unbelievable?"

"You just can't get the idea out of your head that I'm a complete fuckup. You can't fathom that someone like *him* would be interested in someone like *me.*"

And I thought, then, that I understood what all of this was about. It was a statement of her worth, another dare, to see if I would object to the idea that she could attract the attentions of someone as powerful as the governor.

"That's not it," I said, feeling sorry for her. "It's just — all these stories. You met Jimmy Carter in the shampoo aisle?"

"Yes. I don't know, maybe it was the candy aisle — whatever."

"And the one about Kevin Bacon? Seriously."

"Okay, maybe the guy only looked like Kevin Bacon. But this time, I'm not pulling your leg." She gripped the armrest and laboriously got up from the couch. "You'll never admit it, but you can't get out of your mind the person I was five, six years ago. Well, I'm not that person anymore!" She opened the door of the closet and tugged her Vera Wang coat from the hanger.

"You can't leave," I said lamely. "We haven't even eaten."

But she did leave. We were back to square one. I went to bed exhausted and angry with myself. How had I managed, in the space of a few hours, to alienate the two people I cared about most?

When I woke up at three in the morning, Tom still wasn't home, and he wasn't answering his cell. He finally arrived as the sun was coming up. I'd assumed he'd gone on a bender, but the clothes he'd been wearing the night before were clean and un-wrinkled, and he was freshly showered.

"Where the hell have you been?"

For a moment, he looked as though he wasn't going to answer me, but then he shrugged and said, "At Derek's place."

"Derek?"

He peeled off his shirt and threw it over the end of the bed. "We were playing video games, if you must know."

"What?"

"We spent the night drinking beer and

playing Madden football."

I couldn't help smiling, imagining him and Derek playing video games like high school kids. "I don't want to fight," I said.

"Neither do I." He finished undressing and climbed under the covers.

I scooted up against him. "It's Sunday. Let's stay in bed."

He didn't answer, but he did pull me close. We were so different. In the early days of our marriage, it was such a breath of fresh air. He wasn't like anyone I'd dated before. He didn't have an uptight bone in his body. He was great at enjoying life, at discovering new things. He had a talent for relaxing that I'd never mastered. He had a gift for making people fall in love with him; he was so much fun, so genuine and easygoing, everyone wanted him around. But maybe, over time, our differences had taken their toll.

31

Most of the seats in the ER waiting room are occupied. There's a young man who looks like he just crawled out of a bar fight, a small child with an ugly rash squirming in her mother's lap, an elderly Chinese woman shivering with fever, not to mention a dozen patients whose ailments are less obvious, their faces betraying varying degrees of misery. There was a time when I'd walk into a room like this and feel a crushing sense of duty, mixed with equal parts compassion, but I'd be lying if I said the years haven't worn me down. Now a roomful of patients strikes me as a series of problems to be solved, diagnoses to be made, prescriptions to be written. It's not coldness that takes over so much as professional exhaustion.

I text Kim to let her know I'm here. Then I call Heather. To my relief, she picks up. "Where are you?" she asks.

"It's slow going, but I'm on my way. How are your contractions?"

"Manageable. Still pretty far apart. Just don't make me have this baby without you."

"I won't," I promise. And then she hangs up.

Moments later, the phone dings. *Meet me at 4th floor nurses station.*

When I get off the elevator, she is already waiting, looking like Snow White in scrubs: long black hair, red lipstick, pale skin. She glances at my foot, frowning. "What happened to you, Miss Graceful?"

"Somebody moved the curb."

She leads me to an empty room — a glorified storage closet with a gurney shoved against the wall. I sit on the taut paper sheet and lift my foot. "Have you voted?" she asks carefully, rolling up my pant leg and removing my sock.

"No. You?"

"I'm working a double. They'll have to decide the fate of California without me." She gently prods my foot and ankle, which are swollen and tender to the touch, myriad shades of purple and black.

"Does this hurt?"

"Yes."

"This?"

"God, yes."

"On a scale of one to ten —" she begins.

"Seven? Although I've always wondered about the accuracy of the pain scale. I've had patients with canker sores who rated their pain as a nine and a half," I say. "Meanwhile, some guy down the hall who just had a triple bypass calls it a four."

"Well, this sure looks like a six, at least," she says. "You're not going anywhere. We've got to get this thing elevated. You'll need an X ray. And a whole lot of drugs."

"No time. Heather's in labor at the VA."

She gives me a questioning look. The last time we talked, Heather had just returned to town, and Kim had taken Tom's side, advising me not to get involved. "Long story," I say. "Just fix me up with a splint and some crutches and a bunch of Tylenol."

She reaches into the supply cabinet. "Suit yourself."

"What's new with the kids?" I ask, trying to distract myself from the pain as she applies the splint.

"Sally just started band. Clarinet."

"I can't believe she's old enough to play the clarinet. The baby shower was yesterday."

"Speaking of baby showers, are you guys still trying?"

"Hard to follow the ovulation calendar

when your husband lives in a different zip code."

She looks up, surprised. "Sorry, I didn't know."

She pulls the bandage tight, and I suck in air through my teeth.

"Now he wants to get back together, but if he can just pick up and leave, what does that say about us?"

"Maybe it was some sort of midlife crisis. It's not like he cheated on you." She glances up. "Did he?"

"Well —"

"That fucker. Who was it?"

"An old college friend."

"Isn't it always an old college friend? Don't tell me: they hooked up on Facebook."

"No, worse. It was a funeral that brought them together. The guy who died was Tom's roommate at UCLA, and the woman, Lily, lived in their dorm. The three of them had been tight in school, and the guy who died had remained close with both of them over the years, but Tom and Lily hadn't kept in touch. So when the guy died, his sister asked Tom to play the organ at the service —"

"Tom plays the organ?"

"He plays everything. Anyway, the dead

guy's sister recruited Lily to sing. They got together the day before the funeral to practice, and when I asked what she was like, he shrugged and said, 'Just regular.' "

"Red alert," Kim says.

"Precisely. When we got to the funeral, I spotted her before he even introduced us. She's totally Tom's type: red hair, bangs, very petite. Wearing this wacky black dress with fur around the collar, like she just stepped out of Betsey Johnson. The pastor does his thing, and then Tom and Lily get onstage. He's on the organ, and she's standing beside him, holding the mike like she's auditioning for *American Idol*. She exudes this self-congratulatory aura, like she's got Jesus on speed dial. You should have seen the look on her face after she sang the 'Hallelujah' hymn."

"Can she sing?"

"Unfortunately, yes. So the next song they do is 'Open,' by Mike Scott. Do you know it?"

Kim shakes her head. "Never heard of it."

"It's supposedly a religious song, but it has this sexual subtext. So Tom's up there onstage, rocking out on the organ, very intent on the music. She's standing beside him, and she can't take her eyes off him. Even though it's an incredibly sad occasion, she looks like she's thinking about something else."

"Did you talk to her?"

"Yes. At the reception. She goes on about how lucky I am to have landed such a good one, how Tom hasn't changed in twenty years. Apparently, she just moved back to the Bay Area, she's a fan of *Anything Is Possible,* she'd been meaning to call him and catch up, et cetera, and then, voilà, she gets the call from the sister. Tom seems kind of unaware the whole time, like he doesn't even realize she's into him. But as we were standing there in this dreary room of the church after the funeral, next to a table decked out with those sad little round Costco brownies and sweaty rectangles of cheese, I was thinking, *This can't end well.* He swears nothing happened until after we were separated, but a couple of weeks after he moved out, I saw them together."

"No. Where?"

"I was running errands on Cole Street after work. As I was walking by Zazie, I just happened to glance in the window and see him. He wasn't alone. At first I couldn't tell who he was with. I figured it was some sort of work thing. There were plates on the table, glasses. I started to go inside, but as I got closer, I realized that it was Lily.

261

"It felt as though I was witnessing some private moment. The way he was sitting, with his arm draped over the back of his chair, the way he fiddled with the salt shaker, even the way he'd snagged the coveted window seat at prime dinner hour — it was all so familiar. It was the same way he acted with me, that same casual intimacy. I tried to tell myself it was nothing, but it didn't look like nothing. Then she reached over and picked up his glass and took a sip from it, and he didn't react. That's when I knew something was off."

"I probably shouldn't tell you this . . ." Kim says.

"What?"

"I always thought it was a little odd — the two of you. I mean, he's very charismatic, and he's great at what he does. I get that. It's just, you're so different. Did you know that in medical school, a bunch of us took bets on how long your relationship would last?"

I raise an eyebrow. "How long did you give me?"

"Two years," she says, shrugging. "Sorry — though I was at the high end."

"Well, I proved you wrong," I say. "You totally owe me a martini."

"Let's set a date."

A familiar announcement comes over the intercom, and I instinctively snap to attention. So does Kim.

"Shit, I've got a code." She thrusts the end of the bandage into my hand.

Code. Though I've heard the word a thousand times, it never fails to startle me. It's a strange word for cardiopulmonary arrest, someone at death's door, requiring the instant summoning of a whole team of doctors and nurses. After a while you get used to the codes, but for me, there's always that first second when the beeper goes off or the announcement comes over the loudspeakers, a switch flipping in my chest, sending my own heart rate through the roof. It's the immediacy that gets to me, I guess — the fact that, minutes later, a person's fate will have been decided, and their life will have either resumed or ended. Precious, excruciating minutes during which everything you do counts exponentially. If everything goes just right, you save a life. Screw up, and you've lost one.

"Dmitri will bring you some crutches," Kim says, disappearing out the door.

"I owe you," I say to her back. Strange how a code can put everything, instantly, in perspective.

I finish wrapping the bandage from toes

to ankle, up to my calf, tight but not too tight. I'm taping it in place when a stocky young man with a ponytail taps on the open door. "Dr. Walker?"

"Yes?"

"These are for you." He leans a pair of crutches against the bed and hands me a cup of water, some small white pills, and a stretchy sock to cover the bandage.

"Thanks." I pull on the sock, tuck my useless shoe into my bag, and swallow the Tylenol.

Passing the nurses' station, I hear a snippet of sound from a radio, turned down low. "The exit poll numbers are starting to roll in," Tom says, "and it could go either way."

A young woman in pink scrubs stands by the radio, shaking her head. "I don't believe this," she says. "Do you believe this?"

My ears are alert, waiting to hear what song Tom will choose next. Last night, he was still trying to figure out the right songs to play in case he was on air when the results of the vote were announced. Ultimately, he decided on Al Green's "Let's Stay Together" if the voters rejected secession, Tom Petty's "California" if the vote was yes. "Petty grew up in Florida," he explained. "He's this southern guy who moved to L.A. and made it big. That's what

California's about, really. You've got people like me, who are so proud of being born and raised here, but the essential character of California is that it's a destination, a golden ideal. People come here from somewhere else, with their big dreams. Maybe the dreams work out, maybe they don't; either way, people stay and make their lives here. Like Tom Petty did. Like you did."

Secretly, I'm hoping to hear Al Green.

32

"Tell me something," Dennis says, almost playfully.

"What?"

I picture the gun in his hand. I picture Rajiv and Betty. I try not to think about Eleanor. Last year, when all those people died at the mall shooting in Missoula, CNN interviewed several survivors who said the same thing: as it was happening, it felt more like a movie than real life.

This, on the other hand, feels startlingly real. Fifty-one minutes have passed since I knocked on Heather's door, and still we've got no crisis response, no hostage negotiator. No nurse. Heather is pacing the small room, moaning quietly. I struggle to quell a rising sense of hopelessness.

"That time I came in the VA with the stomach pains," Dennis says. "You remember how I asked you out, right?"

"Yes."

"I'm just wondering, if you weren't with Tom, would you have said yes?"

I'd like to believe the answer is no. I'd like to believe that if I hadn't met Tom, I would have met and fallen in love with someone else who was responsible and kind. I'd like to believe that I would have established some equally meaningful life. But the answer isn't so clear. It was luck that brought me face-to-face with Tom that night at the Fillmore — one of those chance meetings that might just as easily not have happened. But what if I'd never gone to that particular concert, smoked a joint, and felt myself floating through the air? What if I'd never been lifted out of the crowd by a stranger?

What if, on the day Dennis came into the VA, I'd been single? I remember how it felt, moving the paper gown aside and touching his skin. I remember the electricity in that touch, the swift and inappropriate pulse of lust. And now, all these years later, I remember the decision I made, without looking back, to walk away from anything beyond a platonic friendship with him. I had already chosen Tom.

There are so many paths a life can take. So many ways it can go right, and infinitely more ways it can go wrong. Sometimes the only thing standing between us and disaster is a fortunate accident.

"Well?" Dennis persists. "Would you have gone out with me?"

"Probably."

"I would have treated you really well, you know."

"Yes, Dennis, I know."

33

Outside the hospital, I pull the red Bakelite out of my bag and adjust the dial. After a few seconds of static, Tom's voice comes through loud and clear. "I'm getting reports that there's a tent city growing in Golden Gate Park near the Conservatory of Flowers," Tom says. "The group is organized by Geeks for a Free California. Rumor has it some of the biggest names in Silicon Valley are there. Of course, this isn't the first time Golden Gate Park has been home to a tent city."

He's talking about 1906, when the park became a massive refugee camp for victims of the earthquake. I turn the volume up just a bit to hear the beginning to Gil Scott-Heron's "The Revolution Will Not Be Televised." I drop the radio into my bag, grab the crutch handles, and start moving, the rhythm of the song propelling me

269

forward. The crutches dig at my underarms, but I like the feeling of lifting and falling, lifting and falling, the unnaturally long strides.

I'm matching Gil Scott-Heron word for word, moving along with the beat. And even though Tom didn't say it, I know this song is for me, too. This is the man who made an art out of creating music mixes for me to run by. He knows that when I hear this song, I always move a little bit faster. The song comes to an end, and my husband's voice cuts in: "No disrespect intended, Mr. Scott-Heron, but I'm watching CNN as we speak, and the revolution is definitely being televised."

My ankle is swelling against the bandage, the pressure adding a peculiar new twinge to the pain. From here I can see the crowd still gathered in the middle of the road, growing bigger. I turn up the volume on the radio, hoping for more music, anything to keep me going, anything to keep my mind off the pain.

"Here's to the one who knows me best," Tom says. "And, as always, here's to Joe. It's Little Steven, singing 'Inside of Me.'"

A long time ago, Tom told me that the secret to being a good radio host is that you never speak to the audience at large. "When you lean in to the microphone, you have to imagine that you're speaking to just one person," he said. "For years, I've had this picture in my mind of some lonely guy named Joe sitting in his flat on Potrero Hill, lights off, kicking back with a beer. It's weird, but I can sort of see the guy, jeans and a wrinkled T-shirt. He needs a haircut, he needs a whole new outlook on life."

Sometimes Joe would randomly make his way into our conversations. "I wonder where Joe is tonight," I might say over dinner.

"He has a date," Tom would say, "with this girl he just met at the gym."

"He's going to the gym now, is he?"

"Yes, he got a membership. He's getting in shape, getting his life together. He's even looking into investing in an IRA."

"But first he'll need a better job."

"Didn't I tell you? He just got a promotion."

"Good for him," I'd say. "Here's to Joe, and to new beginnings." And we would raise our glasses in a toast to Joe, the ideal listener.

Joe had become such an oft-mentioned topic between us that he almost felt like a real person, like some friend you haven't seen in years, the one who's always planning to visit next summer, who lurks on the fringes of your life. And in his mind, when he was on the air, Tom really was talking to Joe. The trick must have worked, because when I listened to my husband on the radio, it felt as though I were eavesdropping on a conversation he was having with someone else, a conversation in which, at any moment, some intimate secret might be revealed.

I'll never forget the morning, about a year and a half into our marriage when I was driving to work, my car radio tuned to KMOO. Lloyd Cole was in the studio, doing a promo for a show he was playing with Jill Sobule that night at the Great American Music Hall. When Tom asked him about one of his songs, Lloyd Cole said the lyrics had been inspired by the work and life of Václav Havel, the great Czech playwright, revolutionary, and, at that time, president of the Czech Republic.

"I met him once," Tom said.

"Oh, yeah?"

I waited for Tom to clarify, but he didn't. Instead, he asked Lloyd Cole to sing "Music in a Foreign Language," and then the station went to a commercial break. When Tom came back on the air, Lloyd Cole was gone, and the subject of Havel with him.

When I got home from work that night, Tom had dinner on the table. "What's the story with Václav Havel?" I asked. "You didn't actually meet him."

"I did," he said.

"How? Where? When? Why didn't you tell me?"

"Prague, a couple of years before I met you," he said, heaping green salad onto my plate. "I was there for a writing workshop."

"You attended a writing workshop in Prague?"

"Sure. I applied by sending in a manuscript, and someone had the poor judgment to let me in. You go and spend two weeks drinking Czech beer and sitting around a table tearing people's stories to pieces."

"Since when do you write stories?"

"I don't. I was just kicking the idea around back then, and I thought I might as well give it a go. Anyway, the guy who led our workshop had us read *The Garden Party* and *Temptation*. He claimed that Havel was a personal friend of his, but I didn't believe him. Lo and behold, on the final day of our workshop, the president himself pays us a surprise visit."

"Amazing," I said.

"In hindsight, I guess it was. But when you're young, you don't realize you've had

273

a once-in-a-lifetime experience until long after the fact. Anyway, after class, everyone else headed off to the bar for a drink, but I decided to wander around the building, because I'd heard there was a room somewhere on the fourth floor that housed the original manuscript of Milan Kundera's *The Book of Laughter and Forgetting.*"

"Did you find it?"

"No, but I did find Mr. Havel."

"What?"

"The building had these labyrinthine staircases," Tom began, "and I got hopelessly lost. At one point, wandering through this weird, dark tunnel of a hallway, I came upon two large, well-dressed men, standing outside the men's room. It was sort of creepy, but I really needed to relieve myself, so I put aside my reservations and went in. As soon as I stepped through the doorway, I realized one of the men had followed me inside. My heart stopped — I thought I'd walked into some strange trap — but then I saw the president standing there at the urinal, and I realized the men were his bodyguards."

"What did you do?"

"Well, that's the funny thing. The bathroom was tiny. It only had three urinals, and between each urinal, in some bizarre and pointless attempt at privacy, was a concrete wall that was only about three feet high — which seemed obscene, because instead of hiding anything it drew attention to things. Mr. Havel stood at the urinal to the far left, so naturally I stepped up to the one on the far right. 'You won't want to do that,' Mr. Havel said pleasantly. I apologized, assuming he wanted his privacy. I turned toward the door to leave, but the bodyguard was right there, blocking my path. I was trying to figure out a graceful way to get past him when Mr. Havel said, 'The pipe is disconnected.'

"I looked at the urinal where I'd been standing, and he was right. On the face of it, everything looked fine, but upon closer inspection I saw that the pipe that was supposed to connect the urinal to the wall was missing. So I stepped up to the middle urinal. There we stood, the president and I, peeing side by side, separated only by this pointless concrete wall, while the bodyguard stood against the door, eyes fixed discreetly on a tiny window that looked out onto Prague Castle. And I remembered what my mother used to say when I was growing up, an awkward kid with all these grand visions in my head of meeting Keith Richards and Bruce Springsteen and Iggy Pop. I had posters of these guys all over my walls, I followed them in the magazines, I wrote fan letters that invariably went unanswered — except Bruce. Bruce actually answered one, but that's another story. And my mother would often say, 'They have to go to the bathroom just like the rest of us, you know.' Standing there beside Mr. Havel, I realized she'd been right.

"A few years after that, I was working at KMOO, and these rock stars were coming in all the time. Whenever I got nervous about meeting or interviewing a musician I admired, I'd prepare myself by visualizing Václav Havel at the urinal, relieving himself."

Tom was smiling mischievously.

"You're pulling my leg," I said.

The smile vanished, and he looked utterly earnest. "No, all true."

"Why didn't you ever tell me?"

"You never asked."

It was one of the things about Tom that both mystified and disturbed me. Anytime something about his past came up, some surprising story that I thought I should have been privy to before, he would excuse his failure to tell me by saying, "But you never asked." The problem with this logic was that the questions would have been impossible to formulate, because any question that would solicit one of his stories would have to be so specific that the only way to ask it would have been to know the story in the first place. This strange, disconcerting catch-22 was built into my life with Tom. I never knew the right question, so I had to wait for the stories to come to me, unbidden, in bits and pieces, often over the public airwaves.

Every now and then over the years, the subject of Václav Havel would come up during some other argument. "It's like the whole thing with Václav Havel," I would challenge him. "You're so private. You never tell me anything."

And Tom would sigh and say, "You know everything about me, Jules. What you see is what you get."

But I never really believed him. There always seemed to be something lurking just beneath the surface, some story yet to be told, some bit of his past — or, worse, his present — on which he was holding out. Every time I turned on the radio, whether I was aware of it or not, I was waiting for some new layer to be peeled away.

34

"We're the same, you and me," Dennis says.

"How's that?"

"I lost my daughter. You lost your son. That's something you never get over. It's like, everything you see reminds you of your kid."

"When was the last time you saw Isabel?"

"It's been three months. They moved to Texas."

"I'm sorry, Dennis. I didn't know."

"Even after I lost custody, at least I knew I could see her every now and then. I could go to her softball games, and if her mother was feeling generous, they'd meet me for pizza. But now, she's so far away. It's like I have no idea what's going on in my daughter's life. The other day, I realized I'm not even sure what grade she goes into next year — sixth or seventh."

"That has to be hard," I say. "I wonder about Ethan, too. I worry whether he has friends, and I wonder what subjects he's studying, if he plays sports."

We fall into silence. *If I can just hold him off a little while longer,* I think desperately, *until help arrives.*

"Dennis," I venture.

"Hmm?"

"How is everyone?"

"Oh, we're just dandy. A little crowded in here, but other than that, it's one big party. Want to talk to Rajiv?"

My heart lifts. "Yes."

He laughs cruelly, and instantly I understand that it was the wrong response.

"The last few times I came in to see you, they pushed me off on Rajiv. You two are attached at the hip, aren't you?"

"I'm his attending physician," I explain, battling panic. "That's all. If anything goes wrong with one of his patients, it comes back to me."

"She's pretty good-looking, isn't she, Rajiv?" Dennis's voice is muffled; he's no longer talking into the receiver.

There's no response. "Answer me!" he shouts, and my breath catches.

"She's my boss," Rajiv replies.

"Hell, that never stopped anyone, did it?"

"Dennis," I cut in desperately. I remember a crucial piece of advice they told us in the crisis seminar: try to lighten the mood. It's risky, but I don't know what else to do. "Ask Rajiv who does his laundry."

Dennis repeats the question to Rajiv.

"My mother," comes the muffled reply.

"See?" I interject, trying to make my voice light. "He's just a kid. Besides, he's not my type."

Dennis laughs. This time, the laughter is more relaxed. "I had you going, didn't I?"

Shaking, I collapse into the chair. Suddenly, Heather is standing beside me, her palm on my face.

"It's gonna be okay," she whispers.

I grip her hand, and she squeezes back, hard. Everything's backward. I should be the one comforting her.

35

On a rainy night in April, I was sitting in my office, immersed in the file of a patient for whom diagnosis was proving maddeningly elusive, and I had lost track of the time. It was something I'd been doing a lot ever since Tom moved out. As long as I was at work, I could delay the moment when I walked through my front door into an empty house.

There was a light tap on the half-open door. It was Heather, her belly stretched taut against a silky black top. I hadn't seen her since the argument at my house almost three weeks before, when she'd told her crazy story about the governor.

"Knock knock," she said.

"Who's there?"

"Holy crap," she said.

"Holy crap who?"

"No, I mean really, holy crap. I can't think

of a single joke. I'm drawing a complete blank."

"It's called mommy brain," I said. "All the blood rushing to your uterus."

She eased herself into a chair. "Actually, I think it's called IED brain."

I set aside the patient file. "I left a bunch of messages."

"I know."

"How are you feeling?"

"Fine. Some trouble sleeping, leg cramps, nothing monumental. Wait, I just remembered one." She paused for a moment to think. "Right, so this dashing young taxi driver is taking a pretty woman to JFK. He looks in the rearview mirror and says to her, 'You know, you're the fourth pregnant lady I've taken to the airport.' And she says, 'But I'm not pregnant.' And *he* says, 'Yes, but we haven't reached the airport.' "

I couldn't help smiling. "Good one."

She glanced out the window. "This view is amazing."

"I know. Hard to believe I kept those blinds closed for years."

"Why on earth?"

"Look down and to the right."

She did. "There are kids everywhere," she said. Then it appeared to dawn on her and she bit her lip. "Oh, it's a school," she said quietly.

"When Ethan was with us, I used to go to that window and look down at the school a dozen times a day. After we lost him, I shut the blinds so I wouldn't have to see it. But then, a couple of years ago, a young resident was in here with me. I was called to the floor, and I left him alone for a few minutes. When I came back, he was standing by the window, and the blinds were open. For a couple of seconds I felt furious — as if he had breached some invisible boundary. The sun was pouring in, and I could see the tip of the Golden Gate Bridge far in the distance. It was a shock to look at the view again from that particular spot — not just the bridge but the wooden play structure down at the school, the sandbox, the orange roof. And it suddenly occurred to me that I'd been denying myself that beautiful view of the ocean for two years, just to avoid thinking about Ethan. But the thing is, I think about him anyway. He's just there; he's in my mind all the time. Since then, I've kept the blinds open."

Heather picked up a framed photo on my desk: Tom, Ethan, and me, playing chess on a giant chessboard at a seaside inn in Monterey. After I'd opened the blinds, I'd allowed the pictures back into my life, too

283

— an attempt to remember the good, instead of remembering only the loss.

Heather placed the picture gently back on the desk.

"Did I ever tell you about Camp Leatherneck?" she asked.

"No."

"I was there on my second tour. Imagine turning sixteen hundred acres of burning sand in the middle of nowhere into a huge base. It's like something out of a sci-fi movie. You've got dozens of bulldozers out there, moving around these massive walls of sand, and lines of soldiers, hundreds of them, swinging hammers like a chain gang. And there's the issue of water, right? There just isn't enough water to support all this construction. We were building this massive parking lot for choppers, not to mention a runway, and the dirt had to be packed down before these huge sheets of metal could be laid on top of it, but it's the middle of the desert — it's not like you can just tap into some magical water line. So you've literally got soldiers out there with buckets, collecting water from the kitchens and showers to use to compact the dirt on the building sites. But one freezing cold night, the guy who's supposed to make sure the water's running at a trickle in my section of the camp forgets to do so, and when we wake up the next morning, the pipes are frozen. We can't brush our teeth, we can't cook, and that might all be okay, except for the fact that we can't build the runway, either. We've got no water to compact the dirt. Even during the day, the temperature doesn't get above thirty-two degrees Fahrenheit. It takes three days for the pipes to thaw, three days that we're just sitting there freezing our asses off, twiddling our thumbs, because one guy forgets his piece of the puzzle."

I nodded, unsure where she was going with this.

"Anyway," she said, "I've been thinking about Leatherneck a lot lately."

"Why's that?"

"I guess I'm just stuck on the idea that there's this monumental machine, and we're all part of it. Most of the time, we don't even stop to think about how it works. We just go about our business, doing our part, trusting that everyone else will do their part, and the machine will keep functioning. But all it takes is for someone to come along who isn't thinking straight, someone who's not paying attention, or worse, hell-bent on self-destruction, and everything turns to shit."

285

There were tears in her eyes, and she was looking at me intently. "I'm trying to say something here," she said, "but I don't know how to say it."

I stared at the floor, focusing on the coffee stain on the carpet that had been there for more than a decade. A familiar point of reference. "We don't have to go there," I said.

"But we do, Jules. I'm so sorry. About everything. If I could take it back, I would."

"I know."

"I thought the army would make me forget. But in the middle of all of it — the patrols, the firefights, the endless days of boredom — I'd find myself remembering how much I'd hurt you and Tom."

She picked at her cuticles and looked at me pleadingly. I looked at the coffee stain again. I didn't know what to say.

"I don't deserve it, Jules, but I need you to forgive me."

The hem of her skirt was frayed. Under the beautiful Vera Wang coat, she'd been wearing the same skirt the last few times I'd seen her — she said it was the only thing that didn't make her uncomfortable. Why had I never thought to buy her another skirt?

"I'm trying," I said. "I'm really trying."

She wanted to know that I forgave her. Why couldn't I give her this? I realized that maybe that was what she'd been waiting for all along, maybe that was why she came back.

Later that afternoon, we found ourselves on the cliffs at Lands End at low tide, the time of day when that frigid stretch of coast is prone to giving up its secrets.

"What's that?" Heather asked, pointing to a bit of steel poking up from the shallows about a hundred yards offshore.

"There are dozens of old shipwrecks around here," I said. "That's most likely the *Lyman Stewart,* or maybe the *Ohioan.* The one that's always fascinated me is one you can't see, the *Rio de Janeiro.*"

"Yeah?"

"It was a foggy morning in February 1901. The ship originated in Hong Kong with two hundred and ten passengers and crew. It hit a submerged rock at Fort Point at about five o'clock in the morning and disappeared within a few minutes. Two hours after the wreck, an employee for the Merchants' Exchange who was waiting for the *Rio de Janeiro* at the port of San Francisco saw a life raft emerging from the fog."

"There were survivors?"

"Eighty-two."

Heather absentmindedly laid a hand on her stomach. "Any kids?"

"It was mostly the men who survived. Years ago, Tom gave me a book, *Great Shipwrecks of the Pacific Coast.* I sort of got hooked. One of the passengers who died was a mail-order bride — Mary Catherine Carraher — on her way to marry Tom's great-grandfather."

"I guess it's lucky for Tom she didn't make it."

"Long story short, the *Rio de Janeiro* vanished. A few bodies washed up onshore after it happened, and over the years, bits and pieces of it floated to the surface, but the hull was never found. All sorts of stories circulated about treasure buried at the bottom of the sea, but to this day no one knows where the wreckage is located. Now whenever I'm out here, I find myself subconsciously searching for the *Rio de Janeiro.* Somewhere in the back of my mind, I have this fantasy that one day, I'm going to make a great discovery."

36

10:01 a.m.

A couple of blocks downhill from St. Francis Memorial Hospital, I stop in front of a motorcycle shop. A single light shines inside, casting its glow on a dozen bikes, chrome gleaming. The door to the motorcycle shop swings open, and a man pulls out on a Harley. He looks to be in his late forties, with blue eyes and close-cropped brown hair.

I hobble over, and he cuts the engine. "Please tell me you're not an apparition," I say.

"Unfortunately, I'm really here. Picking up my money pit."

"I thought Harleys were indestructible?"

"Not quite. My wife says that's what I get for having the poor taste to indulge a midlife crisis. I'm a marine biologist in my real life." He gives me a once-over, his eyes settling on my bandaged foot. "Looks like you've got your hands full."

"I don't suppose I could ask you a favor?"

"Let me guess: you need a ride."

"It's kind of an emergency. I have to get to the hospital at Forty-third and Clement to deliver my sister's baby."

He adjusts the rearview mirror. "Sure. We're going to have to jog around the roadblocks and see how we do. I can't make any promises, but I should at least be able to get you a few blocks west of here."

"Great. Thanks so much."

"No problem. We'll just strap your crutches down." He winds a bungee cord around the crutches. "I'm Ted, by the way."

"Julie Walker."

He tightens the cord. "That should do it. But you're going to need a helmet." He runs inside the shop and comes out with a hot pink helmet. "Sorry," he says, smiling. "I take it you're not a hot pink kind of lady."

"I love it." It feels like some brilliant disguise, like trying on a new life, if only for a minute. I pull the strap tight and climb on behind him, bracing my hands on the back of the seat.

"Don't take this the wrong way," Ted says, "but you might want to hold on to me."

I wrap my arms around his waist, feeling timid at first, but once we get going I lean into him, surprised by how much I like the unfamiliar sense of dependence, my own safety entirely out of my control. I think of Paul, a pediatric oncologist I've known for years. A few days after Tom revealed that he had slept with the "Hallelujah" woman, I ran into Paul in the hallway after my weekly lecture at UCSF. He asked if I wanted to go out for coffee. Over cappuccinos at Reverie, he told me he'd just gotten divorced. He and his wife had two children in middle school, a house in Millbrae, a vacation home in Tahoe, season tickets to the Giants, sixteen years of marriage under their belts. Tom and I had attended their Christmas party a few months earlier. The wife was the principal of a public high school; the children were polite and smiling. Even the dog, a golden retriever named Zito, seemed made-for-TV perfect. From the outside, everything looked fine.

"It hit me like a ton of bricks," Paul said.

"I know what you mean."

He looked at me as though a light had switched on in his brain. "Hey, you want to have dinner with me this weekend?"

"Why not?"

As I was dressing for the date, putting on my best lingerie, I realized I was more nervous than I'd been in years. The last time a man had seen my naked body for the first time, it was Tom, and I had been twenty-five years old.

As it turned out, we didn't go to bed together on that date. But a couple of weeks later, we met for drinks at the Claremont in Berkeley. Well into our third glass of wine, Paul looked at his watch and said, "If we don't leave now, we're going to miss our reservations. Chez Panisse Café doesn't tolerate tardiness."

"I don't really feel like dinner," I said.

We skipped the dinner reservations and checked into a room at the Claremont. It started off steamy and sexy, but once we got past the kissing and unzipping, it quickly turned awkward. Even though Paul was in great shape and knew all the right buttons to push, I didn't have much fun. I felt too self-conscious, as if we were following a script in which we had both decided to cheat on our cheating spouses but we'd been miscast.

The next morning, when I rolled over and got my bearings — registering the small shock of finding myself in bed with another man — I realized that I was going to ask Tom for a divorce. This decision had little if anything to do with Paul, who, I realized, was merely a diversion, a mildly pleasurable means to an inevitable end. Paul and I showered separately, dressed, and went down to breakfast, where we agreed that, while it had been a good night, a therapeutic night, we didn't want to turn it into a relationship.

"Just promise me one thing," I said, raising my mimosa in a toast.

"Hmm?"

"It won't be weird when we see each other at work."

"Other than the fact that I'm going to imagine you naked every time I see you, it won't be weird at all."

And, oddly enough, it wasn't.

We hit roadblock after roadblock, slowly winding our way west. Even with my poor sense of direction, I can tell we're getting closer to Forty-third Avenue, but farther from Clement. By the time Ted pulls over to the curb across the street from Golden Gate Park, it feels as though something with very sharp jaws has taken hold of my ankle and won't let go. Ted cuts the engine, climbs off, and helps me with my crutches. "I'm really sorry. I wish I could have gotten you closer. Good luck with that baby."

I thank him and turn to face the crowd. As Ted and his bike rumble away, I have the sinking feeling that my best chance for getting to Heather on time has just vanished. A brick wall sections off the park at Stanyan and Fulton. In order to enter, I'll have to navigate the two crowded blocks to the Arguello Gate. I think of Rilke again, his pregnant woman making her way along the wall in the middle of the bombed-out city. The world doesn't stop for a baby, but surely, it does at least make some concessions.

37

In early November, after daylight savings kicks the clock back an hour, it is already dark when I leave work just after five. From the parking lot of the VA I can see across the quiet avenues of the Richmond, over the long green swath of Golden Gate Park, and beyond that, the lights of the city glittering on the layered hills. Some nights it is warm, and the children at the school on the edge of the campus are getting in their last few minutes of play before their parents arrive to pick them up.

In the first few days of early darkness, the playground vibrates with excitement. The children chase and squeal and whoop it up, as if they think they're getting away with something, being outside with their friends after dark, when, by the looks of things, they ought to be in bed.

One of my most vivid memories is of the playground at that particular time in that

295

particular season, five years ago. It had been a difficult day at work. I had lost a patient — Mr. Drager, a Korean War vet, very frail. His wife and daughter were by his side when he died, and I was there, too, along with his favorite nurse, a middle-aged woman named Paula who used to cut Tootsie rolls into tiny pieces so that he could suck on them — his favorite sweet, something remembered from childhood. A few days before he died, his daughter watched him smile as the candy was placed on his tongue. She had flown in from Sweden two months before, expecting to stay for a weekend, but had found she couldn't leave her father; she needed to be with him until the end.

His death was a good death, as deaths go, and yet, that afternoon, I was feeling the grief of losing him. With some patients, I'll admit, I feel no such thing. But I had liked Mr. Drager very much, had enjoyed hearing his stories of his childhood in the thirties in Chicago, where his father was a union man and his mother was a seamstress. He had been injured by a grenade, which left him with a metal plate in his left hip, a nail in his left knee, one blinded eye, and a permanent, pronounced limp. But he didn't regret it. "I did my bit for my country," he told me once, "and ever since, my country has been taking care of me in one way or another."

Mr. Drager had been coming in for years, since long before I began working there — sometimes for a couple of days at a time, sometimes weeks. His final stint had been his longest. In the end, we simply unhooked everything. It was what he had approved in his paperwork back when he was able, and something I had discussed with him at length when he was still lucid. When it came time to turn off the machine, my hand shook. I had done it many times; I knew it was the right thing, what he wanted, what his family wanted; and yet it was with deep sadness that I carried out his orders and watched the EKG go flat. He died at two forty-six in the afternoon. After that I still had rounds to make, patients to talk to, a brand-new intern to supervise.

After work, I left the hospital and walked over to the school to collect Ethan. There were plenty of fancier child-care centers in the city, but Ethan was happy here, and I liked having him nearby. It made me feel complete, to have my working life in such close proximity to my home life. Picking him up was always my favorite part of the day, but that evening, as much as I wanted to see him, I would have given anything for half an hour to sit alone in a quiet room with a glass of wine and process the day's events.

As I walked across the parking lot, I could see the children on the playground, could hear their happy squeals. I stopped just outside the tall chain-link fence and spotted Ethan, pushing a plastic tractor through the sandbox. "Garbage guy is coming," he said to no one in particular. "Out of the way, garbage guy coming through." My heart flooded with joy. I lingered outside the fence, watching him, until another child spotted me and called, "Ethan, your mommy's here!"

Ethan dropped the tractor and ran to the fence. I opened the gate and stepped inside, and he rushed into my arms, pressing his face against my shirt. Then he stepped back and asked me very seriously, "Am I on vacation?"

"You're not on vacation," I said. "You're at school. Does it feel like vacation?"

"Look!" he exclaimed, pointing up at the sky. "It's dark. There's the moon! I never go to school at nighttime before!"

"The time changed," I explained. "Now that winter is coming, it gets dark earlier."

"I know!" he said. "Let's have cake for dinner!"

I scooped him up into my arms. "Good idea. We'll make one when we get home."

Suddenly, I no longer felt that I needed half an hour alone. I only wanted to be with Ethan, this sweet boy who had been delivered under such terrible circumstances into my life. I loved the way he saw the world. I loved the fact that the smallest change in routine could become an event, worthy of celebration. From an early age, ambition for me had been a slow burn, the thing that kept me going and gave me pleasure, the thing that marked my place in the world. As I carried Ethan to the car, I understood how it happened that well-educated women suddenly abandoned hard-won careers, devoting themselves to domesticity; something about mothering a small child softens the edges of ambition, mutes the desire to race ahead. When I was with Ethan, I wanted to stop time.

Later that night, watching Ethan devour the chocolate cake we'd made from a box when we got home, I thought of Mr. Drager's daughter, who had traveled thousands of miles to be with her father when he died. Ultimately, wasn't this what it meant to have a child? You raise them up, you suffer every time they suffer, you're happy when they're happy, you make cake together, you

marvel at the moon, and the reward is this:
when you are old, you don't have to die
alone.

38

"I like the pretzels," Dennis says, "but the M&M's were better. Why'd you switch?"

On the other end of the line, I can hear him chewing.

"Health kick," I reply.

The truth is, Betty, who swore off sugar last year, had been giving me a hard time about the candy jar on my desk. "You're pushing forty," she'd reminded me a few months ago as she'd dumped the M&M's into the garbage and refilled the jar with pretzels. "One of these days, you won't be able to count on your metabolism."

"I run," I reminded her.

"Your patients don't. You're supposed to set an example, remember?"

I smile at the memory. Betty's always been a little bossy, but not in an irritating way. Something about her delivery softens the blow. I wish I could go back in time, some-how head Dennis off at the pass. "How is everyone?" I ask.

"Oh, we're fine. These two are quiet, but they were getting a little jumpy, so I had Betty tie up Rajiv's hands and feet. Then I tied up Betty. Just in case they got any ideas."

"Dennis," I begin, but I don't know what to say next. If anything happens to Betty and Rajiv —

"You been to church lately?" Dennis cuts abruptly into my thoughts.

"You know I don't go to church, Dennis."

"That's right. I witnessed your crisis of faith."

I don't remember how I ended up sitting in the back row of the VA chapel, hoping for some revelation or, at the very least, some comfort, two days after we lost Ethan. But I do remember the chaplain's patronizing words as he patted me on the hand: "We don't always understand God's plan for our lives."

I thought of all the patients I'd sent to him, thinking he might be able to help ease their burden. Was this the kind of spiritual fluff he was peddling?

After leaving the chapel that day, I ran into Dennis in the cafeteria. "Coffee?" he asked.

"Actually," I replied, "I could really use a drink."

Half an hour later we were sitting in sticky vinyl booths at the 500 Club in the Mission, and a couple of hours after that I was plastered. I left my car parked on the street, and Dennis, who was on a carb-free diet and had stuck with club soda, drove me home. In the street in front of my house, before I got out of the car, he held me close. Drunk, I sobbed into his shoulder. I knew, as I did so, that I should be leaning on Tom instead. But he was hurting so much already. I didn't want to burden him with my grief, too. Losing Ethan felt like a shared failure; being with Tom only intensified the sadness. On top of it, there was my own guilt to contend with: it was my sister who had caused everything.

39

In the Southern Baptist church Heather and I attended as children, forgiveness was held up as the ultimate act of Christianity — so essential to the faith, it was included in the Lord's Prayer: "Forgive us our trespasses, as we forgive those who trespass against us." We recited the prayer on Easter morning, and on Sunday night four times a year before commemorating the Lord's Supper with grape juice and oyster crackers. Even now the taste of grape juice takes me back to those hushed evenings in the humid, crowded church, the clink of tiny shot glasses and the rustling of the deacons' suits.

Before Ethan was taken from us, my capacity for forgiveness was never really tested. Until that day, I would have insisted that I could forgive Heather for anything.

She was visiting San Francisco, staying with us for a couple of weeks. Since flunking out of college, she had followed a meandering, often rocky path. She'd moved back home for a few months, then followed one boyfriend to Atlanta, another to Nashville. She spent a couple of years there, singing with the boyfriend's band and waiting tables. When the relationship fell apart, she left the band and returned home to Laurel, where she'd been living ever since, working retail at Sears and picking up hostess shifts at the Catfish Cabin.

At the time of Heather's visit, though, she was in unusually good spirits. It was as if something had finally clicked, and she had decided to get her life on track. "I woke up one day and realized I was twenty-five years old, living with my mother, smoking pot five times a week, and selling heavy-duty bras at Sears," she told me. "It might not have registered if it weren't for the fact that Carl Renfro showed up one day and asked me to drop acid."

"Renfro?"

"He was standing there on the lawn in cutoff shorts and no shirt, just like the last seven years hadn't happened. He hadn't changed a bit, and it occurred to me that I hadn't, either.

"All that mess I was involved in, that's behind me now," Heather said. "I want this." She spread her arms and looked around to indicate my house, my dishes, my books, my family, everything. "I admit I've spent a lot of years thinking that I got dealt a shit hand. But you were dealt the same cards, and it never seemed to bother you. It was as if you were only half there, as if your head was always ten years in the future. Mom always knew you would leave. That's probably why she let me get away with so much."

"I didn't mean to leave you," I said, feeling that old guilt flood back. "I just meant to leave our situation. If I didn't get out, I'd have gone insane."

"I don't blame you," Heather said. "Not now, anyway. I'll never forget the morning some jerk showed up to repossess our car, and I watched Mom standing there in that old First Federal T-shirt she used to sleep in, begging him not to take it. Instead of feeling sorry for her, I just felt ashamed. And mad. I'd always known we were poor, but it wasn't until you left that our lives really started to fall apart."

"I'm so sorry." It was too little to say, it did her no good, but I *was* sorry. And yet, I knew that if I were faced with the same decision again, I wouldn't change anything.

"For years I had this fantasy in which my dad walked into my life and fixed everything," Heather said. "I imagined he had a very good explanation for why he'd been gone all those years — like he was running from the law, or he never knew he had a child, or he'd been sending me letters all along and Mom had been tearing them up. In my fantasies, he would show up from out of the blue and he'd be loaded." She laughed. "He'd be driving some fancy car, he'd hand me a wad of cash and tell me to go buy myself something nice, and Mom would suddenly become a happy person."

"God, Heather," I said. "I had no idea."

"How could you have known? By the time I was old enough to begin to process any of it, you were long gone, Jules. I love Mom to death, I know she did her best, but I hated not having a dad, I hated how hard she worked, and I especially hated that winter when someone from the Daughters of the American Revolution came by on Christmas Eve and gave us a box of toys and clothes."

That I remembered. Mom standing in the doorway with a strained smile on her face, saying thank you, but after the woman left, while Heather and I silently arranged the presents under the tree, Mom went into her bedroom and shut the door. I was sixteen, mortified by receiving charity. I recognized one of the sweaters, a pale blue cardigan with yellow daisies embroidered on the yoke. It belonged to a well-to-do, horse-faced girl in my class named Sarah Bender, who had always been particularly mean to me.

"For a long time all of that stuff has been my excuse for everything," Heather said. "But you and I came from the same place, and look at you. Somehow, you figured it out. You've gotten everything you wanted. The job, the husband, Ethan."

"I won't breathe easy until all the papers are signed, the judge has made his decision, and Ethan's completely, legally ours."

"You're almost there," Heather said.

"Knock on wood. What about you?"

"I've been dying to tell you," she said, smiling. "I'm going back to Southern Miss in the fall. I'm not slowing down until I have that degree in my hand. I already applied, and I'm turning in my financial aid forms next week."

College. I liked the sound of it, and I hoped this time she'd follow through. She did seem more mature than I had ever seen her, far more responsible. She had arrived at the airport bearing gifts for Ethan: a pack of Crayons, a pop-up book about dragons, a Nerf football. During her visit, she didn't drink, she'd even given up cigarettes. On previous trips to San Francisco she would always wander off, meet some guy, and come home drunk or stoned at some ridiculous hour, or not at all. But this time she was totally different. She seemed mature and confident and ready to face the world.

A week into Heather's stay, having seen how good she was with Ethan — a perfectly responsible aunt — I made reservations for the night of our wedding anniversary at a small hotel in Napa.

"Heather's going to babysit," I told Tom excitedly, showing him the photos of the hotel online.

"Are you sure that's a good idea?" He looked worried.

"They'll be fine," I assured him.

We left at six o'clock on Friday night and planned to return on Saturday afternoon. It was our first overnight since Ethan came into our home. I've returned to that decision a thousand times, from a thousand different angles.

40

It takes me ten minutes of pushing and shoving to get from Stanyan to Arguello. The sidewalk is blocked by a gang of teen-aged boys clad in identical T-shirts bearing the slogan ANARCHY IS THE ANSWER.

I pull myself onto the wall at the Arguello Gate in order to see over the crowd. The throng stretches blocks down Fulton. It will be impossible to get through using the road. Even though it's a longer route, I'll have to go through the park. The strap of my messenger bag is cutting painfully into my shoulder, and I pause to adjust it. That's when I realize that the zipper is open, and something is missing — my phone. And that's not all. I've lost the Bakelite too. Shit. I search frantically in my bag, scan the ground around me, but they're gone.

It feels as though I've lost something significant, something essential. No more

Tom in my ear. No more Voice of Midnight. No more songs meant just for me, coded messages in a language only we understand. I depended on his music, his voice, the auditory proof of his presence in a booth across town. For so long, I depended on him for so much. There's no denying the fact anymore: I really am alone. Of course, for all intents and purposes, I've been alone for months. And I know I can't blame Tom. It's my fault, too. He's the one who left, but I'm the one who made it so hard for him to stay. When he told me he was leaving, I asked him not to, I suggested marriage counseling — but my protests were half-hearted. By then I was so tired of fighting, so tired of the disappointment I read on his face each day. Our marriage was like a chronically ill patient. It suffered from a cantankerous, nagging pain that wouldn't go away. Our marriage seemed to resist all cures; it had worn us down slowly, over time, exhausting us to the point that both of us, on some level, wanted out.

Nine weeks after he left, Tom said, over a cup of coffee, "If you had begged me to stay, I would have."

"I did ask you to stay," I said.

"You weren't very convincing."

By then, Tom's life had already begun to

change. It was through an accidental slip on the air — or maybe not so accidental — that I discovered just how much. "I spent the weekend in the country," he said late one Monday night. "The only thing better than a picnic under the stars is a picnic under the stars with live musical accompaniment — no guitar, no piano, just a perfect voice. Here's the Lemonheads, with 'The Outdoor Type.' "

I listened to the whole song — one of *our* songs. He'd put it on a tape for me years before. I called his cell.

"Don't tell me you took the singer to Hopland."

His silence confirmed my suspicion.

"How could you?"

"You never liked it," he said, as if that were a valid line of defense. "It was my dream, not yours."

I imagined Tom on his knees in the dirt with the "Hallelujah" woman, pulling weeds and planting seeds. I'd grown up in the country and had happily left it behind; for me, that kind of life held no charm. I needed the city around me, the sidewalks and shops, the lights of passing cars sliding across the living room ceiling at night, the sound of the neighbors coming and going. He was right, in a way. Our dreams did not always match up. How had we not noticed that when we got married? When we met, I loved the fact that he wasn't a doctor, that his work was so different from mine. I knew doctor couples who ended up in a kind of silent competition — one spouse racing ahead, earning accolades and higher and higher salaries, while the other was left behind. I was happy that Tom could have his dreams and I could have mine, and the success of one of us would never feel like the failure of the other. But over time, I began to wonder if we weren't too different, if our marriage didn't suffer from a lack of common ground.

"That wasn't part of the deal," I said.

"What deal?"

"When you moved out for this so-called trial separation, you never mentioned you were going to sleep with someone else."

"It's not like I planned it. It just happened, Jules. It was stupid."

I waited for him to apologize, but he didn't, and it occurred to me that he wasn't sorry.

"Fuck you," I said, hanging up. I immediately felt foolish. For talking like a jilted teenager. For lying awake in the middle of the night, wondering how I might have done things differently, when I had a job to go to in a few hours, patients to care for. For believing him before, when he told me there was no one else on his radar. For screwing up our marriage and then feeling so unmoored when it fell apart.

Later, after the incident with Paul at the Claremont, I told Tom what had happened.

"I guess I deserved that," Tom said.

"Maybe a little."

"Still, I wish I didn't know."

I had thought that telling him would make me feel better. As it turned out, it only made me feel worse.

41

Our wedding anniversary went beautifully: the meal under the stars in Napa; the luxury of a night alone, not worrying that Ethan might wake up; a morning spent in bed drinking coffee and reading *The New York Times.* Tom and I stopped for brunch and went for a short hike before heading home. When we arrived just after three o'clock on Saturday, we found our new caseworker, Marina, sitting on the sofa in the living room, a file folder perched on her lap, a scowl on her face. We'd met her only once. Just weeks before, she had replaced our longtime caseworker, Terry, who had recently moved out of the state. Ethan sat beside Marina, sucking his thumb, watching his favorite show, *Curious George.* The moment we walked in the door, he leapt from the couch and rushed to me, wrapping his arms around my knees. "Mommy!" he cried.

I picked him up, kissed him, held him close. He laid his head on my shoulder, his whole body slack with relief.

The house was chilly, and it reeked of pot. The coffee table was littered with beer bottles. Ethan's Flintstones plate served as an ashtray for the charred ends of two joints.

"What happened?" I asked, my heart sinking. "Where's Heather?"

"I got here twenty minutes ago," Marina said. "I was in the neighborhood, and with your adoption hearing coming up soon, it seemed like a good time to check in. When I rang the doorbell, Ethan opened the door in his underwear. He told me he was making breakfast. It smelled like gas, so I went in the kitchen. The gas was on, but the stove wasn't lit."

My heart pounding, I held Ethan tighter. "My sister is supposed to be watching him."

"You're lucky I stopped by. The boyfriend made a quick exit, but your sister couldn't be bothered to get out of bed."

"The boyfriend?" Tom said.

"Oh, yes, the two of them were very cozy back there," Marina said, looking in the direction of the bedroom. "I took the liberty of putting some clothes on Ethan. He was shivering. Your sister managed to wake up long enough to tell me you'd be home any minute, and she didn't seem to know how to get in touch with you, so I decided to wait."

"Terry had our cell numbers," I said weakly. "It should all be in the paperwork."

Marina shuffled halfheartedly through the file folder. "I only see your home phone."

"This should never have happened." I felt the rage rising in my chest. And shame. All the things we'd done to prove what responsible, caring parents we were, all the love we had showered on Ethan, all the hopes we had for adoption, for giving him a good and stable life. I could see it all being erased before my eyes. "Please excuse us," I said.

I walked back to our room, Ethan clinging to me, Tom following at my heels. Heather was sprawled facedown on the bed, wearing a man's shirt, snoring loudly. She reeked of alcohol. "Heather," I said. "Wake up."

No response.

I shook her by the shoulders, repeating her name loudly. Finally, her eyes opened, red and unfocused.

"You're home . . ."

"You're drunk," I said. "And you had some guy in this house? What were you thinking?"

Ethan started whimpering.

"Dale?" Heather mumbled. "Don't worry about Dale. He's a nice guy. I met him out at Ocean Beach. He surfs." She struggled to sit up.

"Ethan's been on his own all day! And you bring this stranger here! Anything could have happened."

"What are you talking about?" Heather pushed her matted hair out of her face. "It's early still."

Her eyes focused on Ethan, in my arms. "Sorry, little guy," she said.

Ethan dug his head farther into my shoulder, twirling my hair with his fingers.

"Get your things and get out," Tom said coldly.

Heather glanced at him, then at me. "My flight isn't for three days."

Tom took out his wallet and dropped some folded bills on the bed. "This will cover a hotel and cab."

She looked to me, as if she expected me to defend her. "Seriously?" she said. "Lighten up. I gave him a bath and put him to bed, everything right on schedule, like you said. Then Dale came over, and I told him he could only stay for one beer, but then we got to watching this movie —"

Her words trailed off as she stumbled out of the bedroom and down the hall. Ethan had wriggled out of my arms and had wrapped himself around my leg. He wanted me to drag him down the hallway, our old game. I followed her, Ethan laughing now, clinging to my leg.

Heather stopped when she saw Marina sitting on the sofa. "Who's this?"

"You don't remember?" Marina pursed her lips, sighed, and stood, glancing pointedly at her watch. She looked annoyed, as if our incompetence had ruined her perfectly good day. I realized that this tableau, which was so strange to us, must be something she experienced on a regular basis. To her, ours was just another unfit home, nothing special.

Heather raised a hand to her forehead. "Oh, shit." Then she disappeared into the kitchen. With a sinking feeling, I realized she had fooled me. The responsible, re-formed, sensible person she'd presented to us during the preceding week — it was all an act. A very convincing act.

Tom was talking quietly with Marina, trying to defuse the situation. "This has never happened before," he said. "It was our anniversary. Just one night, a few hours — we thought they'd be fine."

To anyone else, Tom probably would have sounded perfectly calm, but I knew him well enough to detect the note of panic in his voice. He was the one person I could always rely on to take things in stride, the one person I knew who rarely worried. The fact that he was worried now terrified me.

"Have you talked to Terry?" I pleaded. "She'll vouch for us. We've never had any kind of problem before. Ethan is so happy here. You can see how healthy he is."

"However it may have happened," Marina said, unmoved, "this is unacceptable. I'll have to write this up, of course."

"I'm a doctor," I said, desperately. "This is a good home. Look at our reports."

Heather was in the kitchen, banging around in the cupboards. I felt something for her then I'd never felt before, a rage so complete it frightened me.

Five days later, our lawyer called to tell us that Danielle's sister, Allison, had filed a petition to get custody of Ethan. I was at work when the call came. I put my chief resident in charge, locked myself in my office, and called Tom. He was in the studio and had just finished taping an episode of *Anything Is Possible.* He was high on adrenaline, as he always was after taping the show.

"There's no way that woman is taking Ethan from us," Tom said. "I won't let it happen."

As if it were that easy, as if he believed the ball was in our court. It was his way to tackle the world with confidence, and he usually won. Life had proved to him that anything was possible. But I understood that this time, we were fighting a battle that might be beyond our power to win. If reunification with biological parents took top priority in the state judicial system, then long-term placement with extended family members came in as a close second. We couldn't afford to make any mistakes.

I looked down at the school, the pale orange roof. It was two o'clock in the afternoon. The children were inside for their afternoon nap. Ethan would be asleep on his blue mat. He would be clutching George, the loved-to-death monkey he'd received as a birthday gift from the secretary at the radio station when he turned three. I could picture him lying there, his dark curls sticking to his forehead; he always perspired when he slept, no matter the temperature. I remembered the night he came to us, the weight of his head against my shoulder when I pulled him from the car, the smell of peaches on his skin. I couldn't lose him; it simply wasn't an option.

I picked up the phone and called Allison Rhodes. She answered on the second ring.

"I'd prefer that you talk to my attorney," she said.

"Ethan is happy here," I said, pleading. "He calls us Mommy and Daddy. You met us. You saw what our home is like, how devoted we are to him."

"Exactly," Allison said. "That's why I didn't do anything sooner. While I may not have agreed with your parenting style, it looked like he at least had a safe home where he would be well cared for. And then this thing happened. You've got people doing drugs in your house while my nephew is left to his own devices."

"It was a terrible mistake," I bargained. "But it never happened before, and it will never happen again."

There was noise in the background on her end of the line, a car door slamming, sounds of traffic, heels on pavement. I realized she'd been driving when I called, and now she was walking. I imagined her in her serious pantsuit, taking care of business, while Ethan's fate lay in her hands. I wanted to scream at her to sit down, to listen, to really think this through.

A door closed, and the traffic sounds subsided.

I was no longer trying to hide my desperation. "This is Ethan's home. Please, I'm begging you."

"Kids are resilient," she replied. "He's so young right now, in a year he won't even remember that he used to live somewhere else."

A sharp sound came from my throat, unbidden. Had she meant for her words to sting so much? "What can I do to convince you?" I pleaded.

"I've made up my mind."

"Please," I said. This couldn't be happening. I needed to start over again, go back to the script. I had to make her understand. But the line had already gone dead.

Forgiveness. The churches of our childhood always made it sound so easy. You take whatever anger is in you, and you give it up to God. But on that day, and in the subsequent weeks as we took our place in court and pleaded for another chance, as we called character witnesses and showed photographs of the three of us together — Ethan and me and Tom, a happy family — I realized that forgiveness is not such a simple thing.

Heather had committed no violence, no act of malice. She had not set out to do us any harm. It was a simple matter of who she was, her inability to think things through, to behave as a responsible adult. Still, the net result was the same.

42

I lower myself carefully down from the wall, into the park, and cry out when my foot hits the ground. A jolt of pain shoots through my ankle and up my leg, a sharp, angry sensation that travels the nerves of my body, sending off red alerts in my brain. I try to visualize the path of neural messages, as if mapping the pain might somehow lessen it. Every pain has its cause, I remind myself. I grab my crutches and begin moving up Conservatory Drive. Here the crowd is thinner. I long for the radio, that small bit of comfort. What I'd give to hear Tom's calm voice of reason, talking me through.

I think of Heather in her room at the VA hotel, gritting her teeth and waiting for me. I remind myself that she knows how to breathe, how to relax, how to brace herself for the contractions. She knows how to stand, knees bent, legs wide, holding on to the back of a chair, letting gravity ease the burden. I attended the Lamaze classes with her, played the dutiful birth partner as she leaned back into my arms, rolling her hips on the giant rubber balance ball. She joked her way through every class, refusing to believe that heavy breathing and a positive attitude could make labor go more smoothly. "Just give me the epidural as soon as possible," she'd say. "And don't tell me to stay calm."

I'm moving faster now, feeling a chill in my bones. My bad foot connects hard with a tough root jutting up through the sidewalk. The pain has an almost auditory sensation, deafening. I take a ragged breath, readjust my crutches, and keep moving.

I remember the day of my father's funeral, when I sat in the front seat of the car with my mother, her perfumed arm draped around me, holding me close. That night, after the guests had left and we were at home alone, in that house without Daddy, she held me in the rocking chair in front of the television. She kept rocking and talking; she talked so much my ears hurt. I wanted to go to bed.

"Mama," I said finally, "be quiet."

She stopped rocking, and her body stiffened. "Sometimes," she said, "you just have to talk yourself through it." And then she started rocking again. She talked all night. I can't remember what she talked about, only that, by the next morning, she'd lost her voice.

43

At the hearing, Marina testified what she had found that day. She described the smell of pot, the beer bottles, the disarray, Heather out cold in the bed. As it turned out, she had an alarming flair for detail.

We made our own case passionately. The director of Ethan's school defended us, as did his teacher and several of my colleagues from the VA. A father of two who worked with Tom at the station described my husband as "the most devoted father I've ever seen."

Allison said that she had been willing to let the adoption go through until she heard about the incident with Heather. "I have three children of my own," she said to the judge, "not to mention a demanding job. I'm not a doctor or a famous radio personality; I don't have the kind of money they do. It won't be easy. But I can promise you that I'll take good care of him. I can't in good conscience allow my nephew to be raised in that kind of home. With me, he'll have his cousins, he'll go to church."

"We can take him to church," I blurted.

The judge tapped his fingers on the desk; he seemed to be waiting for something more.

"We can also provide him with an excellent education," Tom added. His shoulders slumped, and there were dark circles under his eyes. "We have elementary school tours scheduled for the spring, and we've already started his college fund."

The judge looked over at Allison. Was I imagining it, or did he smile at her? She was a single mother, struggling. We shouldn't have mentioned the money, I realized. In this tableau, it didn't matter that we were better equipped to care for Ethan; Allison appeared to be the more sympathetic character.

The attorneys made a few more statements, and finally, the judge shuffled the papers on his desk, glanced first at Allison, then at me and Tom, and said, "Permanent custody is granted to Allison Rhodes, beginning exactly two weeks from today."

It was like a punch in the stomach. Two weeks. I couldn't believe it was over. Just like that. I slumped against Tom, and he leaned against me, and we both broke down.

I called Allison a dozen times, begging her to reconsider, but she was unmovable. "I'm his family," she said the last time we talked.

"*We're* his family!"

"If you continue to harass me, I will be forced to ask for a restraining order. Do not call here again." With that, she hung up.

Ethan had just turned four. Allison's three children ranged in age from seven to thirteen. I worried about Ethan in that house, with those bigger kids. In our house he had his own room filled with toys, his soothing bedtime routines, his shelves of books, our complete attention and affection. How would he fare in a strange place, sharing a bedroom and a mother with three kids he didn't know? Who would make him waffles in the morning and read to him at night?

I worried that he would think I had abandoned him, had simply given him up. I took the next two weeks off from work and withdrew Ethan from the child-care center, so I could spend every minute with him. Tom had someone fill in his shifts and postponed the next taping of *Anything Is Possible*. Everything became magnified in those remaining days with Ethan, his presence sweeter and more painful.

I tried to teach him the things he would

need to know in his new house, where the rules would certainly be stricter than they were in ours. "Share your toys," I reminded him. "And ask permission to leave the dinner table." He cried when I told him that his aunt Allison might not know the night-night song. "You can sing it to yourself when you go to bed," I said. "I'll be singing it too, even if you can't hear me." It was a song that I'd made up, one that I sang to him every night, and when I'd tried to talk to Allison about it, and about the fact that Ethan was accustomed to one of us lying down with him until he fell asleep, she said, "Well, he'll just have to learn to fall asleep on his own. He's not a baby anymore." It made me physically ill to think of Ethan alone in a strange bed, a strange house, with none of his comforting rituals.

"Who's Aunt Allison?" he said once, though we'd discussed it many times. He still didn't understand. "I don't want a play-date with those big kids," he added. And I realized that when I talked about "Aunt Allison's house," he thought he was just going for a playdate.

One afternoon, when he was going to the bathroom on his little plastic potty, I said, "I'll close the door so you can have privacy."

"No," he said. "Stay with me."

"Why?" I asked.

He grinned. "Because I love you."

I sat down on the bathroom floor in front of him, and he clapped his hands on my cheeks, laughing. As I helped him pull up his pants and wash his hands, I thought about how these small ministrations, the daily acts of love, had become all-consuming. Caring for a small child was exhausting, but it also made life immeasurably sweeter. I had wanted so much from life, and I had gotten it; now what I wanted more than anything was this.

On the day we took him to the family services offices to go home with Allison, he clung to me, screaming, "Mommy, Daddy, don't make me go!" He was terrified, too young to understand why we were letting this strange woman take him away.

Overseeing the entire thing was Marina, the stoic-faced social worker with her steadfast belief in rules and reports, her unwavering faith in the supremacy of blood ties. "Please," I begged, as she pulled him out of my arms.

"It's out of my hands," she said — seeming, for the first time, uncertain that she held the moral high ground.

As Tom and I drove home that afternoon, I thought of a vacation we'd taken to

Vieques, Puerto Rico, before we were married. On the fourth day of our trip, on a deserted beach near our small hotel, something had happened to jolt us out of the blissful state in which we had spent our first days there. We were walking hand in hand, talking about the impossible, otherworldly blue of the water, when Tom's grip on my hand tightened, and as I stepped forward, he pulled me back. My eyes had been on the horizon, where a white boat was cutting elegantly through the blue, but now I turned my head and saw what had caused him to stop in his tracks — not ten feet from us, a bull.

The animal was breathing heavily, looking straight at us, and I wondered why I hadn't heard his wet, ragged breath before I saw him.

We backed away very slowly, our eyes on the bull, his eyes on us. I couldn't be sure whether the panting I heard was the bull's or my own. My heart raced, and my hand in Tom's was slippery with sweat. When we had put fifteen yards or so between us, there was a sound in the thicket, a breaking of twigs. The bull lost interest in us, turned toward the sound, and ambled away. As we walked back to our room in silence, I felt exhilarated and frightened, certain that we had just been spared some terrible incident. Our waiter that night confirmed my suspicions. The bulls on the beach had become a serious problem, he said. A tourist had been gored just two months before, and had died.

My life, in many ways, was like the incident in Vieques. I'd grown up with nothing, and then, as it turned out, things had gone so well for me, better than I'd ever imagined they might. I often felt that I had just narrowly escaped some terrible fate, some metaphorical bull in the thicket that I hadn't seen. My own father's completely random and unexpected death had taught me at an early age that terrible things lurked just around the corner. For the longest time, I felt lucky but afraid. How long could this sort of luck hold out?

Now, in the rearview mirror, I could see Ethan's empty car seat. Thousands of times in the past two and a half years, I had glanced up and looked at his reflection. I had taken such joy in seeing him there, had felt such a sense of security and completeness, having him with me, knowing that he was safe. Seeing the empty seat, I understood that the dreaded thing had happened; the bull in the thicket had finally caught up with me.

In the weeks after he was taken away, I

fantasized about rescuing him. At night, unable to sleep, I came up with outlandish plots to whisk him away, back into the safe, loving life we had built for him. We could go into hiding, leave the country, start fresh. Crazy thoughts, but most of the time they seemed more sane than the alternative: life without him.

Everything, during that time, was about Ethan and his absence. I hardly had room in my mind to consider Heather, much less forgive her or offer sound advice. For the first few weeks after the incident, she called repeatedly, always crying, always apologetic, but I didn't want to talk to her, didn't want to see her. A few days after we lost Ethan, she called to tell me she had joined the army.

"Don't," I said.

"It's done."

Soon thereafter, she left for training at Fort Bragg. In a way, it made sense. It was the ultimate act of turning one's life around, the ultimate act of reinvention. And also, I knew, an act of self-punishment. Heather cherished nothing more than her freedom. She didn't like being told what to do, where to be. The thought of her at basic training — rising before dawn, donning fatigues and heavy black boots, standing in line and subjecting herself to the whims of her commanding officer — was unfathomable. I understood that this was her attempt at contrition, her cry for atonement. And I have to admit — a part of me was relieved. I wouldn't have to see her or hear her voice. I wouldn't have to look her in the eyes and pretend I wasn't filled with rage.

44

"Why didn't you try to find him?" Dennis wants to know.

"I did, Dennis. You know that."

"Tell me again," he insists.

On the bed, Heather is lying on her side, her eyes shut tight against the pain. It's getting so close; any minute I will have to put the phone down. But for now, Rajiv and Betty need whatever time I can buy. I think of all the codes I've run, how you quit whatever you're doing, put everything else out of your mind, and concentrate on that single patient, on saving that one life. To be a physician is to be an expert in compartmentalization; every patient, every action, every feeling has its place.

"One patient at a time," Dr. Bariloche used to say.

I don't want to tell this story, I don't want to share anything else with Dennis. But I will. Anything to stall for time. Lives depend on it. On me.

"I went to Glendale a month after Allison took Ethan away," I begin. "She had to let me see him."

"And what were you going to do if she didn't?"

I pause. "I was prepared to do anything."

"What about Tom?"

"He stayed home. He said that if he saw Ethan, he wouldn't be able to walk away."

"And you would?" Dennis asks.

"I hadn't planned that far ahead."

I found an address, made the drive to Glendale in six hours, walked up to the door, and, in a state of disbelief, not knowing what I would say, rang the doorbell. I had no idea how Allison would react, but I knew she wouldn't be pleased.

When an elderly Japanese man opened the door, I felt the beginning of panic. "I'm looking for Allison Rhodes," I said.

"She doesn't live here anymore," the man said. "They moved away."

"Where?" I asked, feeling as if the ground had shifted beneath me. I was too late.

"Arizona?" the man said uncertainly.

After that, I scoured the Internet for Allison Rhodes, but she was impossible to find. I couldn't find her on LinkedIn or Facebook, or any of the other social networking sites, and the people who showed up on search engines bore no biographical resemblance to her. She seemed to have vanished. I paid an investigative service that promised to turn up addresses and all sorts of personal information, but even that led nowhere. How was it possible, in the digital age, for a person to leave no trace?

I contacted our old caseworker, Terry. "How can she just take him away and not even leave a number or address?" I asked. "Is that even legal?"

"I'm afraid it is," she answered. "As Ethan's former foster parents, unfortunately, you have no legal right to see him."

After I finish telling Dennis the story, he doesn't say anything for several seconds, and I recall something else they taught us in the crisis course: if you leave a pause in the conversation, the hostage taker will fill the silence. But it's not Dennis who fills the silence now. Once again, we fall into the old patterns.

"Sometimes I think back to that day in Glendale and wonder what would have happened if I had found them," I say.

"We're not so different," Dennis replies.

Maybe Dennis is right. You think of yourself as one kind of person, abiding by a certain set of rules. And then, something happens to shake that foundation to the core.

45

The summer before I left for college, I sometimes wandered the streets of Laurel for hours in the wet, sticky heat. It was something to do, a way to stave off the boredom. Heather, eight years old that summer, had a new best friend named Molly who lived in a big house with a swimming pool. Most mornings, I'd drop Heather off at Molly's house, where Molly's mom would spend the day doting on the girls, bringing them sandwiches and iced tea. My shift at the Piggly Wiggly didn't start until afternoon. Freed from babysitting duty and school, I found that the day contained endless hours to do with as I pleased.

I loved walking, the way it calmed me, gave me space to think. My new identity — the one I hoped to forge on campus, among people who did not know me — did not come without a sense of guilt. Putting my feet on familiar paths, stepping in the same spots I'd stepped along hundreds of times, took my mind off the fact that I was leaving my mother and sister behind.

At the intersection of two roads — one paved, one a simple country affair of packed red earth — a car pulled up beside me. It was a red Camaro with the top pulled down and, in the driver's seat, a man in mirrored sunglasses.

"Do you need a ride?" the man said. He must have been about twenty-five — which seemed very old to me.

"No, thanks."

"It's a long way to anywhere from here."

"Not really."

I was on guard, but not exactly afraid. After all, I'd just finished my senior year of high school. By then, I knew a few things about boys. I also knew the neighborhood. Just a few yards behind me was a thick stand of pine trees. If I cut through the trees and started running, it would take me less than a minute to arrive at the home of Martin Dilts, who'd been a friend of my mother's since their grade school days, had even proposed to her once. Martin was fiercely protective of my mother, and of me and Heather. In his house, he kept a closet full of guns. Every year at the beginning of deer season, he'd arrive at our house with dozens of pounds of meat, wrapped neatly in white paper, labeled with the date and the cut. He'd pack it carefully in our freezer, then sit with my mother in the kitchen, drinking Coca-Cola and talking. She used to tell me, "If anything ever happens to me, there are two people you girls can count on, no matter what: your uncle Curtis and Martin Dilts."

The guy in the red convertible was good-looking, though I couldn't see his eyes. Clean-shaven, slender, wearing a blue shirt with the sleeves rolled up to the elbows. He had pale skin and a funny accent.

"Where are you from?" I asked. I stayed a good ways back from the car, which idled there at the dirt intersection, the radio playing softly, engine humming.

"Connecticut."

"Connecticut?" I repeated, dumbfounded. "Why on earth are you here?"

"I'm visiting family."

"What family?"

"The Keymans."

"I know them," I said. "Harry went to my school."

Tall, skinny, towheaded Harry, whose parents owned a store that sold ribbons in every imaginable color and fabric, had never struck me as the sort of guy who might have a cousin in Connecticut. It might as well have been Europe, it seemed so exotic.

"Small world," the man said.

"Small town's more like it."

"Where are you going?"

"I don't know," I lied. In fact, I knew exactly where I was going: right on Old Bay Springs Road, right on Twelfth Street, then I'd follow the road past the cemetery, past the Burns place, a big horse property with a grand old house and an elaborate ironwork sign that said THE PONDEROSA, all the way to the west side of town. Eventually, I'd end up at the Piggly Wiggly, where I'd spend the next five hours ringing up bread and milk and Pampers and reduced-for-quick-sale ground beef, counting down the minutes. Back home that night, I'd mark off one more square on my calendar, one day closer to getting out.

"What grade are you in?"

I found the question insulting. I'd graduated, after all. "I'm in college."

"Oh!" He was genuinely surprised, perhaps disappointed. "Where do you go?"

"Mississippi State."

"You live in the dorm?"

"Yes."

"Which one?"

"McKee." In truth, I had no idea whether

I would get a spot in McKee, but I had marked it down as my first choice on the forms I'd mailed in weeks before.

"I'll be damned. That's where my ex-girlfriend lived. Room 215. Whatever you do, don't eat in the cafeteria."

"If you live in Connecticut, why'd you have a girlfriend at Mississippi State?"

"Harry's big brother introduced us. What can I say? I like southern girls." His gaze traveled from my face, down to my breasts, my hips, my legs. I felt my cheeks turning red. "I like the way you walk, like you've got nowhere you need to be. The girls I know back home are always in a hurry."

"Maybe I'm in a hurry," I said.

"You sure don't look like it."

He shut off the engine. His hands were small, his nails manicured. In his left ear he wore a tiny gold stud. From his rearview mirror hung an air freshener shaped like a star.

"Isn't that redundant in a convertible?" I pointed at the air freshener.

"You're funny."

He seemed harmless. His skinny good looks were growing on me. I couldn't imagine him ever throwing a football, much less quoting the Bible, and I liked that. In Laurel, even the bad boys could recite John

345

3:16 in their sleep. I took a step toward the car.

"Take off your sunglasses," I said.

"It's too bright," he replied.

"Take them off," I insisted. "I can't see your eyes."

I imagined myself in another body, another person altogether, the person I surely would be by the time I came home from college the following summer: confident, self-assured, adept at carrying on witty conversations with men who didn't know a thing about me.

He relented. As soon as the glasses came off, I realized why he'd been so eager to keep them on. He was cross-eyed. The right eye looked straight at me, dark green and strangely beautiful, while the left eye pointed down toward his nose. I hoped the surprise didn't register on my face. He put the glasses back on hastily, blushing, and I realized that in that brief moment, with that revelation, I'd gained the upper hand. Everyone has something to hide. Once that thing is exposed, a person is at a disadvantage. The trick I learned at that moment is to discover the other person's secret before he discovers yours.

"How about that ride?" he said. "We can take a little detour through town, have a burger at the Barnette Dairyette."

I thought about what it would be like to ride slowly down Oak Street in the red Camaro next to the handsome out-of-towner. Everyone would wonder who he was, and how we'd met, and whether he was my boyfriend. For a few minutes I'd be someone else.

But something stopped me. My better instincts, maybe. My sense of self-preservation. "I have to go," I blurted.

"Suit yourself." He started the car and peeled away, the star-shaped air freshener spinning in the breeze.

When I told the story that night at the supper table, Heather chewed her butter beans thoughtfully and said, "He sounds nice. Why didn't you get in the car? I would. It would be an adventure!"

Mom reached across the table and slapped Heather's hand. "You most certainly would not get in a car with him or anybody else. Never accept a ride from a stranger, young lady, do you hear me?"

"Yes, Mama," Heather said. But even then, I could see something in her eyes. I knew we were two very different people.

46

One bit of advice I sometimes give my patients who are in acute pain: concentrate on small details around you, the sights and sounds and smells. Focus on something external to distract your mind from the pain. Sometimes it works, sometimes it doesn't. Now I put my advice into practice and notice a small cardboard contraption hanging from a tree, beneath a sign that says, DO NOT TOUCH. SUDDEN OAK DEATH STUDY IN PROGRESS. A plastic Coke bottle is nestled beneath a bush, filled with yellow liquid — most likely someone's urine. A black squirrel scampers so close that the thought of rabies crosses my mind.

All of my body's energy seems to be concentrated at the excruciating intersection of the fibula and the talus. By the time I make it to Crossover Drive, I'm biting my lip so hard I can taste blood. The road, which runs the width of the park north to south, connecting the Richmond District with the slightly bleaker and grittier Sunset District, is free of cars. A few protestors are on the road, making their way who knows where. I exit the park at Fulton. There's no crowd here, but there's something uneasy, not quite right, about the silence. I remember a hurricane in Biloxi, Mississippi, where we'd gone to visit a friend of my father's when I was very small. My parents and I huddled with my father's friend in the tiny closet while the storm raged outside, and suddenly, the wind subsided. "The eye is passing over us," my father explained to me. We stepped into the front yard, into an eerie calm. The yard was strewn with tree limbs, and the front porch swing had been torn off its hinges. My father pulled me closer. The air was still and hot, and smelled beautiful and green. We stood there for a few minutes, feeling awed and fearful, until the wind picked up again, and we rushed inside, back into the closet, to wait out the other side of the storm.

It's like that now. It feels as if I've stepped into the unpredictable eye of the storm, and I don't know what to expect on the other side.

The pain and exhaustion and terror blend

into one; the sun glints off the ocean in the distance. *Swing, step, swing, step, swing, step.* Passing an abandoned bus stop, I find myself thinking of an afternoon in Budapest, when Tom and I, four days into our honeymoon, stood in the rain waiting for a bus to Eger. A woman stood beside us, seeming not to notice the rain, eating bread from a paper bag. The bread smelled wonderful, and the bag was like a canvas, dark spots appearing where the raindrops fell. I couldn't quite wrap my head around where I was, couldn't understand how I had ended up so loved, and so completely happy.

As I move slowly past the avenues, the whitecaps of Ocean Beach visible at the bottom of the hill, it occurs to me that Ocean Beach, like the VA campus, is federal land. This part of town gets a bad rap for the fog, which is so dense in the heart of summer that you can't see ten feet in front of your face. But October always brings a slew of warm, sunny days, so blue and bright you forget that winter is coming. Tom and I used to go to the beach with Ethan on days like that, and we'd build castles and dig moats in the wet gray sand. When we grew tired we would feast on Mexican soda and thick sandwiches from Fredy's Deli. Those were wonderful days. After we lost Ethan, we stopped going. Just a year ago, while cleaning out the garage one morning, I found a stash of Ethan's plastic buckets and shovels, still sandy. One of the buckets was filled with shells and sand dollars. I sat down on the floor, overwhelmed by memories. Tom found me there in the afternoon, still sitting among Ethan's things. Without a word he helped me to my feet. He guided me upstairs and into the bathroom, where he ran water in the tub, so hot the tiny bathroom filled with steam, undressed me gently, layer by layer, and helped me into the water. "Is it too hot?" he asked.

"It's perfect."

He sat on the edge of the tub. "Remember when we used to go there?"

"How could I forget? Ethan loved it."

"No," he said. "Before Ethan, I mean. Just the two of us."

"Oh." The memory slowly returned. He was right. We'd done it many times in the early years of our marriage. We would take a blanket and a bottle of wine, and we would watch the sun go down over the Pacific. Somewhere, there are photographs, in which I tried to capture the incredibly soft, velvet blue of the water. I wonder if I will come upon them someday and regret the path I've taken — away from those perfect moments on that perfect beach.

Finally, I reach Thirty-eighth Avenue. "Please let her be okay," I mutter. I collapse on the bench at the abandoned bus stop and take a deep breath. Five hard blocks, and I'll be there.

47

One Sunday afternoon a few weeks ago, I was supposed to meet Heather at Bi-Rite for ice cream. It was an unusually gorgeous, hot day, and everyone was out in shorts and tank tops. As usual, the line at Bi-Rite stretched down the block. I didn't see Heather, so I got in line and waited. Ten minutes passed. I was sweating. As my turn drew nearer, with no sign of Heather, I called her cell. Getting no answer, I texted. Still no reply. I told myself not to worry — she hated answering the phone. Still, it was unlike her, these days, to flake on me when we had solid plans. When it came to appointments of any sort, she still had a military mindset. I called again and left a message.

A few minutes later, worried, I decided to walk to her sublet apartment just a few blocks up Valencia. I knocked on the door and waited. There was no answer. The curtains were drawn, so I couldn't peek in the windows. I began to feel nervous.

I tried the door. It wasn't locked. Inside, the place was dark and smelled of lavender. I called her name, but there was no answer. The apartment was small — one bedroom with a kitchen, bathroom, and living room. The floor-to-ceiling bookshelves were packed with books. More freestanding bookshelves lined the hallway. It was a terrific apartment, nice hardwood floors and high ceilings. There was a big bay window looking onto the street. I opened the curtains, and the room filled with light.

"Heather?"

The bedroom door was closed. I was about to step down the narrow hallway and knock on the door when a photograph on the table beside the sofa caught my eye. I was sure it hadn't been there before. It was a grainy five-by-seven in black and white, portraying a smiling Heather in desert fatigues, her hair pulled back in a high bun. She looked tired, but at the same time she looked vibrant, happy. The photo had been taken inside a room that seemed strangely palatial, with a high ceiling and a big chandelier, and shot from across a large, gilded coffee table. From the odd angle of the shot, I guessed that the camera had been propped up and set on self-timer mode.

I picked up the photograph, not quite believing my eyes. Heather was sitting next to a man, someone whose face I recognized from other, more public photographs, from TV and newspapers. It was the governor, looking strangely unlike himself behind a three-day beard. He was wearing a denim button-down with the sleeves rolled up; on TV, I'd never seen him in anything other than a suit. He wasn't facing the camera. He was gazing at Heather, as if he was about to tell her something.

"Impossible," I whispered.

I searched the photo for seams, for signs that it had been doctored, inexplicable alterations in light and shadow. I studied the hand draped over Heather's shoulder, the proportions and probability. My first instinct was to marvel at the intricacy of the lie, the precision of the ruse, the bold lengths to which Heather would go to keep her story intact. But then a thought crossed my mind: What if, this time, she was telling the truth?

The bedsprings creaked, a doorknob turned, and Heather stepped into the hallway, her belly huge under an old T-shirt, her legs bare. She rubbed her eyes. "Shit. I'm sorry. I was supposed to meet you for ice cream. After lunch I was so tired I couldn't keep my eyes open. I lay down to take a quick nap, and I was out like a light."

She noticed the picture in my hand. She smiled, as if to say she'd won this round but she wasn't going to gloat. "I'll go change," she said. "The salted caramel cone is calling my name."

She went back into the bedroom. I set the picture down. I had to recalibrate. There was no denying that it was my sister in the photograph. There was no denying that the man beside her was the governor.

As dresser drawers opened and closed down the hall, I thought of Tom's show, *Anything Is Possible.* In the early days, Tom used to try his topics out on me. Invariably there would be a debate — me playing the role of the skeptic, Tom playing the role of the one who believed in endless possibilities: time travel, heaven, ESP, peace in the Middle East. It was almost always easy for me to argue against him, because his topics frequently struck me as absurd, just myths and mirrors, the stuff of imagination, not science. But slowly, over time, Tom began to wear away at my doubt: a general from the NASA Ames Research Center came on the show to explain why we would colonize Mars by 2025; a well-known neuroscientist and former atheist described his own near-death experience, which had caused him to reconsider the possibility of life after death.

I'd grown up in a world where even the most mundane things sometimes seemed impossible, and where dreams were always tamped down by reality. "Medical school?" one teacher had scoffed during my junior year of high school. "Don't get your hopes up. There's a good nursing school in Jackson, though." There was a hometown boy who'd left Laurel in the 1950s and made a name for himself in Hollywood, and he was still revered in the town as a kind of miracle, an anomaly. Another local boy had briefly stood at the helm of a wildly successful Fortune 500 company. The town was proud of these unusual native sons, but also mistrustful. That the actor ultimately met an unfortunate end in a drunk driving accident and the Fortune 500 executive ended up in jail for insider trading seemed fitting; if you aimed too high, you were bound to pay the price.

In my mother's mind, fame and even simple good fortune happened to other people, from other places. After all, she and my father had dared to dream: his job at the bank, the briefly owned Lincoln Continental, the golden ideal of growing old together. None of it had come to fruition. The idea of our family's hard luck was so ingrained in her that when I was accepted to medical school, she told me there would still be a place for me at home "if it doesn't work out." And she really seemed to believe that it wouldn't. She had a certain idea of how the world was supposed to operate for people like us. My life, to her, seemed unfathomable, some fantasy bubble that was bound, eventually, to burst.

I thought I had trained myself not to think like that. My own life served as evidence that it was possible to break the chains of circumstance, that one could rise above expectations. But as I stood in Heather's apartment, looking at the photo of her and the governor, struggling with my own disbelief, I had to wonder if, perhaps, I was more like my mother than I thought. Had I become too doubtful, too closed off to see what Tom liked to refer to as "the endless possibilities of the world"?

Walking to Bi-Rite Creamery, we didn't talk about the photograph. I wasn't sure what questions to ask. I was still processing it, still trying to figure out which part of her story was true, which part was false.

"Cat got your tongue?" Heather asked.

"Sorry. I was kind of lost in thought."

I wondered if it was out of graciousness that she pretended I'd never seen the photo or if, instead, she simply enjoyed the fact that I was so dumbstruck.

The next morning, a strange thing happened. I was driving to UCSF to give a lecture, and as I turned up Cole, I caught sight of the orange Avanti, sitting in front of Reverie Café — the very car, bought with lottery winnings, that had inspired Tom's show all those years before. I might not have noticed the Avanti, were it not for the fact that the meter maid's vehicle was at that moment partially blocking my path, and the meter maid was in the process of slipping a ticket under the windshield wiper of the Avanti. Just then, a man hurried out of the café. It was my husband's friend Wiggins. My windows were down, and I could hear him arguing.

I maneuvered around the meter vehicle and drove on, thinking of the Avanti, a car that was a symbol of all that was possible. I thought of recent items from the news, a whole slew of seemingly impossible things that had in fact come to pass. Scientists had discovered that the universe is crowded with Earth-like planets, many of which had evidence of flowing water. A graduate student in Arizona, meanwhile, had proved theoretically that life could begin with arsenic, a substance that was previously believed to destroy it, thus exploding our notions of what conditions needed to exist in order for life to form. A sixty-six-year-old woman in India had just given birth to triplets. There was a hole in the ozone over Antarctica the size of North America, the glaciers were disappearing more rapidly than anyone had ever imagined, and the rainbow toad, believed for nearly a century to be extinct, had been found alive and well in the Ecuadoran rain forest. And then there was California, the thirty-first state, suddenly hell-bent on independence.

I had to wonder: Was Heather the irrational one, or was I? Which was more willfully blind: To believe it was possible to win the lottery? Or to insist, despite firm evidence to the contrary, that it wasn't?

48

12:02 p.m.

The first block — Fulton to Cabrillo — is manageable. With each painful step I'm grateful that the street's incline is slight. The white buildings of the VA hospital tower at the top of the hill, the large American flag snapping back and forth in the wind.

These days, I work fairly regular hours. But during my residency and in the first few years of my practice, there would be a point in every double shift when the work became purely mental, when the body, left to its own devices, would simply give out. When that happened I would picture the end of my shift as a finish line and repeat to myself, over and over, "Almost there, almost there, almost there." For the last couple of hours, these two simple words would keep me going. The next few blocks are no different, the finish line so near I can taste it.

I pass a ramshackle playground where a

group of teenagers sit on the swings, smoking and laughing. A woman in a long skirt, hair covered with a black net, chases two little girls up the slide. On the other side of the playground, half a dozen men are shooting hoops. While the rest of the city deteriorates into chaos, in this quiet neighborhood built on sand dunes, it almost feels like an ordinary day.

I turn left on Balboa and make my way down to Forty-third Avenue. Balboa to Anza is more difficult. It's all uphill, and the block seems to go on forever. Every few steps I look up at the Stars and Stripes flapping over the VA — my finish line. I'm moving as fast as I can: step with the right foot, swing on the crutches, step, swing, step, past the tall, narrow houses.

And then, suddenly, I'm on the ground, cheek to the pavement, flat on my stomach on the sidewalk, staring into an open garage that's packed with cases of bottles, stacked all the way to the ceiling. I curse, startled by the volume of my own voice on the quiet avenue.

An older woman is standing inside the garage. She looks at me, surprised, before rushing to my side. Warm blood gushes from my nose. I taste salt, iron. I reach up and touch my face; my forehead is bleeding too. The woman tugs at my arm, her grip surprisingly strong, and with her help I am able to push myself up on my palms. Then, with a few excruciating movements, I manage to get to a standing position.

"Come inside," she orders, picking my messenger bag up off the ground.

"I can't," I say, wiping blood from my face. My hands are covered with it. I'm dizzy, light-headed.

"You must."

My nose keeps gushing. The cut in my forehead is pumping blood so fast, it's difficult to see.

"Come!" she says again, and this time she is dragging me toward her house. I stumble after her, trying to see through the blood. I follow her through the garage, to the side stairs. She sets down my bag and props my crutches against the wall. "I will help you," she says.

I put one arm around her shoulders, clutch the banister with the other hand, and together we proceed slowly up the stairs. Then she leads me through a door into a warm kitchen. Something is cooking on the stove, the lid of the pot noisily lifting and lowering, sending out puffs of steam. From another room comes the sound of children's voices.

She takes several paper towels from a roll and hands them to me.

"Thank you," I murmur, pressing the towels to my nose, my forehead. I pinch the bridge of my nose between my thumb and forefinger. It takes minutes for the bleeding to stop. What is happening to Heather? I have to get out of here.

The woman takes an unlabeled bottle from the freezer and pours a bit into a small blue glass. "Drink this," she orders. "You will feel better."

I shake my head, but then she's pressing the glass to my lips. The cold vodka stings going down.

"I will show you the bathroom," she says.

I follow her out of her kitchen, past a large living room, where seven children are standing in a line, waiting their turn. In the middle of the room is a balance beam, and at one end of it stands a man of about sixty, giving orders in Russian to a boy no more than five, who is making his way along the beam. The boy looks up, sees me, and falls off. Then all of the children are staring at me, wide-eyed. The man glances up too, and on his face is a look of shock. The woman says something to him in Russian, he claps his hands, and the children stand at attention.

"Day care," she tells me. "Please excuse the children for staring."

In the bathroom, one glance in the mirror explains their reaction; there's so much blood, I look like a crime scene. My lip is cut and has already started swelling.

The woman wets a washcloth with warm water and cleans my face.

"Oh!" she says, smiling, when the blood is gone. "This way you are much prettier."

Then she opens the medicine cabinet and pulls out a box of Band-Aids and a spray can of Bactine. "Close your eyes," she says. She sprays the cut on my forehead. It stings. She covers the cut with a large Band-Aid. "Much better."

I thank her for her kindness.

"With pleasure," she says, leading me back down the stairs and into the fog. She hands me my crutches and puts the bag over my shoulder. "Sorry I don't have car," she says. "If I have, I give you ride."

Now I go more slowly. *Step, swing, step, swing, step, swing.* This city never ceases to amaze me. Behind every door, it's as if there's another, secret country. In many ways, San Francisco already is what California wants to be: a world unto itself.

My foot feels like a dead weight dangling from my leg. Every sensation in my body is concentrated there. I sing to myself to try to get up the hill. It's a song Tom's been playing on the radio lately, so insanely catchy I haven't been able to get it out of my head — "Save Me, San Francisco," by Train. I don't care who hears me. I don't care who sees me. All I care about is getting to Heather.

I keep hobbling uphill, the song keeps playing in my head, and when I come to the last line I remember what Tom said this morning: "You never needed me to carry you anywhere." He couldn't be more wrong.

And then I'm at Anza, looking up the impossibly steep hill toward Geary, the clock ticking with each step. The waves pound the shore in the distance, the foghorns bellow. It takes me a good ten minutes to get up the hill. Finally, I set off across the wide, empty road. Ahead, at the top of the hill, the flag above the VA keeps flapping in the wind. By the time I reach the other side, my heart is beating wildly, and I have to catch my breath.

The next block, Geary to Clement, is a blur of pain and exhaustion, and then I'm standing at the foot of the VA campus — one last, steep flight of steps between me and the finish line.

"Almost there," I chant under my breath. "Almost there."

49

The Father of Mississippi Secession, according to my childhood textbooks, was a native New Yorker with a strangely apropos name: John Anthony Quitman. At the age of twenty-one, Quitman moved from Ohio to Natchez, where he practiced law and married well. A few years after his arrival, he purchased a large plantation called Monmouth. He would go on to a career in the state senate and the U.S. Congress, abandon politics briefly to command U.S. troops in Mexico, and eventually serve a year as governor of Mississippi. During his decades in politics, he was a fierce proponent of Mississippi's independence. But before Quitman was a secessionist, he was an expansionist. If he had had his way, Cuba would have joined the union as a slave-holding state.

The Monmouth Plantation, which remained in the Quitman family for nearly a century, is now a luxury bed-and-breakfast with twenty-six acres of lushly maintained grounds. I know, because Tom and I have been there. Years ago, he insisted on taking a driving tour of the Southeast. He wanted to see where I'd come from — not just the town but the region. Plus, he wanted to taste grits and butter beans and fried okra in the land that had made them famous. So we flew down to New Orleans, rented a car, and made our way up I-59, through Slidell and Picayune, Poplarville and Hattiesburg. We spent two nights with my mother and Heather in Laurel before setting off through the driving rain for Natchez.

We arrived at Monmouth just as the thunderclouds were clearing. We stayed in the main house, which is said to have been saved from the torches of the Union troops by two of Quitman's daughters. It is an essential element of the southern belle mythology: grand old plantation homes salvaged from Union savagery by acts of female bravery, while the loyal slaves looked on in admiration at their proud and fearless mistresses. During the time of our stay, the owners were renovating the old slave quarters — windowless two-story brick buildings built on the edge of a mosquito-infested pond. Each year I receive a newsletter about goings-on at the former plantation. The most recent one included photos of the old slave quarters, now called Garden Cottages, frilled up with antique dressers, goose down comforters, and gleaming hardwood floors.

"It's all been scrubbed clean," Tom remarked that night in bed. "Like it never happened."

"We southerners are good at that," I said. "Erasing the past, sweeping everything under the rug for outsiders, while obsessing over it in private."

I, too, had wiped the slate of my own history clean. No one in my current life could look at me and know I'd gone whole weeks as a kid eating sandwiches of Wonder bread and ketchup, or that I'd had a second cousin, an angry sheriff's deputy with a stunning resemblance to Elvis, who'd served seven years at the Mississippi State Penitentiary for beating a black teenager to within an inch of his life. An important part of creating a new identity was gradually erasing the old one. You plant new stories like seeds, water them, tend them, until they take root.

History is made not of facts set in stone but of the stories we tell. As a child in Mississippi, I read textbooks that referred to the War for Southern Independence. In my teachers' telling, the heroes of that war were Robert E. Lee, Jefferson Davis, and Thomas "Stonewall" Jackson. Of Abraham Lincoln, we learned only that he was a brilliant but misguided man who sought to force his own views on an unwilling people by way of violence.

A few decades from now, how will the rest of the country construe this moment in history? Will California be remembered as a sovereign state exercising its constitutional right of secession? Or as a rogue and foolish populace bent on destroying the union? What stories will have to be erased to make way for our new narrative?

Our state history — a mere 160 years old, almost laughable in its brevity — is no match for the long history of this land. We keep building and renaming, erecting our buildings and batteries, our signposts and flags, clearing paths and reimagining the landscape: new trees to replace the old ones, new plants to fight off the never-ending erosion.

It would be tempting to say that we've been stupid all along, that we just keep making the same old mistakes disguised as new ones. One might argue we don't deserve what we've been given, and that the moment the planet burns or freezes or hurtles into some black hole is the moment we've been driving toward since the first man crawled out of a cave. But I'm reluctant to ascribe this endless pattern of starting over to human folly or mere hubris. There is more to it than that. We are always looking to do better. The fact that we fail, again and again, the fact that so many of our efforts are deeply misguided, does nothing to diminish the significance of the impulse itself. It is human to start over. It is human to begin again.

Will California secede? Nothing seems outlandish anymore. I think of Tom peeing side by side with Václav Havel. I think of the orange Avanti. I think of the Prague Spring, which tried and failed to overcome communism in the Czech Republic. Twenty-one years later, Berliners brought down the wall. Twelve years after that, horrifyingly, the Twin Towers fell. Nearly another decade passed before the Arab Spring erupted. History seems slow until you're in the middle of it, watching the world come apart at the seams, restitch itself country by country, continent by continent, until the map you once took for granted no longer applies.

50

12:33 p.m.

My legs burn. My foot feels like a dead weight holding me back. I finally reach the top of the hill, sweat pouring down my neck, heart pounding. Ethan's old school stands in front of me. Past the school is the hotel. To the right is Lincoln Park, its slender patch of forest separating the VA from the Legion of Honor.

A quick movement to the right catches my eye. It's a coyote, silver and slim, standing no more than five yards from me. He's so still, so alert, it sends a shiver up my spine.

Cautiously, I take a step. The coyote stands there, watching me. I make my way across the asphalt, past the empty schoolyard. The school is closed today, out of "an abundance of caution," according to the memo that went out to VA staff last week. A row of Big Wheels is lined up against the playground fence. In front of the school, the children have planted a garden. Vegetables are growing there, each seedling labeled with a little wooden stake: HIROMI — BEANS, NIRAJ — CARROTS, KAI — ARTICHOKES.

Cautiously, I proceed toward the hotel. Suddenly, a figure emerges from behind a parked police car. My heart skips a beat.

"Get down," he commands.

It's a policeman, impossibly young. He can't be more than twenty-three. His face is red, and in his shaking hands he holds a gun, pointed toward the ground.

"Down!" he repeats.

I crouch down beside him, feeling fire in my ankle. "What's going on? What's wrong?"

"We've got a situation."

"What?"

"A gunman."

Shit. My first thought is, *This can't be real.* It must be some sort of emergency drill. But I look at his face and see panic; with a sinking feeling, I realize it is real.

"My sister's in there right now." I point to the hotel. "She's going to give birth any minute. I have to get to her."

He shakes his head. "Trying to cross that parking lot would be suicide."

"Where's the gunman?"

"He's holed up in there." He nods toward the main hospital building.

On the second floor, a window is open. The breeze lifts the blue curtains up and outward.

"Where are all the police?"

"You're lookin' at 'em. I called for backup, but there's a lot of shit going down all over the city."

"Do you know who it is?"

"Some crazy vet apparently came by looking for a doctor. When he couldn't find her, he went batshit."

My mouth goes dry. "Which doctor?"

"Walton maybe?" He shakes his head.

"Walker?"

"Yeah, that's it."

In that instant, I know who it is.

"Has he been in the hotel?"

The policeman nods. "He brought a lady out at gunpoint —"

Oh, no. *Not Heather. Please don't let it be Heather.* I struggle to my feet.

"It's not safe," he warns.

But he must realize I don't have a choice, because he lets me go. I arrange my crutches and begin walking, as fast as I can go. *Swing, step, swing, step.* The hotel is only fifty yards away, but the distance feels vast. I

375

glance up at the windows of the hospital. Nothing but the fluttering blue curtains.

Seconds pass. *Swing, step, swing, step.*

I move faster, but it feels as though I'm pushing my way through mud. I'm just ten yards from the hotel now. Five.

I'm standing at the door. I try the knob, but it won't open.

I'm so very close. I put my shoulder against the door and push, putting my whole body behind the effort. The door gives beneath my weight, and I fall. There is the sound of a gunshot. As my shoulder hits the floor, a terrifying question sears itself into my brain: *Is this how it ends?*

51

Two weeks ago, Heather showed up at my place at four A.M. "Get up," she said. "Get dressed. We're taking a road trip."

"You can't," I said. "You're about to burst."

"I'm fine. I need a change of scenery."

"Where are we going?"

"It's a surprise."

"I can't just pick up and leave in the middle of the night."

"You have the day off."

"Still."

It had been a very long time since I'd taken a day off from work, even longer since I'd taken a spur-of-the-moment trip, but she was right; there was nothing in the world to keep me from doing it now. If my sister could be spontaneous while carrying around forty extra pounds, just weeks from giving birth to a married man's child, then surely I could manage a road trip to an unknown destination.

"Do I need anything special?" I asked, climbing out of bed. "A swimsuit? Hiking shoes?"

She gestured toward her enormous belly. "A swimsuit? Honestly?"

"Okay, no swimsuit. What, then?"

"Dress for comfort. I'll go put together a snack for the road. You have twenty minutes."

"What's the big hurry?"

"If we leave soon, we can get there right on time."

"Get where? On time for what?"

"It's a surprise."

I quickly showered and dressed. In the kitchen, Heather was rummaging through the cabinets. "Do you seriously not have a cookie anywhere in this house?"

"Lorna Doones are always above the stove."

"Now you're talking." She found the brand-new box and ripped open the cellophane. "God, this takes me back. That is the best smell, ever. Someone should bottle it. Eau de Lorna Doone."

Minutes later, we were on the road. Heather was too big to fit comfortably behind the wheel, so she rode shotgun and gave directions.

"Just get on 101 and keep going," she said.

"Petaluma?" I guessed. "Healdsburg?"

"You'll know when we get there."

Golden Gate Bridge was wrapped in a blanket of white, the massive orange towers hovering over the bay. To our right, the island of Alcatraz floated in the fog, ghost-like. We drove past the houseboats of Marin, and the hills of Tiburon, dotted with multimillion-dollar homes. Past San Quentin, through the brown hills of San Rafael. Heather kept me company for a while, telling funny stories about her long-ago stint in Nashville, with her boyfriend's failed band. An hour into the drive, she drifted off to sleep, and I turned on the radio. I'd forgotten how much I loved driving in the dark, with few other cars on the road, just the eighteen-wheelers rumbling by with their mysterious payloads. I'd forgotten the thrill of flipping stations, looking for an unfamiliar signal. It was strange how many country stations and evangelists one could discover in the middle of the night.

At dawn, I reached over and shook Heather gently. "Hey, wake up. How will I know when we get there?"

"Where are we?" she asked groggily.

"Cloverdale."

"I have to pee."

I pulled over at a McDonald's, where we bought coffee and sausage biscuits. After Heather scarfed hers down, she dusted the crumbs off her lap and announced, "We've got a ways to go. Wake me up in an hour."

I put in a CD that Tom had made for me years ago and listened to old favorites — Luna, the Jayhawks, Nick Cave and the Bad Seeds. We passed the sign for Hopland. I had to admit the countryside was pretty here; for the first time, I understood why Tom loved it.

When the clock struck seven-thirty, I turned the music up, and Heather jolted awake.

"We're just outside of Rio Dell," I reported.

"Jesus, how fast are you going?"

After that, she didn't fall back asleep, so I knew we must be getting close. We'd just passed the first exit for Fields Landing when she said, "It's the next one."

I swung onto the exit, taking the ramp too fast.

"Good Lord, you'll kill us before we get there," she said, clutching the door handle.

"Eureka? What are we doing in Eureka?"

She pulled a piece of paper out of her purse and started reading off the directions. To our left was the Pacific Ocean, draped in fog. To our right, the little shops and houses of the town. While Eureka was colder and bleaker than San Francisco, the coastline looked similar: rugged beaches dotted with ice plant, steep cliffs plunging toward the ocean. We drove past a laundromat and a taqueria, a karate studio with a broken front window, and then we were in a residential area, not very nice, chain-link fences and flat one-story houses fashioned of red brick. The houses gradually got better — not fancy, by any means, but nice enough, two-story stucco affairs with well-maintained lawns and newly paved streets. We were in a development, one of those dime-a-dozen tracts that had sprung up like crazy in the boom years, now featuring foreclosure signs on every block. After a few minutes the houses thinned out a bit. We passed a park, a small community center, a row of churches. "Here," she said. "Pull in right here."

We were in front of a school.

"What are we doing?" I asked, suddenly feeling uneasy.

"Just wait."

She glanced at her watch. "Give it ten minutes. All mysteries will be revealed."

I fiddled with the dial, growing more and more anxious. Finally, a bell rang, doors were flung open, and dozens of children spilled onto the playground.

"What are we *doing*?"

"We're spying," she said.

"On whom?" My first thought was that it had something to do with her baby. "Are you about to reveal that the father is really nothing more scandalous than a middle school teacher?"

"This isn't about me, Jules."

"Then what?"

"Don't get mad."

I understood, then, why we were here, and who I should be looking for. I felt dizzy.

"How did you —"

I couldn't finish. My breath quickened. I was elated and terrified at the same time, not knowing what I would find. The one thing I knew for certain was that I was utterly unprepared for this, for whatever might happen next.

I looked around. Dozens of kids, barely distinguishable from one another, running around like wild. But then a dark-haired child in a red T-shirt caught my eye. His back was to me. The child began flapping his arms. It lasted only seconds. As abruptly as he'd begun, he stopped, dropping his arms by his sides. And I knew instantly, in that gesture, that it was Ethan.

I don't know what I said, if I said anything. I only know that I ached for him. I wanted to see his face, to hold him. I willed him to turn around, but his back remained to me. I pulled the door handle, because all I could think of at that moment was running to him.

"Wait," Heather said.

She was right. I couldn't very well rush up to him on the playground. I'd scare him. It had been so long since the caseworker had pulled him out of my arms in the family services office in San Francisco; Allison had been his mother for twice as long as I had. He probably wouldn't even know who I was. He was so close, I couldn't believe it.

Ethan stood for several seconds, half a minute maybe, on the edge of the playground, watching the other children. He seemed so isolated, so alone, it was heartbreaking. A cluster of teachers stood by the swings, talking among themselves. Why didn't any of them come to help him, to usher him into the group?

Then Ethan raised one arm into the air and shouted, "Over here!"

"He sounds different . . ." My voice caught in my throat.

A group of boys looked up from the game they were playing and ran over to him. Finally, for a moment, he turned so that I could see him in profile — his sweet face. "Oh, God," I breathed. "It really is him."

The children gathered around, and he began talking animatedly. I couldn't hear what he was saying, but I imagined he was explaining to them some new game he was making up, right there on the spot. When he was very little, he was always coming up with games, complete with his own complex system of rules and rewards. He gestured this way and that, and the boys paid close attention. Finally, from his pocket, Ethan pulled out a small bouncy ball. He tossed it into the air, and the boys scrambled for it. I was overcome with happiness.

"Look at that," Heather said. "He's the ringleader." She reached over and put her hand on mine. "Jules?"

My face was wet. "It's really him."

I got out of the car and went toward the fence; it felt as though a magnet were pulling me. I wanted to be closer. I stood there watching him play, hearing his sweet, wonderful voice rise up from the din of the playground. His beautiful curls had been cut short — I ached to touch his hair, remembering how he'd loved to run his fingers through it, a way of soothing himself to sleep. His face had changed, too. It was thinner. His whole body was leaner. He was all boy now, no traces remained of the baby he'd been when he first came into my life. He was strong and athletic, and he moved with confidence. He was smiling, laughing, shouting orders.

"Oh, my God," I murmured, laughing. "He's bossy." Of course, he'd been bossy even when he was little. Why would that have changed?

Another child bounced the ball hard. Miraculously, it came flying in my direction, and Ethan pivoted and started running toward me. He was within five feet of the fence when he caught it, and for a moment he glanced up at me and smiled. There was the slightest pause, a flicker of recognition, I thought. I opened my mouth to speak to him, but before I could decide what to say, he wheeled and ran back to the group. Of course, would he even remember my face? The last time he saw me, he was four years old. All those sweet days I'd spent with him, those days that formed the most vivid chapters of my own life, could only be, for him, blurry memories. Was it true what Allison Rhodes had said, just weeks before she took custody? "In a year," she had told me, "he won't even remember that he used to live somewhere else."

I stayed by the fence and watched until

the bell rang and the kids lined up to go inside. Ethan was the last one in the line, and as the teacher gave instructions, he stood staring at the sky. I looked up. A blimp moved across the horizon, advertising some local circus. I remembered a circus Tom and I had taken Ethan to — a ramshackle affair in a shabby tent at the San Mateo County fairgrounds, featuring acrobats in awkwardly revealing clothes and a small dog dressed in a miniature elephant costume. It had been a perfect day.

Ethan pointed, said something, and all the children looked up. The teacher clapped her hands and called them to attention, and the children began to file into the classroom. I was grateful that he stood at the end of the line. I willed the children to walk more slowly, so that I could watch him a second longer. I tried to drink in every detail. I knew I would never forget the little tag sticking out of his T-shirt, which I longed to tuck in. I would never forget what he looked like, pointing at the blimp in the sky. I would never forget that, on this day, he was happy.

Back in the car, I rested my head against the seat, hardly able to believe what had just happened. "How did you find him?" I asked. "I've spent a million hours on the

Internet."

"I told you I had friends in high places," Heather said, winking. "His aunt remarried right after she got custody. She changed her name. Then she and the husband adopted Ethan and changed his name, too."

"What does he do, the husband?"

"Pharmaceutical sales. Coaches Little League."

"Ethan's in Little League?"

Heather nodded. "Little League, band —"

"What does he play?"

"The trumpet."

"The trumpet," I echoed in amazement.

"Oh, and he's in the Junior Beachcombers' Club," Heather added.

"What's that?"

"They get together every couple of months to look for treasures on the beach. They've adopted a sea turtle named Boris. There's a picture of the club on the school website. I got copies of the yearbook from the last three years. He's well-represented. You said you didn't have recent photos of him, so —"

I leaned over the seat and put my arms around my sister. "Thank you," I whispered. "Thank you so much."

52

2:07 p.m.

"How's your sister?" Dennis asks.

"Not great." I decide to take a risk. "What about Betty?" After his earlier outburst, I don't dare ask about Rajiv.

"She's fine," he says. Laughs. "Probably a bit bored of me."

I allow myself a shaky laugh, trying to mirror his mood.

"I remember when Lucy had Isabel," Dennis says. "I drove down Geary at three A.M., running every red light until we got to Kaiser. There was nowhere to park, so I pulled right up to the emergency room. I was in such a hurry, I forgot to turn off the engine, and when I came out later the car had run out of gas. When the nurse put Isabel in my arms, it was like the floor had dropped out from under me. She was so tiny, and I was instantly in love with her, but I was terrified, too. Like my whole life was suddenly about keeping her safe. For the first few weeks, I wouldn't let Isabel out of my sight. When I had to go back to work, I couldn't concentrate. I just kept thinking, *What if something happens to her?*"

"But nothing did," I said. "You took good care of her. You did what you were supposed to do."

For all his mistakes, I know this: Dennis always tried to be a good father. He loves Isabel more than anything.

"I'm tired," he says.

"I know."

"I just want it to all be over with."

My throat tightens. "That's not the answer," I say. And then I say the thing I should have said to Danielle years ago, the words I always wish I had spoken to her, the words I now know she so desperately needed to hear: "You have something to live for."

He snorts. "What would that be, exactly?"

I don't have an answer. He lost his wife. He lost his daughter. He has no job and no prospects, his parents want nothing to do with him, and any kind of decent relationship seems to entirely elude him. Now he has killed someone. When this is over, he will go to prison.

389

"One day," I say, "Isabel will want to know you."

"No. She won't. She thinks I'm a monster."

"Prove her wrong."

He laughs quietly. "It's a little late for that, isn't it?"

"I'll get you help, Dennis. It's not too late. Let them go. Please."

"That thing with Eleanor," he sputters. "No one will believe she made me do it. It doesn't matter what happens to the others, because she's already dead."

"It matters," I say gently. "Eleanor wasn't premeditated. It was spur-of-the-moment, you lost it, there were extenuating circumstances, you were under severe mental stress."

"Supposing you're right," he points out bitterly. "Then I end up in a psychiatric hospital. That's your big fix, Doc? I get to go live with the crazies?"

"I can't predict what's going to happen," I admit after a moment. "But I know you don't want to hurt anyone else."

"How do you know what I want?"

"You like Betty. You said it yourself."

"True, but I don't give a shit about Rajiv."

I freeze, afraid to say anything, afraid *not*

to say something.

"Come over here," he says. "To your office. Come over right now, and I'll let them both go. A simple trade: you for them." I can't be sure, but it sounds as though he is crying.

"I can't leave my sister, not yet."

"Afterward?" he asks. "Will you come over after?"

"Yes. I promise, Dennis. As soon as I deliver the baby, I'll come over."

"We can talk face-to-face?"

"Yes, we can talk face-to-face. I promise."

I go over to the bed and hold Heather's hand. The contractions are so close now, the pain must be unbearable. "You're almost there," I say to her. "I'm so proud of you."

And I am. How could I not be? To see my sister, engaged in this most basic struggle, this ancient, life-giving thing, is awe-inspiring. I know she's been to war. I know she's seen things that would horrify me. I know that, in many ways, she has moved beyond me, into a realm of experience I can only imagine — and yet, at this moment, she is above all my baby sister.

"Fuck Eve," she growls.

It comes back in times of crisis: all that religion we soaked in during our formative years, Brother Ray's dogma like a swarm of mosquitoes you can't shake from your skin. "It was woman who committed original sin," he must have said a hundred times. "Woman who led the entire human race down the path of unrighteousness."

"No," I reply. "Fuck Adam."

Heather lets out half a laugh.

"What's funny?" Dennis says.

"It was a joke about Adam and Eve." I try to explain, but something is lost in translation.

Another contraction comes. Heather lifts up on her elbows, groaning.

"Time to push," I say.

She does so, tears streaming down her face. She's just come off a minute-long contraction and is catching her breath when the building starts to quiver. Instinctively, I brace myself.

"You've got to be kidding me." I look up at the ceiling. "Is this a joke? An earthquake?"

Heather motions toward the phone and puts a finger to her lips. I don't dare mute the phone. Instead, I take it into the bathroom, set it down beside the sink, turn the water on, and quickly return to Heather's side.

She spins her index finger. I still don't get it. "Chopper," she whispers. The vibrations increase. "I'd know that sound anywhere. They must be landing in Lincoln Park."

"Who?"

"SWAT."

I go back into the bathroom, turn off the water, and pick up the phone. "How you doing, Dennis?"

"Where've you been, Julie?" he demands. His voice crackles: he's angry.

"I had to go to the bathroom. I turned the water on for privacy."

"What was that noise?"

"News chopper," I say, hoping I'm wrong.

And then, there are footsteps on the roof.

I give Heather a questioning look.

She gestures furiously toward a pen and notepad on the desk. I hand them to her. She writes a single word: *Sniper.*

Her face contorts. But Heather doesn't yell — she just makes these intense, keening moans. It occurs to me that she knows exactly what she's doing, knows how to keep her head low and choose the safest possible action in an unpredictable situation.

"Push," I urge. "You can do it, push."

After the contraction ends, she grabs the pen and scribbles furiously. *Get him 2 window.*

"Why?" I whisper, but I think I understand.

She stabs at the words on the pad: *Get him 2 window.*

I shake my head. "I can't."

Ys! U can!

I think of all the times I sat in the cafeteria with Dennis, chatting over coffee. I think of the confidences we shared. Of the night we spent together at his apartment, his utter tenderness. At that moment, all those years ago, when I was alone in San Francisco, unsure of my decision to leave everything I knew behind and try to make an entirely new life for myself, he was exactly what I needed. There's one thing I learned in church that still holds some ring of truth today: when you sleep with someone, you give him a little part of yourself. It was intended as an admonishment, a call to celibacy until marriage, but for me it has always meant something very different. There are certain people in this world with whom I share a unique and somehow un-breakable bond. Over the years, each time I have chosen a partner, even if it was only for a single night or a few weeks, I have been aware that I was entering into a kind of contract. Each time, upon making the deci-sion to sleep with someone, I vowed to myself that I would always remember him; I hoped he would remember me as well.

Whatever Dennis has become, however our paths have diverged, there was a moment in time when I chose him. A moment when I looked at him and felt the full force of this possibility. And there were many afternoons after that when I said so much, when I looked into his eyes and saw a friend.

The footsteps on the roof again, a shuffling sound.

"Now," Heather whispers.

I think of the oath I recited with my fellow students at the white-coat ceremony during my first week of medical school. There were many families in attendance, but mine was not among them. The night before, I had lain awake in my studio apartment, turning the words over in my mind until they were seared into my memory, especially one strange, unsettling passage: "If it is given to me to save a life, all thanks. But it may also be within my power to take a life; this awesome responsibility must be faced with great humbleness and awareness of my own frailty."

It may also be within my power to take a life. As I'd stood in front of the audience of strangers, feeling somewhat lost in the short white coat, I had stumbled over the words. What did they mean, exactly? And would I be able to fulfill that part of the oath, if and when I was called upon to do so?

I think of a phrase Dr. Bariloche taught us in our very first class: *primum non nocere* — first, do no harm.

"The modern manifestation of this," Dr. Bariloche explained, "is non-maleficence. Given an existing problem, it may be better not to do something, or even to do nothing, than to risk causing more harm than good."

What I want more than anything at this moment is to do nothing. To pretend I didn't hear what Heather asked of me, her utterly logical and unthinkable solution. To pretend there were no footsteps on the roof.

And then I think of Rajiv. His bride-to-be. His mother. The years he's spent getting to where he is now. I think of Betty, and I remember her pride when she told me about one of her grandkids not long ago, valedictorian of Lowell High School, on her way to a scholarship at U.C. Irvine. I think of Eleanor.

I limp over to the window. "Dennis?"

"Yes."

"I'm going to set the phone down for a minute so I can move everything away from the window."

"Why?"

"So I can see you."

"I don't believe you," he says.

396

"Listen."

I set the phone down, take the duffel bag from atop the bureau, lean my back against the heavy furniture, and push. The extra weight on my foot is excruciating. How did Heather have the strength to put it here in the first place? When the bureau is clear of the window, I pick up the phone, push the curtain aside, and peer out.

"Did you hear that?"

"Yes. You're at the window now?"

"I'm right here. But I can't see you. Where are you?"

"Do you think I'm stupid?"

"Of course not. Why would you say that?"

"Who's feeding you orders? Who told you to tell me to come to the window?"

"No one, Dennis. I swear. It's just me and my sister here. No one gives me orders in my own hospital. I want to see you. We've been talking, how long —"

The hand I'm holding the phone with is shaking.

"One hour, twelve minutes, nineteen seconds — give or take," he says, with a slight laugh.

"Okay." I'm at a loss for what to say. "You remember how much I hate talking on the phone, don't you?"

Silence. What is he thinking?

"I remember. You always preferred face-to-face."

"That's right. Face-to-face. Just me and you, Dennis."

Across the way, the curtain flutters. His face peeks out, a flicker of white.

"That's better, Dennis, much better." My heart is hammering. Should I continue? Will it anger him if I press further? I look over at Heather. She gives me the thumbs-up.

I turn back to the window. "I still can't see you, Dennis. You've got to stand where I can see you."

"Maybe I will," he says. "If you do something for me."

"What's that?"

It's quiet for a few seconds. I can hear Dennis breathing.

"Go out on the balcony and lift your shirt."

"What?"

"You heard me. Lift your shirt."

"Lift my shirt?"

"I want to really see you. All the way. Out on the balcony."

It's about control, I remind myself. Control and loyalty. He wants to show that he's calling the shots, and he wants to see how far I'm willing to go for him.

"Okay, Dennis. But you have to promise

me that if I do it, you'll stand where I can see you. I want to see your face. You'll give me that, won't you?"

I can hear the smile in Dennis's voice. "Scout's honor," he says.

I move in front of the window, my heart beating wildly. I try the latch, but it won't budge.

"You're stalling," Dennis says.

"No, I'm not. This window probably hasn't been opened in ages. It's stuck."

"Hurry up," he says, sounding agitated. I bang on the latch with my fist, and I'm almost dizzy with relief when it won't open. Still, I push once more and, finally, it gives. I open the window. Terrified, I limp out onto the flimsy platform, which shudders beneath me. My chest seizes up with fear. He has a clear shot. If he wants to pull the trigger, he can.

"Now," he says. "Your shirt."

A sudden gust of wind lifts the flags on the pole. I shiver in the cold. The foghorns bleat in the distance.

I begin to lift my sweater. The humiliation is almost too much, but I do it. The curtain moves on the window of my office. Down in the parking lot, the young policeman is still crouched beside his car. His gaze travels from my office window, over to me. And then I see someone in full-on SWAT gear, coming up behind the cafeteria. On the roof above me, shuffling sounds.

"Higher," Dennis says.

I lift it higher.

"Take off your bra."

"Dennis."

"We made a deal, didn't we?"

I don't dare look back at Heather. I'm on my own now. It feels, in some strange way, as if it really is just the two of us, Dennis and me.

I set the phone down, lift my sweater over my head, and drape it over the balcony railing. I reach behind my back and find the hooks of the bra. I close my eyes and, in one fumbling motion, release the hooks. A memory comes to me: the way he laid me down on the bed and moved over my body so slowly, so gently, the way he kissed my breasts. Slowly, I bring the straps forward and, for a moment, I hold on to an illusion of privacy, my arms folded in front of my chest, before letting the bra fall to my feet.

I pick up the phone and bring it to my ear. On the other end, silence. I glance left, where the avenues of the Outer Richmond slope down toward the sea.

Here I am, on the eve of forty, soon to be divorced, possibly jobless, entirely alone, standing half-naked on the balcony of a run-down hotel room, looking out over my adopted city, my home. There is no room left for humiliation or remorse. Here I am.

For several seconds, my mind simply goes blank. And then I feel the warmth of the sun, a gust of wind blows across my bare skin, and I smell the briny smell of the ocean, taste salt on my tongue.

"That's nice," Dennis says.

There's a tinny clicking sound on the roof above me.

I hear Dr. Bariloche's voice in my head: *"Primum non nocere."*

And then I see myself, all those years ago, standing in front of the audience of strangers, the words strange on my tongue: "It may also be within my power to take a life."

Which is it? Do no harm or take a life? In medical school, why did no one ever offer an answer to these contradictions?

There was a time when Dennis and I might have been a couple, a time when our paths could have merged, but I had the good luck to meet Tom instead. I am responsible for what happened to Eleanor. I am responsible for what happens to Rajiv, and Betty, and, yes, to Dennis. I don't believe in divine intervention. I believe in cause and effect, the domino power of choice. If we

401

hadn't reached for the same novel at a bookstore on Clement Street all those years ago, Dennis would not be here, holed up in my office, with a gun in his hands and a murdered woman by his side. He might have gone off the rails somewhere else, at some other time — but not right here, not right now.

Primum non nocere.

I could step inside right now; I could let this play out some other way. What kind of person does what I am about to do?

"I can't see you," I say.

"What?"

"We made a deal."

Suddenly the curtain flutters, and there he is, standing in front of the low window, smiling. Dennis Drummond. Even from here I recognize his face. Even from here, even now, I see in him what I saw that first day, when we stood side by side, reaching for the same book. He's a good-looking man, always was, even at his most down-and-out. If I were up close, I know I would be startled, as I am each time I see him, by the perfect blueness of his eyes.

Then there is the crack of gunshot. I wait for the sting in my chest, the pain, but it doesn't come. Dennis's mouth opens in shock, our eyes lock, and he begins to bow toward me.

Primum non nocere.

A red flower blooms on his forehead, and he folds forward completely, over the windowsill, and it is strangely graceful, the way his body falls from the window and seems to pause for a moment before landing on the soft green grass below.

Oh, God. What have I done?

Heather moans. I step inside and move toward her in a kind of trance.

"Just a few more," I say. It is all so surreal. And yet it is really happening.

Heather yells for the first time, really yells, a guttural, primal wail of pain and determination. Moments later, the baby's head begins to crown.

"You can do it," I urge her, still trembling.

I picture my mother on the cold cement floor of a grocery store in Laurel, the tornado raging around her. I think of her the day she brought my infant sister home. "Everything's falling into place," she had said, placing Heather in my arms.

Heather is making no noise now. Her face is red with the effort of pushing, small blood vessels leaving marks across her cheeks.

"Just once more," I promise my sister.

Then there's the final push, a howl of joy and pain, and this tiny living thing slides into my waiting hands. Heather is crying, pushing herself up on her elbows to see, her face flushed and glowing.

"Is she okay? Julie?"

"She's perfect."

I swab the baby clean and lay the perfect, naked infant facedown in Heather's arms. I cover them both with the soft blue blanket. Then I gently rub the baby's back, and she begins to cry. Moments later, she latches onto Heather's nipple and begins to suck greedily.

53

There's more noise on the roof, more shouting and commotion down below. Heather and the baby lie quietly, a world unto themselves. The soft sounds of the baby's sucking feel real, strangely distilled, while the chaos going on outside this room seems distant, like a movie playing on a screen in some far-away theater.

I retrieve my sweater from the balcony, put it on, and wash my hands.

There are footsteps on the stairs, followed by pounding on the door. "SWAT!" someone calls. "Anyone in here?"

"We're here," I answer.

The door begins to open, then slams into the desk. Someone throws his body against the door, forcing the desk aside. A man stands in the doorway, dressed in full black gear.

"Everybody okay?"

Then he sees Heather, lying there with

the baby in her arms. He speaks into his walkie-talkie. "Medical! One woman with a newborn and another woman with —" He looks me up and down. I imagine how I must appear: crazed, or broken, or both. "Just get medical."

Minutes later, the room is filled with people. The SWAT guy, Greg Watts, and, to my relief, Sandy Bungo, sporting her trademark navy scrubs, pushing an empty wheelchair.

A nurse-practitioner, Sandy was at the VA when I started here, all those years ago. I'd trust her with my life.

"Is Rajiv okay?"

"Yes."

"Thank God. Betty, too?"

She nods. For the first time in hours, I feel as though I can really breathe. "You look like hell," Sandy says. "Want me to take over? I brought the essentials."

"Please."

"A little privacy, guys," Sandy yells at the men in uniforms. Then she runs the Apgar test, clamps the cord, checks the baby's heartbeat, and massages Heather's stomach to release the afterbirth. Finally, she stitches my sister up, then takes her into the bathroom and helps her bathe while I hold my tiny, beautiful niece.

Minutes later, Heather is dressed in a clean flannel nightgown. Sandy helps her into the wheelchair, and I lay the baby in her arms. Downstairs, I grab my crutches, and we make our way across the parking lot. People have come out of the cafeteria and the hospital and are wandering around, looking dazed. Some are in hospital nightgowns, plus a few staffers in scrubs.

At the entrance, I find Rajiv standing over to the side. His shirt is dark with blood. He's smoking a cigarette. He quit two years ago.

"You go ahead," I say to Sandy.

She nods. "We'll be in room 312."

As she wheels Heather into the hospital, I walk over to Rajiv. I put my hands on his shoulders and pull him toward me, and for several seconds we stand there, leaning into each other in an awkward embrace. When I pull away, my sweater is damp with blood.

In the lobby, I wait for the ancient elevator. On the third floor, Mr. Fairchild is wandering down the hallway, clutching his walker, which is decorated with little red pom-poms — his granddaughter's handiwork. "You look like shit," he calls out cheerily.

"How's your heart holding up?" I ask.

"So far, so good, Doc. Hey, it was Dennis,

wasn't it?"

I nod.

"Figured." He shakes his head and shuffles on.

I grab a clean top from a cart of scrubs in the hallway and duck into the staff lounge to change out of my bloody sweater. A few rooms down, I find Heather in bed, Sandy by her side. "Would you like to hold your niece?" Heather asks.

I prop my crutches against the window and ease myself into a chair. Sandy places the baby in my arms. Wrapped tightly in the soft green blanket Heather bought for just this day, the baby looks like an alien washed up on a distant shore. I slowly rock back and forth, mesmerized by the strange face peering out from the covers.

"This should help," Sandy says, dropping two pills into my palm. I put the Percocet on my tongue and wash it down with water from a paper cup. "I'll be back," she says, closing the door softly behind her.

Soon, Heather is sleeping. She can sleep anywhere, in any situation; it has always been that way. "I never knew what a gift it was," she told me recently, "until I went overseas. If you can sleep, you can escape anything for a few hours."

I rock the baby back and forth, relieved to

finally be alone with my sister and my niece. The normal hospital noise has given way to a disconcerting quiet. Through a small opening in the window above me, I can hear the waves crashing below. The foghorns up and down the coastline continue their random litany. It is hypnotic, that sound. Beneath it all is a steady hum, a tumble of words and song: the radio, turned low, in some other room — my husband's voice. Even though I can't make out the words, I recognize him through the rise and fall of it. Those foghorns, that voice: the sound of my life.

I half-expect to hear Mr. Yiu in the background, calling out, "Buster boy! Buster boy!" The Percocet and the exhaustion work their voodoo on my brain. I think of Danielle sitting in my living room, nervous and shaking, holding Ethan in her arms. I remember my husband's strong arms lifting me out of the crowd, setting me gently down. How could I not make a life with him, in this beautiful place, in the home we shared? How did I allow it to go wrong?

I rock the baby slowly, quietly. I want to savor this moment. I look at her sweet face, and for a moment I'm lost in a time warp — I am ten years old, holding Heather on the sofa in Laurel. I am startled to see a resemblance to my own baby photos. I tell myself that I am only imagining this reflection through the looking glass of four decades, but I know the similarities are in fact there. There are Heather's eyes, my mother's chin. And somewhere, surely, an echo of Heather's father, that unknown quantity.

It is something astonishing, the sleep of a newborn baby, so deep and still. And then the infant opens her tiny eyes, and a bewildered gaze falls on my face. I know she can't really see me yet. In her eyes, for now, there is only the difference between light and dark, vague shapes hovering close by; and yet she appears to be looking into my eyes. I am amazed and confused. It is as if she can see right into me. If there is such a thing as déjà vu, then there is also this: an unexpected moment, completely new, unlike anything I have experienced before.

Before the world intervenes, it seems I should take a moment to tell my niece something important, to impart some sort of wisdom or, at the very least, a series of simple life lessons. Six months ago, a year ago, I might have known what to say; I might have found the perfect pronouncement for this profound moment of beginnings. But things have changed, and now I am unsure. Everything I once believed to be permanent has revealed its transience.

There are footsteps in the hallway — quick, short bursts, followed by a light tapping at the door.

"Come in," I say. At the sound of my voice, Heather stirs.

A man steps into the room. He's dressed in jeans and a black sweater. Taller than I imagined, less tan. His hair is perfect. He smiles at me, and for a moment I imagine that I'm dreaming.

He glances at the bundle in my arms, and his eyes fill with tears. "Can I hold her?"

"Of course."

He leans down to take the small, squirming bundle. "She's beautiful," he says. He walks over to the bed, kisses Heather on the forehead, and together they admire their child.

Staring, at a loss for words, I quickly recalibrate the world as I knew it. For years, it seemed as though my life was charmed, all the parts falling into place: the husband, the career, the child. Meanwhile, Heather's world unraveled. But when I wasn't looking, everything reordered itself. Now it seems we have undergone some strange reversal. In our backyard in Laurel, we had a rickety seesaw where Heather and I would sometimes sit. I can't help but feel the same principle has been at work all along: one rises, the other falls.

"Julie," Heather says, smiling, "meet James. James, meet Julie."

54

Sandy appears in the doorway of Heather's room. Once again, she's pushing an empty wheelchair. She glances at the governor, does a quick double take.

"But you're —"

"Late," he says. "I was in Sacramento when I got the call. We had some trouble landing at SFO."

It's the first time I've seen Sandy nearly speechless, but she quickly recovers. "Congratulations," she says. "Get in," she commands, pulling the wheelchair up beside me. On our way out, she turns back to the governor. "Just so you know, I voted for you."

"I hope I didn't disappoint."

"Jury's still out," she replies.

In the X-ray room, I climb onto the table. Sandy arranges the lead blanket, places the cold plate beneath my ankle, and positions the machine. "Lie still," she says, stepping behind the wall. The machine clicks and hums. "I'm not going to ask you about that man I just saw with your sister," she says. "But just so you know, I *can* keep a secret."

"Believe me, I'm as surprised as you are."

"I doubt that." She comes back to the table and removes the X-ray plate. "In some ways we're lucky the whole city is in chaos. Otherwise, we'd be in the middle of a media storm by now." And then she disappears.

I prop myself up on my elbows and gaze out the window. A wall of fog hangs over the ocean. It begins to rain, gently at first, and then it pours. The wind blows the rain in great horizontal sheets, and I'm glad not to be out there. Glad to be here, in this warm place I know so well, my second home. I realize that my fingers are crossed, that I'm wishing for something. I'm wishing for unity — a grand statement that things can work, that we can all, somehow, get along.

Sandy returns, shaking her head. "Girl, you're not going to like this picture."

The X ray shows a medial malleolus fracture, which explains why I've been in so much pain. "Maybe walking across the city on it wasn't such a great idea."

"You think?"

I suck in air through my teeth as she applies the cast. Then she wheels me into an empty room and helps me onto the clean, hard bed, propping my injured ankle up on pillows. When she leaves, everything is so quiet. Too quiet. Two boats somewhere in the distance call out to each other. Another ship adds its response, and another. The wind subsides slightly, and the rain stops suddenly. Three hundred and ninety billion gallons of seawater rush in and out of the bay each day, and yet, for the moment, I hear nothing. Just silence. I consider that split second between high tide and low tide when the water is still, unsure which way to go, as if the world, for a moment, has stopped.

I lie back on the bed beneath the thin blanket and try to push thoughts of Dennis out of my mind. And Eleanor. She wasn't married, but there must be someone I should call to offer condolences. It startles me to realize how little I knew her.

I got through this, I tell myself. *We* got through this. Rajiv is okay. So is Betty. Heather delivered a healthy baby girl. A perfect baby girl.

People are dying right now all over the country, all over the world, right here in this city. You can't save everyone. Death is a fact of life. It's terrible, but it happens. I'm a doctor; I know this. And yet, I was in no way prepared for what happened today.

I think of those first moments when I fell through the door of the hotel, my world split open by gunshot. I think of the long trudge up the stairs and down the hallway, not knowing what I would find. *We made it,* I tell myself again.

But when I close my eyes, I picture Eleanor's bloodied corpse. I see Dennis, lying on the grass. The wound in his forehead, the blood soaking his hair. I clench my fists and tell myself to hold it together. All these years, I've been trying to hold it together. And through everything, any time I felt the temptation to crawl into a corner and weep, or go outside and scream, I've always believed I was holding it together for someone else: my patients, my students, Ethan, Heather, Tom.

But now I understand the truth. The resilience on which I prided myself was never selfless. I shut down my emotions because I was terrified what might happen if I let go, even for a moment.

Now the tears come, slowly at first, and then torrential. Sobs tear through my body, and ragged guttural sounds emerge from my throat. I pull the blanket tightly around myself, curl into a ball, and close my eyes. What have I done?

55

I wake to a San Francisco sunrise — more the suggestion of sun than anything else, a vague yellow glow emanating from the fog.

The hospital is eerily quiet. I slowly make my way to my office. The room smells of cleaning fluid, but blood still stains the floor. In the center of the desk is a small box wrapped in red paper. It has been opened — by the police or FBI, I imagine — and taped back together. Inside the box is a small card. I recognize the handwriting: *Happy birthday from your old friend.* Beneath the card is a slender gold bracelet inset with a tiny pearl — my birthstone. I lay the bracelet and card back in the box, close it, and place it carefully in the top drawer of my desk.

Tom's red Panasonic Toot-a-Loop is perched on the bookcase. You can tell a lot about a marriage by the objects it accumulates. With our marriage, it was radios.

I'm not sure what that says about us, but I do know there's something comforting in the feel of the dial beneath my fingers, the static fuzz as the receiver works to pick up the signal from outer space. A song is playing on KMOO, something I don't recognize.

I go over to my window and pull open the blinds. Once again, I find myself looking down at the rooftop of the school. My gaze follows the line of the roof over to the hotel, to the balcony where I stood yesterday. Out there, everything looks the same — the hills of Marin, the ocean meeting the bay, the grand orange bridge spanning the divide. I think of the ships that lie buried beneath the water, their cargo and all those lives relegated to a distant past.

The song comes to an end, and Tom's voice flows from the radio — a voice so sweet, so familiar, the sound of my life. And it occurs to me that yesterday, while I was on that crazy journey across town, I kept wanting to talk to him. This morning, my first urge was to call him and say, "You'll never believe who showed up to see the baby." I wanted to tell him about the beautiful baby girl. I wanted to tell him how surprised I was when the governor walked into the room. Invariably, after the truth set in, Tom would ask about the governor's hair, and I would assure him that it was perfect.

More important, though, I wanted to tell Tom about Eleanor, and Dennis. I needed to tell him what I had done. I needed to tell him about the choices I made.

All these months he's been gone, and yet he's still the first thing I think of when I wake up in the morning, the last name to cross my mind before I go to sleep at night. When I was falling through the door, Tom was the one I longed for.

For so long I believed that we needed a child of our own. After we lost Ethan, having a baby seemed like an essential measure of our love — the ability to combine our DNA and pass it on to another person, who would carry that imprint forward into the world; the ability to completely join our two selves together. But I failed to see the truth: Tom is a part of me already.

I think of the cross-eyed stranger that summer in Mississippi, the one who urged me to get into his car. I think of all the chances I had to try something different, to do something totally unplanned, but didn't. How might the arc of my life have been altered if I had accepted his peculiar invitation, or any number of other invitations over the years? What if I had veered from my chosen path? I guess this could be the part where I lament my lack of adventure, the part where I wish I'd lived a different life. But I don't wish any such thing. The straight and narrow suited me. I chose my path and took it. It led me to this particular life in this particular place, to a career I love and to a marriage I don't regret.

I never expected to find myself here, on the edge of the continent — forty, childless, possibly jobless, with broken bones and a broken marriage, citizen of a broken country. But here I am, and I must make something of it. That's really the only choice one has: make something of it, or don't — a choice my mother failed to make after my father died, a choice my sister has completely embraced.

I picture my mother on the grocery store floor in Laurel, the baby in her arms. "She'll be an ambitious one," the store manager had said, to which my mother replied, "Lord, I hope not. There's pain enough in this world without getting your hopes up." But what if it turns out, instead, that the pain lies in not hoping — in refusing to believe that anything is possible?

In the days before I first left for medical school, my mother walked around in a cloud of sadness. Although I knew it would never happen, one night I suggested that she and Heather come with me to San Francisco. I remember the look she gave me, as if I had said the most ridiculous thing in the world. "Sweetheart," she said, "I could never leave this town, I could never leave your father."

I was confused, concerned for her. "Daddy's not here."

"Yes, he is, silly. Every time I walk into the Arabian Theatre, where we had our first kiss, he's there waiting. Every time I wander through Pinehurst Park, where we had our first fight, I sense him around me. He's here for me sometimes when I need him, and sometimes when I don't."

Years later, when Tom and I had flown in to help Heather out of another jam, I finally understood what she meant. We were in a rental car, driving in from the airport, when I saw the Barnette Dairyette up ahead, under the crackling neon lights. I asked Tom to pull over so I could pee, but at first, I couldn't bring myself to get out of the car. "Is everything all right?" he asked. I couldn't explain to him that this was the very essence of the life I had known, the very essence of awkward high school nights and happy childhood days. Hesitantly, I got out and headed inside. The bathroom key was in the same spot on the blue counter, still tied to the same big mixing spoon. I unlocked the door and stepped inside the tiny bathroom — same medicinal smell, same weird, dark lighting, probably the same graffiti. As the heavy door slammed behind me, I felt paralyzed; it was as if not a single day had gone by since I was last there. It was as if nothing had changed at all.

"Remember whose you are," my father used to say. And after he died, my mother said it, too — an admonishment to remember that my words and actions reflected on the parents who raised me, and on the God they raised me to believe in. Good advice, but it needs a simple addition: Remember *who* you are.

Two nights ago, as I drifted in and out of sleep on the couch at the radio station, Tom leaned down and mumbled into my ear, "What are you dreaming about?"

"The Barnette Dairyette."

"Oh, I remember that place," he said, surprising me. "Great milk shakes."

When I left Mississippi, I believed that I could slice my life neatly down the middle. Between my past and my future, there would be a clean divide. But there is no such divide. I will always carry this inside me: the truth of my origins. Tom is a part of me, but so are my mother, my sister. I am a doctor, but I am also a teenager on Christmas Eve, staring into the charity box that contains the old, used sweater of a girl who never liked me.

I have been a mother, a wife, a sister, a physician. The layers accumulate, the layers fall away. Not everything fits. Some things drift away. Others hold tightly.

I don't know if I still have a job. I don't know what will happen to my state, my country. But I know I'm going to buy those tickets to Norway. I know now that I was the one who pushed Tom away, and it is my responsibility to try to bring us back together. I know that, through everything, he never stopped loving me. We'll begin at the Grand Hotel in Oslo, where Ibsen often held court. We'll take the Flåm Railway through the mountains, stop overnight at the tiny village of Aurland. We'll take a boat through the fjords. And finally, we'll drink hot chocolate in Bergen, just like we planned, all those years ago. We'll begin there, and see where it leads.

Eighteen years ago, alone and new to California, I wandered along the cliffs of Point Reyes in the freezing fog, and stood gazing out at the roaring Pacific. I followed a picket fence for several hundred yards, curious where it led. And then, without warning, the fence abruptly ended. A narrow ditch ran perpendicular to the fence, splitting the ground in two; on the other side, some distance away, the fence continued. A middle-aged man stood on one side of the ditch, a boy of about seven on the other. They held hands across the divide. I imagined the earth moving in one swift, startling motion, rearranging everything in an instant. You wake up one day, and you're forty, and nothing is the way you'd planned. The ground shifts. It comes together, it pulls apart, and there's nothing to do but dig in and grab hold of something, whatever is closest and best.

I think of my infant niece, surely asleep in my sister's arms. And now I know what it was that I wanted to say to her. There is a simple truth, and it is this: Somehow, we must move forward, always carrying with us who we are, always looking forward to who we might be.

ACKNOWLEDGMENTS

I would like to thank my wonderful agent and friend, Valerie Borchardt, for her intelligence, persistence, great sense of humor, and ongoing faith in my work. I'm also indebted to my amazing editor, Kate Miciak, for pinpointing the heart of this story, encouraging me exactly when I needed it most, and shining a light in the labyrinth.

Thanks to Caitlin Alexander, who read many early drafts of this novel, and to Bonnie Thompson and Janet Wygal. Thanks to the Random House family for providing a supportive home for my work, and to the amazing independent booksellers who make Northern California such a good place to be a writer and a reader.

Gurpreet Dhaliwal, MD, graciously allowed me to shadow him and his residents at the San Francisco VA Medical Center. My friend Ted Morton provided insight into military life.

The epigraph at the beginning of the book is from my former mentor John Balaban's translation of "Spring-Watching Pavilion," collected in *Spring Essence: The Poetry of Hồ Xuân Hu'o'ng*.

For resources and information on issues affecting veterans, visit craigconnects.org/military-families-and-veterans.

As always, thanks to Kevin, for everything.

■ ■ ■ ■

GOLDEN STATE
MICHELLE RICHMOND

A READER'S GUIDE

■ ■ ■ ■

A CONVERSATION WITH MICHELLE RICHMOND

Random House Reader's Circle: Why did you decide to set the novel against the backdrop of a vote for secession?

Michelle Richmond: I am fascinated by the fact that so often things that seem impossible are actually very much within the realm of possibility. Every day in the news, there's something else that completely explodes our expectations. Tom's radio show, *Anything Is Possible,* is a tribute to that notion, and I hope this novel is a tribute to that notion as well. Personally, to be clear, I *don't* think that California should or will go anywhere, but there's been so much secession talk on the fringes for years, from states as diverse as New York, Texas, Colorado, and California, that it seemed worth exploring what would happen if the concept of secession moved from the outermost fringes to the mainstream.

I also am interested in the way characters live out their lives against the backdrop of the larger world, which is what every one of us does, every day. Only days after moving to California, I experienced my first tremor. I'd been in hurricanes and tornadoes, but this was the first time I'd felt the ground move beneath my feet. It sent a powerful message: that stability is an illusion, and that we have no way of knowing when everything is going to change.

Fifteen years have passed since I felt that first tremor, and I've felt hundreds of them since then. I am accustomed to them, but I don't imagine I'll ever be immune: every time the house moves — whether it's a quick jolt or a slow roll — I'm reminded that we live on a fault line. To me, this seems like an apt metaphor for marriage in particular and for life in general.

RHRC: In *Golden State,* as in *The Year of Fog,* the couple is suffering from the loss of a child. Can you talk a bit about this theme and why you are drawn to it?

MR: The worst thing I could imagine as a child was being separated from my parents. Now that I am an adult, I see this fear of separation from the other side. As a child, you fear the loss of protection, but as an adult, you fear the inability to protect a child who is in your care.

In my mind, Julie is deeply in love with Tom, and always will be. But there is something about the love for a child that is very different and more fierce than romantic love — I believe it must have something to do with the need to care for those who are incapable of caring for themselves.

RHRC: You have said in the past that you never outline, and that you don't know where a book is going when you begin. How much did you know about this story when you began writing it?

MR: Well, I knew from the start that it would be the story of a marriage. I am always intrigued by what holds a couple together, and by what it takes to sever the bonds that, at some point, were strong enough to justify a vow of lifelong commitment. For Julie and Tom, there is this deep love and passion and mutual respect that have kept them together for so long, but things happen, things largely beyond their control, to threaten that love. Will the center hold? That was the question I began with, and I had no idea when I started writing what the answer would be. But it was important to me that Julie and Tom both be characters as decent as they were flawed.

I also knew, when I began writing the novel, that three relationships would be central to the novel: the marriage, Julie's relationship with her sister, and the couple's relationship to the lost child. It was only much later — years into the writing of the book — that Dennis became a strong force. He sort of took me by surprise and added a new element to the novel. This is where the author-editor relationship comes into play; in this case, my editor noticed a character that had been lurking fairly quietly on the sidelines and basically said, "What's the deal with this guy?" It was a good question, one that forced me to look at the story from an entirely different angle.

When I began exploring Dennis's role in Julie's life, I thought about all of the relationships we enter into sort of blindly over the course of our adult lives. And I thought about how much of ourselves we make known to people, and how easily we sometimes trust others with our deepest secrets and fears. What interested me about Dennis were the long-term repercussions of that trust.

RHRC: There's a lot of music in your book. Do you listen to music when you write?

MR: I'll sometimes listen to instrumentals, but I never listen to music with lyrics while I'm writing. It gets in my head. When I'm not sitting down writing, though, there's always music in our house. My husband used to DJ at UCLA when he was in college, and he's always on the lookout for new acts, or new albums by people you haven't heard of in twenty years. In our house, I buy the books and he buys the albums, and then we share.

RHRC: How did you research this book?

MR: Well, I spent a lot of time driving, walking, and taking the bus up and down California Street! Most people in San Francisco never use the cable cars, and when I started writing this novel, I'd been living in San Francisco for years but hadn't ridden a cable car since I was there on a family vacation when I was thirteen.

Sometimes, some of the research happens before the idea of the book ever takes hold, and that was the case with this novel. At the time I began writing it, my little boy attended the preschool on the campus of the

Veterans Administration Hospital in San Francisco. It's this amazingly beautiful place, and I felt so fortunate to drop him off there every day. But I was also aware that the hospital served a population of veterans who had seen the very worst of war. This was also at a time when the patient population was beginning to change, and when many veterans were coming home with terrible wounds that would not have been survivable in previous wars.

A general internist at the hospital generously allowed me to shadow him and his residents. I took copious notes, but it goes without saying that much of what I witnessed on rounds and in the lectures went over my layperson's head. When it comes to the actual medical terminology of the book, I should emphasize that any failures in logic or procedure are, of course, entirely my own!

I also read a lot of first-person accounts by veterans of the wars in Iraq and Afghanistan and talked with friends in the military. We expect so much from our service members, and when they come home, I think we civilians sometimes feel awkward around them. There is this sense of not knowing quite what to say, of being curious but afraid to ask questions that would be intrusive or would force them to recount what they've been through. I tried to capture that in the relationship between Julie and her sister: Julie knows that Heather has been through a great deal, but she also knows that it's something she will never entirely be able to understand.

RHRC: If you hadn't become an author, what career would you have pursued?

MR: Well, I am endlessly fascinated by outer space. I spend a lot of time reading about newly discovered planets and the Martian atmosphere. I do weird things like attend the SETI (Search for Extra-terrestrial Intelligence) conference and stay in the hotel with all the Artificial Intelligence people just to soak up the conversation. I ask my son at least once a month, "Honey, do you think you might like to be an astronaut?" I've made my husband sit through the planetarium show at the California Academy of Sciences more times than I care to admit, and it has never once failed to move me to tears. So, I would love to say that I would have become a physicist had I not become a writer, but that simply would not have been possible. We are not always given the brains that we would choose. I am very, very happy to be a writer, and I am keenly aware that my gray matter supports the writing life quite well but would not be particularly well suited for a life observing the unknown universe. I must stick, then, with the known universe, and spend a lot of time staring at the stars.

MICHELLE RICHMOND'S
GOLDEN STATE PLAYLIST

Golden State began with the idea for a single scene: a husband and wife at the end of their marriage, spending their final night together in a San Francisco radio station, where the husband works as a late-night deejay. As the story developed, the one thing that remained constant in my mind was the sound of the music from the radio station. Early drafts of the novel contained a number of songs that didn't make it into the final draft. Here are the songs that, for me, capture the spirit of the novel and of the place that has become my home:

Admiral Radley, "I Heart California"
California has inspired many great songs over the years, and, like "California Dreaming," this one is a personal favorite. The product of a one-off local California indie super-group combination, comprising members of Grandaddy and Earlimart, this song

is an unapologetic celebration of the true spirit of California.

Josh Rouse, "Sweetie" This one comes from Rouse's 2007 record, *Country Mouse City House.* For me, the best love songs contain just a pinch of melancholy. When I picture Julie and Tom working through their complicated relationship, I always hear this song and think of Rouse's great line "crooked couple standing side by side / Is that you? Is that me?"

Tom Petty, "California" Like Julie, Tom Petty is a transplant to California from the South. For years, his identity was intertwined with his birthplace in Gainesville, Florida, and his stories seemed to emanate from there. Listening to his albums over the years, I've always been interested to hear how his southern identity has slowly evolved and reconciled itself with his adopted home. With the short, direct, and brilliant "California," from 1996, the evolution seems complete. This song is highly personal for me. Like Petty, my roots are deeply southern, but I have made my home and my adult life on the West Coast.

Norman Greenbaum, "Spirit in the

Sky" Another California transplant, Greenbaum moved to California at the age of twenty-three. He wrote and recorded this classic four years later in San Francisco. A Jewish kid from Massachusetts, Greenbaum reportedly penned his fun, funky, celebratory "friend in Jesus" song in less than fifteen minutes. By some accounts, he was never really sure what the song meant. I can never figure out what it means either. I don't know what it would've been like to live in San Francisco during the Summer of Love, but I imagine that the vibe was very similar to what is captured in this song.

Scorpions, "Wind of Change" Written by Klaus Meine during a trip to Russia in 1989, this song celebrated the imminent fall of the USSR. Since then, of course, it has become an anthem for large-scale movements that topple unjust regimes. At the heart of *Golden State,* for me, is the idea that huge, unexpected political and social shifts often seem inconceivable and impossible until the moment they happen. More important, though, this song rocks. I dare you to listen to it without feeling inspired. Long live the Scorpions.

The Mendoza Line, "Aspect of an Old

Maid" As the radio plays throughout *Golden State,* I wanted to establish the melancholy soundtrack of mature breakup songs. No one does a bittersweet, super-complicated breakup song like the Mendoza Line. If we lived in a world where all things were fair, the Mendoza Line's classic album *Lost in Revelry* would have sold as many copies as Michael Jackson's *Thriller.* This is one of their later songs, and it comes from their last disc, *30 Year Low.*

Kirsty MacColl and Evan Dando, "Perfect Day" Though the Lou Reed original of this song is a classic, I'm always drawn to this version by MacColl and former Lemonhead Dando. You can find it on MacColl's disc *From Croydon to Cuba.*

Steve Forbert, "Goin' Down to Laurel" I can't imagine anyone other than Steve Forbert being able to write a great song about Laurel, Mississippi. I first saw Forbert at Mercury Lounge in New York City, then at Maxwell's in Hoboken (which now, sadly, is closed). Years later, I saw him play at a little church in San Francisco's Noe Valley. Forbert has a gift for writing heartbreaking songs and delivering them with his unforgettable voice. He's another musician with one foot in the South (he's from Meridian, Mississippi) and one foot in the wider, urban world.

Aidan Moffat and Bill Wells, "The Copper Top" For me, this is one of the saddest songs ever written. Everything is getting older.

Dire Straits, "Telegraph Road" Lasting more than fourteen minutes, the storytelling in this song covers a span of well over a hundred years and tells the tale of a single Detroit, Michigan, road from beginning to end. When I first started writing *Golden State* (which was originally titled *California Street*), this song was on a mix disc in my car. At the time, my son, in the back seat, always wanted the volume louder, and whether we had arrived at our destination or not, we always had to sit there until the song was over. Someday I will clean out the car, and when I do, I hope to find this disc among the Tootsie Roll wrappers and lost tubes of lipstick — and in working order.

Badly Drawn Boy, "The Way Things Used to Be" Quick, obvious songs of infatuation (think early Beatles) have never done it for me. I'm always drawn to songs about long, messy, complicated relationships (isn't that the only kind of relationship worth having?). In that category, this Badly Drawn Boy number is one of the best.

Elbow, "August and September" What can I say? I love cover songs, and this is one of my favorites. It's a cover of the nearly-as-good original by The The, and I found it seven years ago on a *Q* magazine 1986 tribute disc. It's another sad breakup song, and although it didn't make the final edit of *Golden State,* it always seemed to fit in well with the sound the novel made in my head.

Graham Parker, "Anniversary" Another song celebrating a long relationship. The words are so nice and happy; why, then, does the song sound so ominous and desperate? During the early period of writing *Golden State,* I had a CD in my car with a collection of Graham Parker songs, and the mood and spirit of this one, "You Can't Be Too Strong," and "Haunted Episodes," seemed to seep into the mood of the book somehow.

Johnny Cash, "Further On Up the Road" Johnny Cash singing a Bruce Springsteen song about graveyard boots and looking for a light up ahead . . . what could be better?

Lambchop, "Let's Go Bowling" This one is from the 1994 Lambchop album with the confusing mix of two different titles — *I Hope You're Sitting Down* and *Jack's Tulips.* Although the record was their debut, it appeared with a rustic, world-weary sound that made it seem like it had been around forever. The story is a nice, foggy piece about a couple on a trip to Greece, taking pictures, wandering through the ruins of their life.

Lesley Spencer, "Childhood Revisited" My husband frequently plays this song while doing the dishes. I often hear it oozing out of the kitchen, working its way downstairs to my writing room. I love instrumentals that somehow tell a story, as this one does.

Mark Mulcahy, "A Smack on the Lips" How does love happen? What's the magic, unnamable thing that brings two people together? I was twenty-four when I met my husband. We've been together for most of my adult life. While my husband is definitely not Tom, and *Golden State* is "purely a work

445

of fiction," as they say, the passion and stability of a long-term partnership is something that, fortunately, I know well. If you want to tell your spouse you'd do it all over again, play this song!

The Handsome Family, "A Thousand Diamond Rings" Albuquerque's Handsome Family seems to know a thing or two about complicated relationships. For me, this one and "So Much Wine" are classics.

Richmond Fontaine, "A Letter to the Patron Saint of Nurses" I would love this great Portland band even if we didn't share a name. "A Letter to the Patron Saint of Nurses" is a weird one, almost spoken word. It's a nice tribute to the importance of being able to remember the high points in a relationship, especially when you are at a low point.

Woodpigeon, "Enchantée Janvier" Canada's Woodpigeon was an infatuation I had during the early versions of *Golden State.* If you're in need of a great, uplifting song, this is it.

Tracey Thorn, "Sister Winter" This is a pretty cover of the lesser-known Sufjan

Stevens not-exactly-happy Christmas song.

Billy Idol, "Sweet Sixteen" I fell head over heels for Billy Idol as a fifteen-year-old girl in Alabama. My bedroom was pretty much wallpapered with pictures of him. It was like running into an old crush when, quite by accident, he walked into *Golden State.* This song goes a bit further than his others — it's catchy and hummable, yes, but also sad, with an indescribable vein of melancholy weaving its way through. For years, I thought this song was about a guy who's in love with a sixteen-year-old girl. Only recently did I come to realize that this is a song about the long haul, about a man who has loved the same woman for a very long time, and who now feels the threat of losing her.

QUESTIONS FOR DISCUSSION

1. The author uses an unconventional timeline to tell her story, moving back and forth between past, present, and earlier that morning. What elements does this add to the reading experience? How would the experience have changed had the author used a strictly linear approach?

2. How are music and lyrics important throughout the story? What does the incessancy of Tom's voice on the radio mean to Julie?

3. Describe how Heather and Julie's relationship changes. What are the most influential moments? If you were Julie, would you have been able to forgive Heather?

4. On page 235, Julie questions her and Tom's relationship by saying, "Without a child, are we even a family?" Ethan un-

doubtedly transforms Julie and Tom's life, but does he prove that children are necessary to have a real family?

5. On page 131, Julie wonders, "Between a marriage one chooses and a blood relation one doesn't, shouldn't marriage be the more powerful bond?" Does Julie find an answer to this question? Which do you think is the stronger bond?

6. What does Julie's mother represent? Why are Julie's memories of Mississippi and her childhood so important? Why might she reflect on them during the stress of the hostage situation?

7. The characters in *Golden State* grapple with the idea of things either happening for a reason or happening due to cause and effect. Julie spends most of the novel defending the latter, but which do you believe in? Why?

8. Explain Dennis and Julie's relationship. How is it possible that Julie could feel remorse for Dennis in the midst of a hostage crisis?

9. Throughout the novel, Julie views her life

as a series of beginnings and endings, rather than a continuum of learning and growing. Does this mindset hurt or help her? Does her attitude change by the end of the novel? Through which interpretation do you view your life?

10. The author leaves certain questions unanswered at the close of the story. If you were to write a sequel, how would you tie up the novel's loose ends?

11. On page 152, Tom says, "We become so used to the way things are . . . we can't imagine things being any other way." What does he mean by this? How does the premise of *Golden State* encourage readers to imagine the impossible?

12. Of all the themes in the novel — forgiveness, family, belief, patriotism, identity, etc. — which was the most relevant to you? Why?

ABOUT THE AUTHOR

Michelle Richmond is the author of *The Girl in the Fall-Away Dress, Dream of the Blue Room, The Year of Fog, No One You Know,* and *Golden State.* She is the recipient of the Hillsdale Award for Fiction and the Catherine Doctorow Innovative Fiction Prize. A native of Alabama's Gulf Coast, she makes her home with her husband and young son in Northern California.

michellerichmond.com